D1242151

Mary Margaret,

Hope you enjoy this one.

All the best,

[illegible]

THREE DEADLY DROPS

Books in the
Donald Youngblood Mystery Series

Three Deuces Down (2008)
Three Days Dead (2009)
Three Devils Dancing (2011)
Three Deadly Drops (2012)

A Donald Youngblood Mystery

THREE DEADLY DROPS

Keith Donnelly

Hummingbird Books
Gatlinburg, Tennessee

Hummingbird Books
A division of Harrison Mountain Press
P.O. Box 1386
Gatlinburg, TN 37738

Designed by Todd Lape / Lape Designs

Library of Congress Cataloging-in-Publication Data

Donnelly, Keith.
Three deadly drops / by Keith Donnelly.
p. cm. — (Donald Youngblood mystery ; 4)
ISBN 978-0-89587-587-7 (hardcover : alk. paper) 1. Youngblood, Donald (Fictitious character)—Fiction. 2. Private investigators—Tennessee—Fiction. 3. Cherokee Indians—Fiction. 4. Special forces (Military science)—Fiction. 5. Revenge—Fiction. 6. Serial murder investigation—Fiction. I. Title.
PS3604.O56325T477 2011
813'.6—dc22

2012018677

Printed in the United States of America
by the Maple-Vail Book Manufacturing Group
York, Pennsylvania

To Tessa

The great ride continues

Prologue

He sat at his desk and wrote the letter in his neat left-handed penmanship. He had finished the cryptic warning notes. Now, he had to write the letter. He needed to get it all out of his system; it had been festering too long. And he had to tell someone. There was only one person who would understand.

Two years ago, his stuttering had come back at the most inopportune time, fueled by stress and fear. He had almost mastered it, had it dead and buried. He had even fooled the army, gone all the way through basic with a minimum of slips that no one noticed. But it was lurking in the shadows like some hideous creature waiting for an unsuspecting victim, and it finally victimized him.

He had applied for the Rangers simply to prove he was tough enough to make it. He made it, all right, and then found himself smack-dab in the middle of Desert Storm. Well, that was okay; it was another chance to prove himself. He hadn't bargained for war, and he certainly wasn't ready to die halfway around the world in some godforsaken desert. But he would make the best of it. He would be a brave soldier.

Then he was selected for the black ops mission. He had no idea why. They were eight in all—a lieutenant, a sergeant, a corporal, and five PFCs. They were all from different companies. The mission was top secret, a rescue. They trained for only a week and were told little. Only the lieutenant and the sergeant were briefed. The rest of them knew squat, except that if they got caught they were dead.

The mission took them into enemy territory. The deeper in, the more stress he felt. By the time the copter landed, he couldn't string two words together without stuttering. The lieutenant thought he was stressing out and made up an excuse to send him back on the copter to command with a message and a progress report. But he knew it was all bullshit, that the lieutenant just wanted him gone. No one said anything, but a few of the other seven gave him a superior look before he left, the cocky bastards. Command sent him back to his unit. Later, he was medically discharged.

He heard the mission was a success. He also heard rumors that something had gone terribly wrong, but it was all hush-hush. The rumors made him feel a little better until he learned that all of them received medals—all seven, the Silver Star, the motherfucking Silver Star. That made him really angry—crazy angry, revengeful angry.

In the two years that followed, the anger had grown to monstrous proportions. It was time to unleash the monster.

So he sat at the big roll-top desk and wrote the letter and outlined his plan to get even. His best friend would understand. His best friend had always understood, had always been there to calm him and offer encouragement; had helped him in high school to find the right therapy. He had the battle won until he got the bright idea to join the army and apply for Ranger School. Then the Gulf War came. Things begin to unravel, and all that hard work and therapy became wasted time and energy.

He was on the second page of the letter now, his left hand moving steadily across the paper. His mind was whirling. If he could actually kill those seven assholes, he wanted someone to know why. He wanted it documented in his own handwriting so there would be no mistake. *You don't fuck with people who have a disability*, he thought. *You don't treat them unfairly.* The seven had to be punished. If anyone would understand, it would be his best friend.

The names were in the letter, all seven. He planned to kill one a year or every two years, he wasn't sure. He would take his time and savor each kill. It would be his black ops mission, and he would award himself a medal—maybe a Gold Star—when it was done. After all, he was a Ranger, and he knew how to kill. They would die, and no one would suspect they had been murdered. He would make their deaths look like accidents or random acts of violence. That was the beauty of the plan. There would be no connection to him.

He took the letter, placed it inside an envelope, and wrote on the outside:

Open only if something happens to me.

Then he placed it inside another envelope and wrote his friend's name and address on the outside and affixed one of his return address labels.

◆ ◆ ◆ ◆

Early the next morning, he drove to a post office in Durham, North Carolina, with the letter and the seven notes, smiling all the way. *I am so clever*, he thought. *Durham is far enough away that no one will suspect me.*

When he got to the post office, he took one final look at the envelopes and dropped them down the mail slot. His decision was complete. *I will have my revenge*, he thought as he pulled out of the parking lot, a horn blowing in the background.

THREE DEADLY DROPS

1

My name is Donald Alexander Youngblood. I used to be a rich, carefree, confirmed bachelor. I used to live with only one black male standard poodle. Those days were simple; those days are gone.

Some years ago, I fled New York City with my best friend, Billy Two-Feathers, and came home. Home is Mountain Center, Tennessee. After filling out the required paperwork, I was granted a private investigator's license by the state, and after completing the mandatory class, a gun carry permit. Billy and I then opened Cherokee Investigations. Billy is a full-blooded Cherokee Indian. He doesn't carry a gun. He carries a knife, or two.

For a while, things were quiet. Then our first big case landed on our doorstep, followed by another and another. Quiet took a permanent holiday.

Along the way, I have acquired a wife, a daughter, and another black male standard poodle. Mary Sanders and I just recently celebrated our first anniversary. Mary is a cop with the Mountain Center Police Department. We adopted Lacy Malone, who decided she wanted to be known as Lacy Malone Youngblood. How she came to be with us is another story. The new poodle is Jake's son, registered name Son of Jake. We call him Junior. Jake went to stud, lucky dog, and I got the pick of the litter. Father and son are doing fine. I am also doing fine, but I must admit there are times . . .

◆ ◆ ◆ ◆

The door leading from my office to the outer office and the reception area was shut. I kept it closed because if I didn't, I would never get a moment's peace. Thanks to all the press I had received on the Three Devils case over a year ago, my private detective business was booming.

Another reason business was so good was because I was a sucker for every Dick and Jane with a sad story. I didn't need the small cases or the money that went with them, but I had a hard time saying no. Some days, I sat around twiddling my thumbs. Other days, the office was like Grand Central Station at rush hour. This particular day would not be a thumb-twiddler.

In the early mornings, to escape the world, I hung a Closed sign on the frosted glass that was visible from the hall. I'd turn on a single lamp in the outer office to let the friends in my inner circle know I was in my office and that they were welcome to join me. Billy had a key, as did my boyhood friend and chief of police, Big Bob Wilson. Roy Husky, a more recent friend who often covered my back even when I didn't want him to, also had a key. And I had recently given one to Oscar Morales, who did part-time work for me.

It seemed like a lifetime ago that I was on Wall Street competing in the daily frantic panic of the investment world, where fortunes were won and lost not in days but in hours, sometimes minutes. The more successful I became on the Street, the higher the expectations rose. I didn't need the money and didn't like the pressure. I finally went back to my hometown with plenty of money and no life and began rebuilding myself.

The buzz of my intercom interrupted my daydreaming that early October Tuesday.

"I'm in," Gretchen said, which meant it was ten o'clock and I could hide from the world no longer.

"Okay," I said. "Pour yourself a cup of coffee and come on in."

Gretchen had been with me for almost a year. She concentrated on the routinely boring private investigator stuff and assisted me with my investment accounts. I took on only those cases that looked to be intriguing and maybe dangerous. Mary had found Gretchen for me when it became apparent I couldn't deal with the phone calls and the flow of people through my office door after the Three Devils case. We were asked to do everything from interviewing accident witnesses to finding lost dogs. Jake and Junior handled the lost dogs.

Gretchen was wise beyond her years. She had a young daughter and no husband. I didn't ask about the husband, and she didn't tell. She worked ten to four five days a week and occasionally came in on Saturdays to play catch-up. She was college educated and smart. I gave her a big salary with benefits. I thought at the time I was overpaying. She soon proved me wrong.

"You have an appointment with the president of National Distributing at one-thirty," she said. "He said he would talk only to you. The Tennessee Insurance guy called and wanted an update on his case, and I gave him one. Oscar is working on that. Dr. Chang emailed to ask your thoughts on a certain stock purchase." She handed me a printed copy of Dr. Chang's email. "And Billy will be here at three."

"Why is Billy coming here?" I asked, surprised.

"He said he has something he wants to talk to you about in person," Gretchen said.

I started to pursue that further, but we were interrupted by the opening and closing of my outer office door. Gretchen was out of her chair and into the outer office like Superman in search of a phone booth. She closed my door as she went. I heard an exchange of low voices. It went on for about a minute. Gretchen came back in my office and shut the door.

"I have a lady out there who says her husband might have been murdered," Gretchen said.

"Might have been," I said.

"Yes," Gretchen said. "Might have been."

"And you told her the police handle murder investigations," I said.

"I did," Gretchen said.

"So I assume the police do not think it was murder," I said.

"You would be correct," Gretchen said.

"What do the police think it was?"

"According to her, the police are incompetent and could not tell a murder from a bad cold," Gretchen said.

"One of those," I said.

"Her husband just died, Don. Cut her some slack."

"Okay, Gretch," I shot back, knowing that would irritate her. "Think there's anything to this?"

"Might be worth hearing her out," Gretchen said, ignoring my jab.

"All right," I said reluctantly. "Send her in."

She turned to leave, got to the door, and whirled around. "And don't call me Gretch," she snapped, shutting the door behind her before I could respond.

◆ ◆ ◆ ◆

A moment later, my door reopened and Gretchen entered, followed by a tall woman impeccably dressed head to toe in black. I stood.

"Mr. Youngblood," Gretchen said formally, "this is Jessica Crane."

"Please sit down, Mrs. Crane," I said, motioning to a chair in front of my desk. "Can we get you a cup of coffee or something?"

"No, thank you," she said as she seated herself.

Jessica Crane, I guessed, was around fifty years old. But with the clothes and the grooming, it was hard to tell. She could have been older. She looked around the office as if she were an interior decorator given the unpleasant task of redoing the place. I was glad I had worn a shirt and tie.

"I think someone might have murdered my husband," she said, returning her gaze to me.

"Tell me about it."

"Six days ago, my husband, Walter, died of an apparent heart attack," she said. "When the county medical examiner finally performed an autopsy, he could not find any evidence of a heart attack. It would seem that, for no apparent reason, Walter's heart just stopped. According to the medical examiner, no trace of anything in Walter's blood or tissues might offer an explanation. Those findings are just unacceptable to me."

She seemed more annoyed than grief stricken, but sometimes grief is hard to read. She waited for me to respond. I could tell she was a woman used to being in control.

"Can you think of anyone who would have wanted to kill your husband?" I asked. "Did he have any enemies?"

"No," Jessica Crane said without hesitation. "None."

"Anyone who would want to get back at you by killing him?"

"Heavens no," she said.

"Could your husband have been having an affair?"

"Absolutely not," she said sharply.

"Sorry," I said. "I had to ask."

"It's okay," she said. "I understand."

"What did your husband do for a living?"

"He was the president of the Blue Ridge National Bank Corporation," she said, as if I should have known.

I wrote "BRNB" on my notepad. I had heard of Blue Ridge National but didn't know much about it.

"What did the police say exactly?" I asked.

"That they saw no evidence of foul play."

"And you think it was foul play."

She slumped in the chair and took a deep breath. "I don't know what to think," she said. "I refuse to believe my husband had a heart attack, especially since there is no such evidence. Will you look into it?"

I ignored that question and pushed on. "Where do you live, Mrs. Crane?"

"We have an estate outside Knoxville off Highway 11-W toward Morristown," she answered.

"Why did you come here?" I asked. "Knoxville is much closer. I know a private investigator there who is very good."

That's right, Youngblood. Pass this one on to Tom Slack, I thought.

"Too close to home, if you know what I mean," she said. "Besides, you come highly recommended."

"By whom?" I asked.

"My attorney," she said.

She told me an attorney's name I didn't recognize, but I smelled Rollie Ogle's hand in this. Rollie Ogle was a friend and attorney who had an office down the hall. I would need to have a word with Rollie, even though he had saved my life once.

"I also had you checked out," she said, pleased with herself. "You're rich, well connected, smart, and tenacious. I think you will find out what there is to find out."

"You may not like what I find," I said.

She leaned forward in her chair. "Believe me, I can deal with whatever you find out. Of course, I'd like to keep it confidential."

"I would share information only with people I feel need to know or could help me in the investigation," I said.

"Very well," Jessica Crane said. "I'll leave that to your discretion."

I nodded. "Did your husband have an office at home?"

"He did," she said.

"Can I have a look?"

"You may," she said. "Call before you come."

"I may need access to private information," I said.

"Whatever you need," she said. "I am certainly not going to hire you and then limit your scope."

"Do you have an email provider?" I asked.

"Of course," she said. "I may be a little older than you, but I do not live in the Dark Ages." She emphasized the word *little.*

"When you get a chance, send me an email so I'll have your address."

"No need," she said, handing me a personal card with her email address and phone numbers on it.

I gave her one of my business cards. She looked at it and nodded.

"When will the county release the body to you?" I asked.

"They are finished with Walter," she said. "He may be moved at any time."

"Have you made plans for services?"

"Not yet," she said. "I thought you might want someone else to take a look at the body."

Jessica Crane seemed to be thinking pretty clearly for a woman who had just lost her husband. I was sure I had more questions, but at that moment I couldn't think of any.

"Okay," I said. "Tell the county medical examiner that Wanda Jones from Mountain Center will call to make arrangements to have the body transferred."

"Does that mean you'll help me?"

"It does," I said.

Who was it who sang that song, "Here I Go Again"?

2

James W. West, president of National Distributing Corporation, was a lean man about five-foot-ten with short, dark hair and icy blue eyes that looked like they could see through walls. I had the distinct feeling his employees walked softly around their boss. We shook hands.

"Call me J. W.," he said.

I didn't care what he called me, so I didn't comment. "Please, sit down," I said.

He sat. I guessed that J. W. was in his mid-fifties.

"Nice chair," he said. "Get people relaxed and they open up. I like it."

I nodded. I didn't want to burst his bubble by telling him I got the big chairs because I had big friends.

"What can I do for you J. W.?" I asked.

"Joseph Fleet recommended I come see you," he said.

National Distributing Corporation was located down the road from Fleet Industries. I wasn't surprised that James W. West and Joseph Fleet knew each other.

"We were having lunch at the club, and I told him about my problem, and he said you could probably help," he continued.

"What do you need me to do?"

"I need to have someone followed," he said. "One of my employees. His name is Jerry Block."

"Tell me why," I said.

He said he thought Jerry Block might be faking a back injury to collect disability insurance. An anonymous tip had come to his human resources manager. James W. West wanted me to prove it. He handed me a file folder.

"Everything you'll need to get started should be in there," he said. "If you think of anything else you might require, we'll provide it if we have it."

He handed me a business card. "My personal cell-phone number is on the back. How long do you think this will take?"

"Hard to tell," I said. "Depends on how dumb your employee is, and if he's really faking it or not. The tipster could have an agenda."

"Maybe," J. W. said. "Jerry's not that bright, according to the test we give during the hiring process. He might think he can get away with it. It would probably never occur to him that we'd hire a private investigator. Also, if the tip is bogus, then I want to know that, too."

I nodded.

"The sooner we can wrap this up, the better," he said. "It's costing me money."

I stood and extended my hand. "I'll get my best surveillance guy on this," I said.

"You won't do this yourself?" He looked disappointed.

I stared at him and smiled.

"No, of course you won't." He smiled back. "Stupid question."

◆ ◆ ◆ ◆

I called Roy Husky. A hard man ten years my senior, Roy had come into my life some years back on my first big case. He had since helped me with other cases, and I now counted Roy among my good and close friends. Roy had also become friends with Billy and my mentor, T. Elbert Brown. Roy was an ex-con turned jack-of-all-trades for powerful Mountain Center businessman Joseph Fleet. Even though our backgrounds were at opposite ends of the spectrum, Roy and I had found common ground in honesty, humor, and like-mindedness in defining right and wrong. He had watched my back on a number of occasions.

"Hey, gumshoe," Roy said, when he answered the phone. "What's going on?"

"A few things that might be interesting," I said. "They seem to come in twos. I need the O-man when he's free."

O-man was our nickname for Oscar Morales. Exactly when we started calling him O-man, or who started it, I can't say for sure. But it stuck, and Oscar seemed to like it.

"I'll tell him," Roy said. "Anything dangerous?"

"Probably not," I said. "If it turns out to be dangerous and I need backup, you'll be the first to know."

"Please," Roy said. "I could use some action."

◆ ◆ ◆ ◆

The rather large frame of my partner, Billy Two-Feathers, sat in the oversized chair nearest the window and waited as I wrapped up a call with one of my financial clients. Since we started our little business, Billy had expanded Cherokee Investigations by opening an office in Cherokee, North Carolina. Along the way, he had acquired a wife and was now a proud papa. Among other things, Billy's contributions to our partnership included a deep understanding of the human psyche, that and an air of danger. He seemed to be in touch with life on a different plane than most people. It gave the partnership a nice balance.

"Good to see you," I said to Billy when I finished my call. "It's been awhile."

Although we talked almost every day, we now saw each other only about every couple of weeks.

"You, too," he said.

"How is Little D?" I asked.

My godson, Donald Roy Two-Feathers, had arrived in March, checking in at twenty-four inches and ten pounds even. Billy's beautiful wife, Maggie, was a slender, statuesque Cherokee woman nearly six feet tall, so Little D, as he was now called, was destined to be Big D sometime in the future.

"Eating, sleeping, pooping, and growing," Billy said.

I smiled. It was still hard for me to imagine Billy as a father. On the other hand, it was still hard to imagine myself as a husband, with a teenage daughter, no less.

"So, what's so important that we couldn't discuss it over the phone?" I asked. "Maggie's not pregnant again, is she?"

Billy laughed. "Nothing like that. Little D will probably be our one and only."

"What, then?"

"I've been asked to get involved in the race for county sheriff," Billy said.

"Sheriff?"

Billy nodded.

I was stunned. "Can an ex-con run for sheriff?"

"There is no record I was ever in prison," Billy said.

I shook my head. Billy never ceased to amaze me. "I don't want to know," I said, although I could guess.

"No need for you to," Billy said. "And besides, I'm not running."

"So what's your participation?"

"Maggie and I are going to help raise funds to finance the campaign and do some campaigning ourselves. If the guy I'm supporting wins, and he should, he'll appoint me as a part-time deputy."

"Why not full-time?"

"I don't want full-time," Billy said.

"Why not?" I asked, smiling to myself. I couldn't believe Billy even wanted to be a part-time deputy.

"I don't want to completely disassociate myself from Cherokee Investigations," Billy said.

"Disassociate," I said, stifling a laugh. "Being married to a schoolteacher is rubbing off on you."

"You might remember that I do have a college degree," Billy said, trying to act insulted.

"Sorry. I forgot."

"You'll still need me to watch your back sometimes," he said.

"Roy and O-man can watch my back."

"Not like I can," Billy said flatly.

Well, I couldn't argue with him there. As good as Roy and Oscar were, they weren't Billy. Billy had a way of being invisible like no one else could.

"Is there time to mount a campaign?" I asked. "You have only about a month."

"More like five weeks," Billy said. "The campaign has been under way for a while. Our guy won the Republican primary. I've just gotten involved in the last few weeks."

"What's Maggie think about this?" I asked; knowing Maggie was probably in the thick of it.

"In case you haven't noticed, Blood," Billy said, "Maggie is somewhat of a social activist in our community. She thinks this is a good way for me to get involved."

I nodded. It was pretty much the answer I expected, but my head was still spinning from the news.

"What about the current sheriff?" I asked.

"He's a good man," Billy said. "He's retiring. He's supporting the guy I'm backing, Charlie Running-Horse. Charlie is the senior deputy."

"What about the Cherokee office?"

"It stays open," Billy said. "I'll divide my time between the two jobs."

"You might have to carry a gun," I said, teasing. Billy did not like guns.

"Maybe, maybe not," Billy said.

Well, gun or not, a six-foot-six, 250-pound Cherokee deputy sheriff would be very intimidating, even if he were just part-time.

"I guess the big question is, do you want to do it?"

"I do," Billy said.

"Why?"

"It's complicated," Billy said. "I want to help the community. I might even want to be sheriff someday. This will give me a chance to get some experience and see if I'm cut out for the job."

Knowing Billy's history, I could imagine how complicated the decision was. It was a further chance to get to know a culture he didn't grow up in but felt part of.

"What do you want from me?" I asked.

"I want to know what you think," he said. "Me, as a deputy sheriff."

"I think you'd be great," I said.

"I don't want to spend much time raising money for the campaign," Billy said. "I could handle the financing myself, but I'm going to have to put a kid through college someday."

I raised my hand and stopped him. Billy asked me for money about as often as Halley's Comet made an appearance. He obviously thought this was important.

"I'll be glad to make a sizable donation," I said. "And you don't need to worry about my godson's education."

"That's why I picked you as godfather," Billy said, smiling.

"So you're a Republican?" I asked, trying to sound serious.

"For the time being, I guess," Billy said.

"Tell me how much you want," I said.

He quoted me a figure, and I agreed to it.

"Of course, I'll expect any speeding tickets I might receive in your county to be torn up," I said.

Billy grinned. "Not a chance."

◆ ◆ ◆ ◆

After Billy left the office with a substantial check in hand, I sat and thought about our conversation. Billy was such a free spirit that it was hard to imagine him as a deputy sheriff. On the other hand, he was the most disciplined person I knew and had an innate sense of right and wrong. He would be tough but fair. I was truthful when I told him I thought he'd make a good deputy sheriff. I was also a little worried. The job could be dangerous.

I glanced at my notepad, which reminded me of Jessica Crane. I picked up the phone and dialed Wanda Jones's private cell. Wanda was a close friend and the medical examiner for the county. She was attractive, probably bisexual (she hadn't completely decided on that), extremely smart, and flirted with me unmercifully, although not as much since Mary and I got married.

"To what do I owe this pleasure?" Wanda asked upon answering. Caller ID took all the fun out of phone calls.

"I haven't talked to you in a while," I said. "I just needed to hear the sound of your voice."

"That's sweet," Wanda said. "And total horseshit. What do you need?"

I laughed. Wanda always told it like it was.

"I need you to look at a body and an M.E. report and see what you think," I said. "It'll be a paid gig."

"I can do that," Wanda said. "Tell me about it."

I told her everything I knew.

"Think he just died for no apparent reason?" I asked.

"There's always a reason," Wanda said. "But sometimes things happen we can't explain. We'll talk after I take a look at the body. Who did the autopsy?"

I told her the county where the autopsy was performed. Wanda knew the M.E. and thought he was highly competent.

"I'll make the arrangements," Wanda said. "He'll probably welcome a second opinion."

"Thanks," I said.

"How is married life?" Wanda asked.

"Great," I said.

"Darn," Wanda said. "I was hoping for a breakup."

"What are friends for?" I said.

Wanda laughed. "Give that good-looking wife of yours a kiss from me," she said. "No, wait. I'd rather do that myself."

"You're incorrigible," I said. "Call me when you know something."

◆ ◆ ◆ ◆

When I reached our condo that evening, Mary was already there preparing dinner. It was unusual for her to be home ahead of me. And most weeknights, she didn't cook. I went into the kitchen and sat at the bar. Mary was preparing a chicken casserole with gravy and rice. A half-full glass of white wine was on the counter. She slipped the casserole into the oven, set the timer, and picked up her wineglass. She walked over to me and gave me a kiss on the mouth.

"Nice," I said.

"Did you have a good day?" Mary asked.

"Very," I said. "Two new cases."

"Want a beer?"

"Or two," I said.

She took an Amber Bock from the fridge, twisted and removed the top, and set it in front of me. I raised it, touched it to her wineglass, and took a drink. It was almost as good as that first drink of coffee in the morning.

"Tell me about these new cases," Mary said.

I did.

"I'll put Oscar on the surveillance case and look into the Crane case myself," I said. "I don't think it will amount to anything, but it's been awhile since I did any investigating, and I need the change of scenery, so to speak." I took a long pull on the Amber Bock. "Where's Lacy?"

"At Hannah's," Mary said. "She'll be home after dinner."

I nodded as I processed the information. At least three hours by ourselves. *Hmm.*

"I have news," I said.

Mary smiled. "About Billy."

"You know already."

She smiled again. "You forget that Maggie and I speak almost every day. She made me promise not to talk about it. Billy wanted to be the first to tell you."

"Is Maggie all for this?" I asked.

"She is," Mary said.

"What do you think?"

"Billy will make a great deputy," Mary said.

"I think so, too," I said, and then paused. "And how was your day?"

"Nothing special," she said.

"Maybe we can change that."

"I'm counting on it," Mary said.

3

"Billy's going into politics?" Roy asked, amazed.

"Not exactly," I said.

"Kind of sounds like it."

We sat on T. Elbert Brown's front porch. Years ago, a drug dealer's bullet had put T. Elbert in a wheelchair. T. Elbert was a former agent for the Tennessee Bureau of Investigation and still had some connection to the agency but was secretive about what that connection was.

"Let's hear all of it," T. Elbert said. "Details, I want details."

We sat in rocking chairs eating blueberry muffins Mary had made and drinking Dunkin' Donuts coffee Roy had brought. It was a cool morning in early October, and I could smell autumn in the air. The leaves on the maple trees were announcing the new season by showing some color that would intensify, and then fade, as the days passed toward winter.

I took a bite of muffin and a drink of coffee and told them about Billy's visit to my office. I knew Billy wouldn't mind. Roy and T. Elbert were in our inner circle.

"Billy will make a pretty imposing deputy," T. Elbert said.

"Very imposing," Roy said.

We sat for a while listening to the sounds of morning and enjoying our bounty.

"How was the ball game?" Roy asked T. Elbert.

T. Elbert had gone to Knoxville this past Saturday to see Tennessee take on an inferior team from the east. The Volunteers had won easily.

"That sophomore quarterback can really sling it around," T. Elbert said. "I think he's the real deal. I just hope he can stay healthy."

Tennessee had already lost its best wide receiver for the year, and a brutal SEC schedule was ahead. I was not optimistic.

A car sped by. We watched it pass going at least twenty miles an hour over the speed limit.

"What are you working on right now?" T. Elbert asked. "Anything juicy?"

Roy smiled and stayed silent.

I told them about Jessica Crane's husband and about the possible disability scam. They weren't much interested in the scam.

"Think the wife is overreacting?" Roy asked.

"Probably," I said.

"Some poisons out there are completely undetectable," T. Elbert said. "Exotic stuff from tropical jungles around the world. Back in the day, one of those secretive government agencies—the CIA, maybe—supposedly had this gun that would fire a poison dart that would kill the victim in seconds and dissolve without a trace."

"Sounds like science fiction to me," Roy said.

"I wouldn't be too sure," T. Elbert said.

"Well, I don't think Walter Crane was assassinated by the CIA or anyone else," I said. "But it might be interesting looking into it."

Roy snorted. "When you look into things, all hell seems to break loose."

"It's a gift," I said.

◆ ◆ ◆ ◆

That same morning, Oscar Morales sat in one of the oversized chairs in front of my desk snappily dressed in a blue blazer and gray slacks and smiling his perpetual smile.

"How are things, O-man?" I asked.

"Things are good," Oscar said. "I am forever in your debt."

"There is no debt, Oscar," I said. "You turned your own life around."

Oscar had once been a drug dealer who avoided jail by giving the feds some valuable information about distribution. He had also unwittingly helped me with a couple of cases I had worked involving drugs. He was now employed almost full-time at Fleet Industries and did some part-time work for me. It was true that I was responsible for the job at Fleet, but Oscar had made the most of it, and as far as I was concerned it was ancient history. His role there was expanding as Joseph Fleet explored new markets in Spanish-speaking countries. Oscar was street smart, tough, a sharp dresser, quick witted, and a fast learner. He had success written all over him.

"So," Oscar said, "what's up, boss?"

Oscar had called me boss ever since he started working part-time for Cherokee Investigations. I preferred it to Mr. Youngblood, at least. All attempts to get Oscar to call me Don had failed. Actually, few people called me Don except for Mary, Lacy, Gretchen, Stanley Johns, and Wanda Jones. I was Blood (to Billy, Big Bob Wilson, and Scott Glass), boss (to Oscar), gumshoe (to Roy), Donald (to Joseph Fleet and T. Elbert), cowboy (to Rollie Ogle and sometimes Mary, when she was in a playful mood), and Mr. Youngblood (to Doris Black). It was a wonder I knew who I was.

"Surveillance," I said.

I handed Oscar the file on Jerry Block and told him about the possible scam. "He lives in an apartment complex out on the highway to Newport," I said. "It shouldn't be too hard to pick him up and follow him. Bring the camera with the telephoto lens and the miniature camcorder. Try to take some incriminating pictures. Buy a newspaper and get the date on camera while you're recording Jerry, if you can."

"No problem," Oscar said.

"Come in on Monday and show me what you got."

"Will do, boss," Oscar said, rising to leave.

"Nice outfit," I said. "You spend more money on clothes than I do."

"When you are a minority," Oscar said, smiling, "clothes can make the difference."

They sure don't hurt, I thought.

◆ ◆ ◆ ◆

After lunch, I did my afternoon check of the Street. The Dow was bumping eleven thousand. I checked my accounts. I had made some nice gains in the last couple of years and taken my clients along for the ride. *My net worth is obscene*, I thought. I supported various charities, owned three well-appointed residences, dined out when I wanted, drove a decent vehicle, and made hardly a dent in my bank accounts. I mostly ignored my wealth, as did Mary and Lacy. We were happy with the status quo—and the status quo by most standards was pretty good.

When the phone rang, all thoughts of money and how to spend it vanished.

"Mr. Youngblood."

I knew that low growl.

"Yes?"

"Carlo Vincente," the voice said.

4

A lunch invitation that involved a two-hour plane ride was intriguing—especially if that plane ride was on a private jet. I originally declined, but when Carlo said it concerned his granddaughter, I heard the angst in his voice. And I was a sucker for young ladies in distress. I was also too damn curious for my own good.

From thirty thousand feet, the landscape below reminded me of my childhood and the model railroad layout my father and I had worked on. From a distance, it looked perfect. Close up, not as good. I enjoyed the comforts of Carlo Vincente's corporate jet, which had picked me up at Tri-Cities Airport early that morning. The coffee was excellent, the Danish fresh, the jet well appointed, and the pilot friendly.

"Find everything you need?" he asked as he came from the cockpit.

"I assume we're on automatic pilot," I said, a bit unnerved.

He laughed. "I certainly hope so." Pilot humor.

"I'm fine," I said in answer to his question, hoping he'd return to the cockpit.

"We'll land in about an hour," he said. "The weather is clear, with unlimited visibility."

"Good," I said. *Now, go back up front*, I thought.

He smiled as if he could read my mind. "Guess I'd better see how far off course we are," he said, heading back up front.

"Good idea," I said. *This guy ought to meet Jim Doak*, I thought.

I settled in with my coffee and Danish and removed a copy of *Rocky Top News* from my briefcase. The Tennessee football team was struggling with a lack of depth. The Volunteers had led almost every game, only to fade at some point in the second half and lose four times—once on the very last play of the game. The new coach promised that help was on the way, but the Volunteer Nation was into instant gratification, and I wondered how long he would last. The basketball program was flourishing, but there was trouble in paradise, as the NCAA was sniffing around. I scanned the magazine cover to cover; finishing about the time the pilot came on the intercom and told me to fasten my seat belt for landing.

◆ ◆ ◆ ◆

We touched down at MacArthur Airport in Islip, Long Island, and taxied to a private hangar. As I came down the stairs from the jet, briefcase in hand, a familiar figure was waiting for me. I had not seen him in a few years, but he hadn't changed one bit.

"Mr. Youngblood," he said, extending his hand. "It's been awhile."

"Frankie," I said. "Please call me Don. How are things?"

"Pretty quiet," he said. "The car is over there."

He pointed to a black Lincoln Town Car. I followed him over, and he opened the rear driver's side door.

"I can sit in front," I said.

"Mr. Vincente wouldn't like it," he said. "And he wouldn't like it if I called you Don. I'm supposed to treat you with the utmost respect."

I nodded, got in the back, and scooted to the right side. The partition that separated passenger from driver was open. The limo pulled smoothly away from the hangar. Frankie exited the airport, found the Southern State Parkway, and headed east.

"How's Gino?" I asked. Frankie had been with Gino the first time we met. Unfortunately for Gino, I had broken his nose. I later redeemed myself, but I didn't think Gino had ever forgiven me.

"He's fine," Frankie said. "Works in the city now."

"How's the nose?"

Frankie laughed. "It bothers him sometimes," he said. "When it does, he curses you. 'That fuckin' Youngblood,' he says."

"Sorry to hear that."

"Not to worry," Frankie said. "He's mostly kidding."

We talked sports, the universal male language, most of the way. Frankie was a Giants fan, and the Giants were having a mediocre year. He loved their quarterback but hated their coach. Fans are fickle—especially fans of winners, and most especially New York fans. It hadn't been long since the Giants won the Super Bowl.

We continued east into the Hamptons, passing Bridgehampton, then East Hampton.

"Are we going to Montauk?" I asked.

"Amagansett," Frankie said.

A few minutes later, we turned off the main road and headed south toward the ocean. We took a left on a road that paralleled the water, then a right into a driveway that led to a recently built house on a premium piece of beachfront property. We parked in front of a three-car garage.

"Nice house," I said.

"Thirty-five hundred square feet, five bedrooms, six and a half baths, and lots of goodies, including a theater," Frankie said. "Acre and a half of beachfront, nineteen and a half mil. I have a room on the first floor."

"Sweet deal," I said, just to say something. Frankie's pride in his boss's house was obvious.

"Yeah, it'd be worth thirty mil on the market," Frankie said. "Somebody owed Mr. Vincente."

I nodded.

"But don't say I said anything," he added hurriedly.

"Not a word," I said.

Frankie got out of the Town Car. I waited as he came around the back and opened my door. I had been well trained by Roy Husky. I picked up my briefcase and got out.

"Follow me," Frankie said.

I followed Frankie around the left side of the house to a walkway with a few steps. Frankie rang the doorbell, then opened the door and allowed me to enter first.

We waited a few seconds in the foyer before the man himself appeared. He was a little shorter than I; trim, with a full head of salt-and-pepper hair. *Attractive and deadly*, I thought.

"Mr. Youngblood," he said. "Welcome to my home."

"Thanks for the invitation," I said. "I assume it's not entirely a social occasion."

"You assume correctly," Carlo Vincente said. "Follow me. We'll join the others."

The others were an attractive silver-haired older woman, the wife; a dark-haired, dark-eyed man in his early forties, the son-in-law; and a good-looking raven-haired woman, the daughter. They were sitting around the dining-room table but stood when we entered. Carlo did the introductions: the wife, Victoria; the son-in-law, Anthony Capelli; and the daughter, Cynthia.

The dining room was spacious. A big picture window looked out over the dunes to the ocean. The ceiling was high. A chandelier hung over a table that would easily seat ten.

"We need you to locate someone," Carlo said.

"Our dumb-ass daughter," Anthony said.

"Anthony," Cynthia said, annoyed.

"Well, she is," Anthony said.

"Be quiet, Anthony," Carlo growled. "I did not invite Mr. Youngblood here to listen to a family squabble about the intelligence of my granddaughter."

Anthony went silent. I also remained quiet.

"We haven't heard from my granddaughter in a couple of weeks," Carlo said. "She is a sophomore at Palm Beach Atlantic University but informed us recently that she was taking some time off and for us not to worry. She is probably with her boyfriend."

"The little wetback," Anthony said.

Carlo shot Anthony a look.

"Mexican?" I asked, looking at Carlo.

"No," Carlo said. "Freddie is from a prominent South American family. Ecuador. His father is a man of means. I think my granddaughter is in love."

"Love," Anthony snorted. "What does she know about love?"

"A heck of a lot more than you do," Cynthia said quietly.

Anthony's face reddened.

"Enough," Carlo said as he stood. "Mr. Youngblood and I are going to my study."

The family meeting was abruptly over.

I picked up my briefcase and followed Carlo down a hall to a spacious corner room that also looked out on the ocean. Carlo's study reminded me of Joseph Fleet's, minus the fireplace.

"Sorry about all that," he said. "Everyone has a different opinion. Anthony would have the boyfriend whacked. My wife says to stay out of it and it will blow over. My daughter just wants to make sure Regina is all right. I am in the same camp as my daughter."

"What do you want from me?" I asked.

"Find my granddaughter and let her know we're worried and need to hear from her," Carlo said. "Let her know that I'll handle her father if she stays in touch. He's the problem, of course."

"What makes you think Anthony won't hire a private investigator on his own?" I asked.

Carlo smiled. "He knows things would not go well for him if he did."

I understood.

"Why me?"

"I know I can trust you, and I know you'll tell me the truth even if you think I won't like it," he said. "You'd be surprised how many people tell me what they think I want to hear."

I probably wouldn't, I thought.

"And I know you have a place on Singer Island," he continued. "I figured you know the area pretty well."

Lunch arrived—a small filet mignon, mashed potatoes with gravy, and broccoli with a white cheddar cheese sauce. We carried on a casual conversation about business, the stock market, the economy, and my latest big case, the Three Devils. I knew Carlo was giving me time to think over his request.

"You made the news awhile back," he said.

"Much to my dismay."

"You got a lot of credit for cracking that serial-killer case," Carlo said. "Saved a girl's life, they said. Made me proud I know you."

"Geez," I said. "I hope I'm not blushing."

Carlo laughed. "You don't appear to be."

We were silent while the lunch dishes were removed. Coffee was served, along with a small slice of carrot cake—one of my favorites. I wondered if Carlo had a hidden camera in my kitchen.

"What can you tell me about Palm Beach Atlantic University?" I asked.

"Nothing," Carlo said. "I've never been there."

"Who initially took your granddaughter to school?"

"Cynthia," Carlo said.

"Can I speak with her?"

Carlo picked up a walkie-talkie on his desk and pressed the transmit button. "Frankie," he growled.

"Yeah, boss," I heard Frankie say.

"Tell Cynthia to join Mr. Youngblood and me in the study," Carlo said.

"Right away, boss."

◆ ◆ ◆ ◆

About the time we finished dessert Cynthia joined us.

I looked at Carlo. "Leave us, please," I said.

"You are a ball-breaker," Carlo said, smiling. He excused himself.

Cynthia took a chair opposite me. She seemed at ease. "My father likes you," she said. "He says you cannot be intimidated. He respects that."

"I think your father values the truth," I said.

"Very much."

Not wanting to talk about Carlo, I took another sip of coffee and moved on. "Does your daughter live on campus?" I asked.

"Yes," Cynthia said. "She lives at the Lakeview Apartments. They aren't hard to find."

"Roommates?"

"Yes," she said. "One."

I waited. She was silent.

"Roommate's name?" I prodded.

"Oh," she said, embarrassed. "Of course. Sorry. Angela Bennett. She's from Melbourne, Florida."

"Boyfriend's name?"

"Fernando Destruge," Cynthia said. "They call him Freddie. A nice young man. She brought him home this summer to meet us. Very handsome. Wonderful manners."

"Do you think your daughter is in trouble?" I asked.

"No," she said. "But Freddie might be."

"Why?"

"When I pressed Regina about leaving school, she said she had to help Freddie with something. She was vague and I thought maybe a little scared."

"When was the last time you spoke with her?"

"Last week," Cynthia said. "She promised to call once a week if I didn't push her on where she was and what she was doing."

"Have you tried to call her?"

"No," she said. "Regina told me not to. She said her cell phone was off most of the time."

"Do you ever text her?"

"No," she said. "I don't even know how to send text messages."

I smiled at that. I could text, but it was a painful process. Lacy, on the other hand, could text under the table with one hand while eating with the other and carrying on a conversation with Mary and me. Technology had passed me by.

◆ ◆ ◆ ◆

I sat in Carlo's study drinking the last of my tepid coffee. Cynthia had departed, and Carlo had returned. Outside, the wind was picking up and blowing sand around the dunes. Clouds were moving in. It was a cool day for October. I knew Carlo was waiting for an answer. He sat patiently behind his desk.

"Regina Capelli," I said finally.

Carlo nodded.

"You have pictures of your granddaughter and her boyfriend, I presume."

Carlo retrieved a letter-sized manila envelope from a drawer and slid it across his desk toward me. I picked it up and put it in my briefcase.

"I'd like her cell-phone number," I said.

Without a word, Carlo wrote it on a notepad, ripped the top sheet off, and handed it to me. I folded the sheet and slipped it into my shirt pocket.

"I'll see what I can do," I said, though I had no idea why I wanted to help a mob boss. "It might take a day or two for me to get down there. I'll give it a week, and then I have to get back to another case I'm working on."

Carlo Vincente smiled. "A week should be enough for a man of your skills," he said. "And the sooner you get started, the better."

"You'll be billed," I said.

"I would expect to be," he said. "Stay in touch, Mr. Youngblood."

◆ ◆ ◆ ◆

I was back in Mountain Center in time for dinner.

"Long way to go for lunch." Mary said after we finished eating.

"Carlo had carrot cake for dessert," I said, as if to justify the trip.

Mary wasn't happy about my involvement with Carlo Vincente. Lacy was in her room doing homework or sending text messages or talking on her cell phone. Mary and I sat at the kitchen bar and shared the last of a bottle of very good red zinfandel, old vine. Still full from lunch, I'd found room for only a Caesar salad at dinner.

"So, are you going to help Carlo Vincente?" she said, already knowing the answer.

I shrugged. "Might as well. It'll be more interesting than the Crane case. I don't think that's going anywhere. Besides, I can stay at the condo."

Mary frowned. This conversation was not going well. *Think, Youngblood.*

"Maybe Tom and Suzanne would let Lacy stay with them, and you can come with me," I said.

The frown disappeared. "You're pretty smart for a private eye," Mary said.

"Smart has nothing to do with it," I said. "I'd just rather be with you, that's all."

"How sweet," Mary said. "I'm touched."

I smiled. Score one for the home team.

"I'll call Suzanne," she said. "If she says okay, you clear it with Big Bob."

"Deal," I said.

"To Florida," Mary said, raising her glass.

5

"I know you," Big Bob said. "You want something."

Besides being the Mountain Center chief of police and my close friend, Big Bob Wilson was Mary's boss.

Suzanne, of course, had said yes to letting Lacy spend a few days with Hannah, so I had invited Big Bob to breakfast at the Mountain Center

Diner, my treat. I knew my invitation would raise a red flag, but breakfast at the diner would put the big man in a benevolent mood.

I smiled. "You're such a cynic. Can't a friend ask a friend to breakfast without having an ulterior motive?"

I was doing serious damage to a feta cheese omelet with home fries and rye toast.

"What is it?" Big Bob said, ignoring my comment and forking in a mouthful of French toast.

Stalling for time, I took a healthy bite of home fries and ate some toast. "I want Mary to go with me to Florida for a few days to help me with a case," I said finally.

"A case," he said with a hint of sarcasm.

I nodded and drank some coffee.

"When?"

"As soon as possible," I said.

"How long?"

"A few days," I said. "A week at the most."

"A week," he snorted. The French toast was disappearing fast. "What's this about?"

"A grandfather is worried about his granddaughter and wants me to look into it," I said. "It shouldn't take long." I dared not mention that the grandfather was a semi-retired New York mob boss.

Big Bob inhaled a slice of bacon. Nibbling was not in his gene pool. "Need some time away from the teenager, I'll bet."

"Nothing like that," I said. "Lacy's fine."

"Lucky you," he said.

Big Bob's teenage sons were a handful, like their father used to be. It didn't help that their dad was the chief of police. He took a long drink of coffee and stared at me. I had known him a long time and understood all the signs. I waited.

"Yeah, go ahead," he said. "And have some fun while you're at it."

"Thanks," I said.

"And no longer than a week," he growled, trying hard not to look like a pushover.

◆ ◆ ◆ ◆

Later that morning, I went to see Wanda Jones. My best female friend other than Mary and a long-ago one-night stand, Wanda was, thankfully, in her office and not cutting someone open.

"Well, well," she said when I walked in, "the famous Mountain Center private detective."

I didn't get the usual kiss and flirtatious attitude. It dawned on me that I hadn't seen Wanda in a while.

"What, no kiss? No come-on?"

"A thing of the past," Wanda said, staying safely behind her desk. "You're out of circulation, an old married man."

"Not that old," I said.

"How's your sex life?" Wanda asked.

"You tell me," I said.

Wanda and Mary shared lunch about once a week and had become best of friends. Mary could be jealous but for some reason didn't feel that way toward Wanda, who was probably the second-best-looking woman in Mountain Center—after my wife.

"Pretty good, I hear," Wanda said.

"Uh-huh," I said, dismissing the subject. "Tell me about the body."

"You're no fun," Wanda said. "I worked on Walter Crane last night, read the reports, opened him up, and didn't find a damn thing. He shouldn't be dead."

"Blood work?"

"I'm having some tests done by a friend of mine at the CDC," she said. "It'll take awhile. The tests won't be high on his list of priorities, but I stimulated his curiosity, and that should be enough to get him going."

"Old boyfriend?"

"Someone I knew in med school," Wanda said.

"And you slept with him, probably once, and he's doing you a favor hoping to get lucky again."

Wanda laughed. "You sure have an active imagination."

I could tell she wasn't in the mood for our usual banter, so I moved on. "What do you think about Walter?"

"I don't know any more than anyone else," Wanda said. "If he was murdered, it was something exotic—a deadly, untraceable poison that was probably ingested. Some poisons out there, two or three drops in a drink will kill you in a minute or two."

"If a poison was put in liquid, how long would its efficacy last?" I asked.

"Efficacy," Wanda said, smiling. "Fancy word for a private eye."

"I'm very well read," I countered smugly. "Answer the question."

"Well, that would depend on the poison," Wanda said. "Could be indefinite, or it could dissipate in a matter of hours. Many new poisons have been discovered recently. And there are all kinds of urban legends about deadly, fast-acting poisons from tropical jungles around the world. If it was an exotic poison, we might never know which one."

"Could he just have died for no reason?"

"There is always a reason," Wanda said. "But a small percentage of deaths each year go unexplained."

"Pardon the pun," I said as I stood to leave, "but I seem to be at a dead end."

"Welcome to the club," Wanda said. "I'm always at a dead end."

"Call me if anything shows up in the blood work."

"I'll do that," she said.

I turned and headed out her door.

"Don," she said, stopping me in my tracks. "Do you have any reason to believe this was not a death from natural causes?"

I shook my head. "Not yet. Right now, all I've got is the intuition of a grieving widow."

◆ ◆ ◆ ◆

Only two banks were in downtown Mountain Center, and they were right across the street from each other—the Mountain National Bank and the Harrison National Bank, which was one flight down on the first floor of my building. Mountain National used to be below me but had moved across the street a few years ago, and Harrison National had moved in. My investigation of Walter Crane had to start somewhere, so that afternoon I took the stairs down to the first floor to see Ted Booth.

Ted, the president of Harrison National Bank, had a few years on me. He grew up in Mountain Center, attended the University of Tennessee, came back home, and took a job as a teller at the bank. Over the years, he had worked his way up to president, proving that patience and hard work could still pay off. He had prematurely gray hair, wore wire-rim glasses, and looked every part of his title.

"You need to come upstairs sometime," I said. "I make good coffee."

Ted smiled. He was a soft-spoken man with a good sense of humor. "If someone saw me in your office, they'd think I was in trouble," he said. "You know how people love to gossip."

"You're probably right," I said. "That would be big news in Mountain Center."

"I'm pretty sure this is not a social call," Ted said. "What can I do for you?"

"Did you hear about Walter Crane?" I asked.

"Terrible," Ted said. "A heart attack at his age."

"Did you know him?"

"Not well," Ted said. "The area bank presidents used to get together once a quarter for dinner. We called ourselves the Association of East Tennessee Bank Presidents. We quit meeting when the economy went south. We'd drink some good wine, eat some good food, have a few laughs, and call it business—completely deductible, of course."

"Of course."

"Walter always came. I talked to him several times. Nice enough guy."

"Did you ever meet his wife?"

"No, but I knew who she was," Ted said. "Walter married well, rich man's daughter. Her father owned the bank and a lot more. She was older than Walter."

"Any rumors floating around your group about him?" I asked. "Affairs, scandals, anything like that?"

"No," Ted said. "Bankers tend not to gossip. We have to worry about confidentiality so much that it carries over into our social lives." He paused as if he just had an epiphany. "Why are you asking me all this? Are you working a case?"

"Confidentially?"

Ted nodded.

"His wife doesn't think he had a heart attack," I said.

"Oh, my," Ted said.

6

Monday morning, we sat on the balcony of our Singer Island condo drinking coffee and watching the sun try to come up. We had flown in the day before on the Fleet jet, which was usually available on weekends.

The sun was having trouble penetrating the mostly cloudy sky. The weather forecast wasn't doing it any favors. A Category 2 hurricane far out in the Atlantic was stirring things up, and the predictions were for more clouds, high surf, and wind. The hurricane did not threaten Florida but had a chance to nip the Outer Banks of North Carolina. The wind was blowing Mary's hair. She had let it grow longer and had it in a ponytail that danced back and forth. I found the look extremely sexy.

She looked at me, and I smiled. "What?" she said.

"You're a damn fine-looking woman, Mrs. Youngblood," I said in my best Irish brogue.

"Thank you, Mr. Youngblood."

I was still amazed that my path in life had intersected hers, and that we had connected, fallen in love, and gotten married. Blind luck or destiny—that was the million-dollar question. Destiny, I decided. *You're a closet romantic, Youngblood*, I thought.

"What's the plan?" Mary asked, breaking the spell.

"Breakfast at Southern Kitchen and then a trip to Palm Beach Atlantic University," I said.

"Want to work up an appetite before breakfast?" Mary asked.

"You bet," I said without hesitation.

◆ ◆ ◆ ◆

Two hours later, well loved and well fed, we sat in our rented Lincoln Navigator in the parking lot of the Lakeview Apartments, where Regina Capelli had until recently resided on the third floor. We had decided that Mary would try to question the roommate about Regina's whereabouts. Mary would play the role of friend of the family. I would sit in the Navigator playing the role of impatient husband and listening to sports talk radio. College football was in midseason, so there was plenty to talk about in Florida.

"Try not to scare the coeds," Mary said as she got out of the car.

I watched her walk toward the apartment entrance. She was wearing white slacks, a lime-green top, and white two-inch heels with multiple straps. The sight of her made me take a deep breath. I found the ESPN network and waited. I heard an interview with Beano Cook, then another with Lou Holtz. I waited some more—a good sign. Mary must have found someone to talk to.

A half-hour later, she came out and got back in the Navigator.

"Any luck?"

"Some," she said.

"Tell me."

"I found Angela Bennett," Mary said. "She was just out of the shower, so I waited. She was cautious at first, but the bottom line is that she thinks the boyfriend, Freddie, is in trouble. I told her my husband's a big, bad private investigator who might be able to help if I knew what kind of trouble. Then she told me Freddie likes to gamble on pro football and may be unable to pay off a recent loss."

"Gambling," I said. "I was hoping it might be something easy, like they eloped."

"Whatever you choose to get involved in is never easy," Mary reminded me.

"True," I said. "Anyway, good work. Anything else?"

"According to Angela, Freddie and Regina are real good tennis players. They've played mixed doubles in some amateur tournaments and have won a couple. They practice at a public park in Jupiter. Freddie teaches lessons there sometimes. Angela was happy to give me directions."

"Which I'll be glad to follow," I said, starting the engine.

7

We slowly cruised into the parking lot for the public tennis courts in Jupiter's Carlin Park. To our left was a large pond. To our right were six hard-surfaced courts fenced off in groups of two. Only one of the courts was occupied. Two young Hispanic-looking men were having a long rally, hitting lots of topspin, and moving freely on the court closest to the parking lot. We pulled into a spot near the fence that separated us from the players.

"Did you get a description of Freddie?"

"Of course," Mary said as we watched the action.

"Well?"

"Over six feet tall, slender, dark, and good looking," Mary said.

"Sounds like me."

"Darker than you," Mary said. "And *much* younger."

The point was finally won by the bigger of the two players, neither of whom was Freddie Destruge, since the taller one couldn't have been over five-foot-eight.

"Your turn to wait," I said to Mary as I got out of the Navigator. "If they attack me with their rackets, shoot 'em."

Mary laughed. "You bet."

I walked to the fence and waited for the next point to end. Tennis etiquette.

"Hey, guys," I said. "Either of you seen Freddie Destruge? He's supposed to give me a lesson later today, but I can't make it."

They looked at each other as if I might be an immigration agent and then cautiously approached the fence.

"*This man does not look like he is after tennis lessons*," the taller one said to the smaller one. "*Maybe he is working with the same men who have been looking for Fernando the last couple of weeks*." He spoke Spanish, oblivious to the fact that I understood every word. I played dumb.

"We haven't seen Freddie in a while," the taller one said in very good English.

"How long?" I asked.

"Maybe two weeks," he said.

I nodded and tried to look concerned. I made a decision. When in doubt, go with the truth. I removed my private investigator ID from my shirt pocket.

"I don't really want tennis lessons," I said, holding up the ID. "The grandfather of Freddie's girlfriend hired me to find his granddaughter,

Regina. I think she could be with Freddie, and I think Freddie could be in trouble. If he is in trouble, I think I can help."

They looked at each other.

"*Think we can trust him*?" the taller one asked.

"*I do not know*," the smaller one said. "*It is up to you. I do think Fernando could use some help.*"

"Who is the lady in your automobile?" the taller one asked.

"My wife," I said. "She's a police officer. She's helping me with this case."

They exchanged glances, not sure what to do next.

I decided to help them along. "If bad men are looking for Freddie, they'll find him sooner or later," I said. "If they do, he could be badly hurt."

The taller one looked at the smaller one, who nodded.

"Two men have come here every day for two weeks looking for Freddie or Regina," the taller one said. "I think he owes them money."

"Why do you think that?" I asked.

"Freddie says he likes to gamble," the taller one said.

"He must not be very good at it," the smaller one said with a nervous laugh. His English was not so good.

"Why would they be looking for Regina?" I asked.

"I think Regina places the bets for Freddie," the taller one said.

"What do these men look like?" I asked.

"One is Hispanic, and one is black," the taller one said. "As tall as you are, and not friendly looking."

"What kind of vehicle do they drive?"

"A gray car," the taller one said.

"Expensive," the smaller one said. "A BMW, maybe."

"What time have these guys been showing up?" I asked.

"Around five o'clock," the taller one said. "When the courts are usually all occupied."

"Thanks," I said. "Don't mention I was here."

"We will not," the taller one said. "We hope you can help Freddie."

The smaller one smiled and nodded.

◆ ◆ ◆ ◆

"What did you find out?" Mary asked when I was back in the Navigator.

I recounted my conversation with taller and smaller.

"So we come back later today and see if we can get a line on these guys," Mary said.

"We do," I said.

"What do we do between now and then?"

I gave her my best leering smile.

"No," she said, hitting me on the shoulder. "The next time I get undressed will be tonight for bed."

"Fine," I said. "I can wait until then."

"That was not an invitation," Mary said, laughing.

I shrugged. *Can't blame a guy for trying.* "So now what?" I asked.

"I have a grocery list," Mary said. "Take me to the market."

We drove out of the tennis court parking lot and went south on State Route A1A, moving leisurely at the thirty-five-miles-per-hour speed limit. The day was bright and cloudless. Runners, walkers, and rollerblade babes sprinkled the oceanside sidewalk on our left. Houses and condos abounded to our right. Mary read her grocery list aloud, and I added a couple of things I couldn't get back in Mountain Center. I watched as a well-built roller babe cruised by. She was blond, tall, lean, and well proportioned.

"Want to turn around for another look?" Mary said.

"I was looking at the ocean," I said.

"You can't see the ocean for the vegetation," Mary said sharply.

"Correction," I said. "I was *trying* to look at the ocean."

"Uh-huh."

I drove to a traffic light where A1A ran into U.S. 1, turned left, and continued south to the Oakbrook Market. I made a left into the parking lot and found a shady spot to park.

"I may be awhile," Mary said. "You listen to the radio and be a good boy. Try not to wear out your eyes on the scenery."

I watched her as she headed into the market and smiled to myself. *You did okay, Youngblood*, I thought. I dialed in ESPN Radio and sat back and listened to sports babble while my eyes followed a parade of proud, good-looking women going in and out of the market. They had lots to be proud of and didn't mind putting it on display. They wore a variety of shorts, jeans, halter-tops, bikini tops, and, invariably, high heels. *High heels in a grocery store. Can somebody please explain that one to me?* I thought.

◆ ◆ ◆ ◆

Mary was gone almost an hour. Meanwhile, I called Jessica Crane. A woman who was not Jessica Crane answered the phone. It took a few minutes, but I finally got Jessica on the line.

"Our medical examiner, Wanda Jones, took a look at Walter's body and autopsy report and agreed with the initial findings," I said. "She's going to carry the blood work a step farther. I'll let you know what she finds. You may have Walter's body picked up any time."

"Thank you, Mr. Youngblood," she said. "I'll proceed with the arrangements."

"I need to interview the people Walter worked with," I said. "Can you tell me where to start?"

"Why do you need to do that?"

"If Walter's death wasn't an accident, then someone went to a great deal of trouble to make it look like one. Walter's workplace is the logical place to start asking questions."

There was silence on the other end of the line. I could feel her resolve being tested. Maybe she was changing her mind about my digging into Walter's life.

"Mrs. Crane," I said, "if I'm going to do this, I have to do it my way. I may have to dig into Walter's past. I may have to ask you some personal questions. If you're not up to that, then I suggest you be satisfied that Walter died of a heart attack and move on with your life."

More silence. I thought the line might have gone dead.

"Mrs. Crane?"

"I'm here," she said.

I waited.

"Walter did not die of a heart attack," she said firmly.

"You may be right," I said. "So do I pursue it or forget it?"

She paused again. I was betting she wouldn't back off.

"Allan Wilton, vice president," she said. "I'll call and tell him to cooperate fully. When can I tell him to expect you?"

"Probably next week," I said. "I'm in Florida working on something that requires my immediate attention. Tell Mr. Wilton I'll call for an appointment when I get back."

"Next week," Jessica Crane said, sounding annoyed. "I was really hoping you could start sooner."

"If you need to hire someone else, I'll understand," I said.

"That's okay," she said. "Sorry to be pushy. Just get to it as soon as you can."

"I'll do that."

"Very well," Jessica Crane said. "And I'll email you Allan Wilton's address."

"Thank you," I said. "I'll call you for an appointment after I've seen Mr. Wilton. Email me your home address. It wasn't on your business card."

"Do you need directions?" she asked.

"No," I said. "I have a very annoying GPS."

8

We sat in the Navigator in a parking lot on the other side of the pond at Carlin Park, where we had a good view of the tennis courts. We had been there a half-hour when a silver BMW pulled in and parked. A tall, slender Hispanic-looking man in a nice suit got out of the passenger side. He proceeded down a walkway between the courts, looking from side to side. Five of the six courts were occupied. Seemingly satisfied that Freddie Destruge was not one of the players, he turned and walked back toward the BMW, slowly shaking his head. Moments later, the BMW pulled out on A1A, heading south. I followed.

The BMW went to the first light and took a right. A left at the next light put us south on Route 1. I kept a reasonable distance but didn't try not to be spotted.

"You want them to make us?" Mary asked.

"Couldn't hurt," I said. "I want them curious."

The BMW went past the market where I had spent an hour in the lot waiting for Mary, then crossed PGA Boulevard. We crossed a short drawbridge and watched as the BMW turned right into North Palm Beach Country Club. I followed. The BMW parked in front of the tennis complex. The Hispanic man got out and went inside the clubhouse. A couple minutes later, he came out and got back in the BMW. As they drove past us, the Hispanic man gave us a long look.

"I think we've been made," Mary said.

"Seems so," I said. "Let's be sure."

I followed, staying a little closer this time, as the BMW continued south. When we reached Blue Heron Boulevard, I took a left and headed back to the condo. The BMW continued south on Route 1.

"Is the game over for today?" Mary asked.

"It is."

"You sure know how to show a girl a good time."

"And the evening's still young," I said.

◆ ◆ ◆ ◆

We had drinks on the balcony overlooking the ocean. Tailing thugs made me thirsty. The sun would soon set, and the soft light of late afternoon brought a peaceful feel to our cocktail hour. The breeze was light, the air warm, and the humidity low. *If I had to be trapped in time,* I thought, *it couldn't get much better than this.*

An hour passed. We said little. We looked at each other from time to time and smiled, connecting without speaking. When words fail to describe what you are experiencing or feeling, it is best to remain silent. As the light receded, I knew this special time was almost up.

"We need to call Lacy," Mary said, breaking the spell.

"We do," I said.

I talked to Lacy for maybe three minutes. When I couldn't think of anything else to say, I passed my cell phone to Mary. They talked for half an hour in earnest detail. I heard my stomach growl. I feigned passing out, and Mary took the hint and wrapped up the conversation.

"Let's go to Johnny Longboats," she said. "I love their grouper in a bag."

"Let's do," I said, remembering my fondness for the fish and chips.

9

We sat in the same spot as the day before, looking across the pond at Carlin Park and hoping the BMW would show up again. The radio was on a country-music station; the volume turned down so low we could barely hear it. Mary was reading the latest *Southern Living*. Every now and then, she read a recipe aloud to get my opinion. I was attentive, remembering how good the food was last night. After dinner, we had enjoyed a long walk on the beach. Taking advantage of being teenager-free, we made love before falling into a long, restful sleep. *Twice in one day, Youngblood,* I thought. *You still got it.*

"What's that smile about?" Mary asked.

"Was I smiling?"

"From ear to ear."

"Just thinking," I said.

"About last night?"

"Maybe," I said.

"Last night was special," Mary said.

I had no witty response for that. No wisecrack. No flip comeback.

"It was," I said.

I have no idea how long we sat there in smiling silence.

◆ ◆ ◆ ◆

"Call from Wanda Jones," announced my cell phone in a very feminine electronic voice.

I reached, but Mary beat me to it.

"Cherokee Investigations," she answered professionally. "Yes, it's me. I'm keeping an eye on him, making sure he's a good boy."

Laugh.

Pause.

"No, not this week," Mary said. "I'm out of town with the big, bad private eye."

Short pause.

"Oh, yeah," Mary said. "Plenty."

Laugh.

"I will. Hold on."

Mary handed the phone to me and smiled.

"What are you up to?" Wanda asked.

"Surveillance," I said.

"Is that what they're calling it these days?" Wanda asked.

"No, really," I said. "We're on a stakeout waiting for some bad guys to show up."

"My friend at the CDC finally called back," Wanda said. "He found something in Walter's blood but has no idea what it is. Unidentifiable."

"Poison?"

"He doesn't know," she said. "Could be. He's going to send a sample to a friend of his who works at a research lab in California to see if they can duplicate it. He'll get back to me."

"How long?"

"Who knows?" Wanda said.

I watched as the silver BMW drove into the lot across the lake and parked in the same spot as the day before.

"Got to go, Wanda," I said. "The bad guys just showed up."

"You two be careful, Don," Wanda said.

"Don't worry about us," I said. "We'll be fine. Call me if you find out anything else."

I disconnected.

◆ ◆ ◆ ◆

This time, a well-dressed black man exited the BMW, did a sweep of the courts, did not find Freddie Destruge, and went back to the car. The BMW drove out of the parking lot and took the same route it had yesterday. Again, we followed.

"These guys are well dressed for collectors," Mary said.

"I noticed. Think they could be cops?"

"I doubt it," Mary said. "But it is curious."

Twenty minutes later, we were sitting in the North Palm Beach Country Club parking lot, facing the tennis courts and trying hard to be noticed. Our efforts were rewarded. As the BMW pulled out and passed us, it slowed, and the black man on the passenger side gave us a long look. I waved. The BMW sped out of the lot, heading south on Route 1, and I followed at a reasonable distance. At Blue Heron Boulevard, I turned left and headed back to our condo on Singer Island.

"How long are we going to play this little game?" Mary asked.

"One more day should do it, I think."

10

The next afternoon, Mary and I bypassed Carlin Park and went straight to the North Palm Beach Country Club. I figured we had a lesser chance of trouble at a busier place. I backed in courtside so I could face the entrance. If the two men in the BMW came to the tennis clubhouse, they would have to drive right toward me. We sat for a while. My cell phone rang. Caller ID told me it was Jessica Crane. Maybe she had news, or maybe she was getting impatient. I let the call go to voice mail. She did not leave a message.

Twenty minutes after we parked, I saw the BMW make the right turn off Route 1 into the club and head our way.

"Wait here," I said to Mary.

"Why do you get to have all the fun?"

"My case," I said as I got out. "You're here for backup—and other stuff."

I thought I heard an epithet as I closed the door, but it could have been the wind. I watched as the BMW pulled into a space opposite ours. I waited for someone to get out. No one did. I waited some more.

Finally, both the men I had seen before got out and walked casually toward me.

I gave them my friendliest smile. "Gentlemen," I said, nodding.

"You seem to be following us," the black man said, taking a wide stance, arms folded across his chest. "Why?"

"I like your car," I said. "Just wanted to know where you got it."

"He likes our car, Henry," the black man said to his Hispanic partner.

"So do we," Henry said.

"What else?" the black man asked, all business. Evidently, he had no sense of humor.

"I hear you're looking for Freddie Destruge," I said.

"What if we are?" the black man said. "No law against it."

"I'm not the police," I said. "But I work for someone who wants to find him more than you do." *Well, not actually Freddie,* I thought. *Freddie's girlfriend.*

"They must want him really bad if they want him more than we do," Henry said.

"How much does he owe?" I asked.

"Who said he owes anything?" the black man said.

"Common knowledge," I said. "I might be able to collect for you."

"We should call the boss, Morgan," Henry said.

"Shut up, Henry," Morgan said.

"Finding people is my business," I said to Morgan, handing him my card. "Sooner or later, I'll find Freddie. If you're interested in getting paid, give me a call. You've got twenty-four hours."

I turned around, got back in the Navigator, and started the engine. The two men backed away as I pulled out. In the rearview mirror, I saw Morgan studying my business card.

◆ ◆ ◆ ◆

Soon afterward, Mary and I went for a twilight beach walk. The temperature was in the mid-seventies, and a light breeze was coming off the Atlantic. Casually holding hands, we walked south toward Palm Beach Shores on hard sand at the water's edge. I wore shorts and a T-shirt. Mary wore shorts and a halter-top that drew surreptitious glances from male passersby. We were barefooted. Occasionally, the tide rolled in a little farther than we anticipated and doused our feet, a not unpleasant sensation.

Mary was uncharacteristically quiet.

"What's on your mind?" I asked.

"What makes you think something's on my mind?"

"You usually have things to say," I said.

"Just thinking," Mary said.

"About what?"

"My life," she said. "Since I met you."

I stopped, picked up a piece of well-worn green sea glass, and slipped it in the left pocket of my shorts.

"What about it?" I asked as we resumed walking.

"I've known you only a few years, but it seems like all my life," Mary said. "At the same time, it seems like only yesterday I was here rehabbing from being shot. It's very confusing."

"I guess when you're in love, time gets distorted," I said.

She stopped and pulled me toward her and gave me a deep, passionate kiss, which I returned with gusto.

"I love you," she said. "You're such a hopeless romantic."

"Interesting," I said as we continued our stroll. "I see myself as a pragmatist."

"That, too," Mary said, laughing. "But you're evolving into a hopeless romantic."

"Hopeless doesn't sound good," I said.

"It was a compliment, silly."

The beach was less crowded as the day grew dimmer. We walked in silence. When we had gone a couple of miles, we turned and headed back. By the time we sat on the balcony of our condo, drinking a nice white wine, the Atlantic was black. We could hear the surf below but couldn't see it.

"I wish I met you sooner," Mary said.

"No you don't," I said.

"Why?"

"What about Jimmy and Susan?" I asked. "Would you be willing to give them up?"

"No, of course not," Mary said.

"Well, there you go. We met when we were supposed to meet."

"You're right," Mary said.

"And we have the rest of our lives."

"Here's to getting old and gray together," Mary said, raising her wineglass.

"And then some," I said, touching my glass to hers.

11

I was having coffee and a bagel on the balcony around eight o'clock the following morning when my cell phone rang. Mary was still in bed. She loved to stay up late and sleep in when we were at Singer. I didn't mind staying up late occasionally, but I could never sleep in. I was always up before seven.

I looked at caller ID. It wasn't whom I expected.

"You're in early," I said.

"I'm often in early when you're away," Gretchen said.

"What's new?"

"Not a lot," she said. "A couple phone calls, that's all. Jessica Crane called. Wanted to know when you'll be back."

I didn't like avoiding people, but I didn't like being pressured either. "Call her and tell her it will be a couple more days," I said.

"I'll take care of it," Gretchen said.

"What else?"

"O-man says he has the goods on Jerry Block. He said to call when you get back. He said to tell you everything worked out fine."

"That's good," I said. "I'd like to hear the details. Tell him I'll be a few more days. What else?"

"One small job," Gretchen said. "Rollie has a little snooping he wants done, so I'll put Oscar on it."

"Fine," I said. "Husband or wife?"

"Wife," Gretchen said.

"Women," I said. "Can't trust 'em."

"That hasn't been my experience," Gretchen said. She was not teasing.

"Do tell," I said. "What has been your experience?"

"That all men are rats," Gretchen said sharply.

"Not all," I said. "Anything else?"

"When will you really be back?"

"Not sure," I said. "I'm not in a big hurry."

"I can understand that," Gretchen said.

"Don't call me unless the building is on fire," I said.

"Hanging up now," she said, laughing.

◆ ◆ ◆ ◆

The call I was hoping for came forty minutes later. Caller ID read, "No data." A throwaway cell phone, I was betting.

"Youngblood," I answered.

"Mr. Youngblood," the voice said. "I have a collection problem that I understand you can help me with."

"Could be," I said. "We need to talk."

"So talk," the voice said. I heard a trace of an accent, but her English was very good.

"In person," I said.

A pause followed.

"Why?"

"I like to see who I'm dealing with," I said. "If you lie to me face to face, I'll be able to tell."

In truth, I was easily lied to by women, but it never hurt to bluff.

"A unique gift," she said. "Where would you like to meet?"

"Palm Beach Gardens Mall," I said. "Macy's side parking lot."

"Eleven o'clock," she said. "Look for a silver BMW. You've seen it before, I understand. Come alone."

"Are you coming alone?"

Another pause.

"No," she said. "Morgan will drive me."

"In that case, Mary will drive me," I said.

"Who is Mary?"

"My driver."

"Your driver is a woman?" she asked. I detected a hint of amusement in her voice.

"Yes," I said.

"Fine," she said. "Don't be late."

◆ ◆ ◆ ◆

We were early. Mary was a little surprised that I asked her to drive but resisted the urge to ask why. We sat in the shade of a tree, one of many dotting the parking lots scattered around the mall. We watched as the silver BMW parked under a nearby tree. Morgan got out and opened the back door and looked our way.

"I think you're being invited to sit in their car," Mary said.

"Seems so," I said. I pulled out my cell phone and brought up Mary's number. All I had to do was press *Send* and her phone would ring. "If I call, come get me with your gun drawn," I said.

"My pleasure," Mary said.

I exited the Navigator and walked toward Morgan. When I heard a door slam behind me, I knew Mary had gotten out of the Navigator—a show of force.

When I reached the BMW, I leaned in the driver's side back door and spied a dark-haired woman sitting on the passenger's side. She had a wide face. Her hair was shoulder length and curly. She was not beautiful, but something about her made her extremely attractive. I felt energy coming from her.

"Mr. Youngblood," she said, a hint of flirtation in her voice. "Join me, please."

I got in, and Morgan shut the door.

The woman extended her hand. "I am Alexandria," she said, now all business. Alexandria was well groomed and well dressed. Her eyes were wide-set, her lips full. She wore black slacks and a white, sleeveless, well-fitted top. She was not unpleasant to look at.

Concentrate, Youngblood, I thought.

"Donald Youngblood," I said, taking her hand. She had a firm grip.

"You think you can collect my debt?" she said. She sounded doubtful.

"I do," I said with an air of certainty. *Well, if worse comes to worst, I can pay it myself*, I thought. But I was pretty certain Carlo Vincente would take care of it if his granddaughter went back to school.

"What makes you think so?"

"Connections," I said.

"Connections are nice," Alexandria said. She had an air about her that signaled danger, as if an invisible tattoo adorned her forehead: *Not to be messed with.*

"How much does he owe?" I asked.

"Fifteen thousand dollars."

"Is that what Freddie will tell me when I find him?"

"No," she said. "Freddie will tell you ten thousand dollars. But he is late, and I have spent considerable resources trying to find him."

"Okay," I said. "Fifteen thousand, and you accept no more bets from Freddie."

She smiled. It was really more of a smirk. She was silent, staring straight ahead. "Who is the blonde?" she finally asked.

"Mary," I said.

"And who is Mary?"

"My driver," I said. "And my wife."

"Wife?" she asked, surprised. "Impressive. She is looking out for her man. I like that. Is she armed?"

"Yes," I said.

"Can she shoot?"

"Almost as well as I can."

Alexandria laughed. "Yes, I heard you can shoot."

She had checked me out. Why was I not surprised? I was all over the Internet after the Three Devils case. She probably knew Mary was a police officer.

"Do we have a deal?" I asked, a little annoyed.

"I'll give you a few days to work this out. We meet here Monday morning at eleven, you give me the cash, and I will do no more business with Fernando Destruge."

"I'll be here," I said, getting out of the BMW.

No doubt wanting to be seen, Alexandria exited the other side and leered at me over the roof of the car. She appeared to be almost as tall as Mary.

"It was nice meeting you," she said with a dazzling smile.

"Likewise," I said without much conviction.

"Morgan," Alexandria said.

Morgan got in behind the wheel, and Alexandria returned to her spot in the back. The doors slammed almost simultaneously. I heard the BMW drive away as I walked back to the Navigator.

"How'd that go?" Mary asked as she pulled out of the parking lot.

"Pretty well, I think."

"Attractive woman," Mary said. I noted something in her voice I could not quite put my finger on.

"She liked you, too," I said.

◆ ◆ ◆ ◆

We had lunch at Paddy Mac's near I-95 at PGA Boulevard. Mary ate a salad with bacon-wrapped scallops, and I had a blackened grouper sandwich with fries.

"What's your next move, Mr. Private Investigator?" Mary asked. I could tell she was having fun watching me work.

"Well, I have no leads," I said, "but I do have Regina's cell-phone number."

"You think she'll answer a call from you?"

"No," I said, "but she might answer a text message, especially if it sounds like I can solve Fernando's problem."

"You're going to text?" Mary asked, laughing.

"Sure," I said.

"Exactly how many times have you sent a text message?"

"I don't know," I said. "A few."

"I'll bet," Mary said. "Give me your phone and tell me what you want to say."

I formulated the text as Mary thumbed my keypad at an impressive pace.

When she finished, she handed the phone back to me. "How's this?" she asked.

I read the proposed text:

> Regina. My name is Donald Youngblood. Private investigator & friend of ur gfather Carlo. I know that Freddie is in trouble w/gamblers. I can help with that. U & F & I need to meet. Call me.

"Looks good," I said. "From now on, you can do all my texting."

"Send it," Mary said, "and I'll take you back to the condo for dessert."

I may not be good at texting, I thought, pressing the *Send* button, *but I know a good offer when I hear one.*

12

The next morning, we had breakfast at Johnny Longboats. I had yet to hear from Regina Capelli. Clouds were blocking the sun and rain was in the forecast, but that didn't make me any less hungry. We sat in the open facing the beach with a gentle breeze blowing in. Patrons were few, and the place was quiet. We were finishing breakfast and enjoying that final cup of coffee when my cell phone made an unfamiliar noise.

"You have a text message," Mary said.

"I do?" I looked. "New text message," the screen said. I brought up the message. It was from Regina Capelli.

How do I know I can trust u?

I handed my phone to Mary. She read the message and looked at me.

"Tell her to call her grandfather," I said.

Mary did the thumb thing. "Now what?" she asked.

"We finish our coffee," I said.

After we paid the bill and were walking toward the beach, my cell phone rang. We sat on a nearby park bench.

"Youngblood," I answered.

"Mr. Youngblood, this is Regina Capelli."

"Your family is worried about you, Regina," I said, getting straight to the point.

She responded with silence. Obviously, my opening comment was not what she expected to hear.

"I'm fine," she finally said.

"I'm glad to hear it."

"Does my family know about Freddie's trouble?" she asked.

"No," I said.

"Will they?"

"Only your grandfather," I said. "What he chooses to do with the information is up to him."

Another pause.

"How can you help us?" Regina asked.

"I can make this go away," I said. "But I'll have some stipulations."

"What stipulations?"

"We'll talk about that when I see you," I said.

"Freddie will never agree to that," she said. I heard panic in her voice.

"Then he's a fool," I said.

"I'll talk to him," she said after another pause. "I'll call you back."

◆ ◆ ◆ ◆

We spent most of the day at the beach. We had a cabana I paid for by the year. Financially, it didn't make sense, but it was convenient, and I could afford it. I gave anyone staying in my condo access. In the past year, Roy Husky, Scott Glass, and Raul Rivera had spent time there. I had tried forever to get Sister Sarah Agnes to come down and take advantage of my place in paradise, but she was always "too busy."

The clouds lingered, but the rain held off. We walked and swam. I was reading *Murder in Pleasant Grove*, a neat little mystery by a relatively unknown Virginia author, J. Russell Rose.

Late in the day, my cell phone rang.

"We'll talk with you, Mr. Youngblood," Regina Capelli said.

"When?"

"As soon as you can get here," she said.

"Where are you?"

"Sarasota."

"Okay," I said. "Let's meet for lunch tomorrow. Do you know a place?"

"I do," she said. "I'll send you a text."

◆ ◆ ◆ ◆

I called Carlo Vincente.

"Mr. Youngblood," he answered.

I need to learn how to block caller ID, I thought.

"I take it you have news," he said. "Good news, I hope."

"Well, it's not bad news," I said.

"Tell me."

"I am meeting your granddaughter and her boyfriend for lunch tomorrow," I said. "They have a problem that is fixable, and I have some suggestions."

"Tell me more," Carlo Vincente said.

I told him all of it—or at least almost all of it. I did not tell him where they were. I didn't want Carlo sending Frankie down to whack Fernando.

"I like your solution," he said. "I'll authorize the fifteen thousand if it comes to that. It may not. I'll make some calls."

The less I knew about the calls, the better, so I didn't ask.

"I'll call you tomorrow afternoon," I said.

"I'll be waiting," Carlo said. "Good work, Mr. Youngblood."

13

The next morning, we drove across the state on Route 70 toward Sarasota. The road was long, straight, flat, and almost devoid of traffic. Lightning flashed in the distance to the south; a thunderstorm was brewing. I needed to make some calls, so Mary put on earphones and listened to an audiobook on her iPod.

I called Ted Booth on his private line.

He answered almost immediately. "What can I do for you, Don?"

"I need fifteen thousand dollars in cash Monday morning. Can you make the arrangements?"

"You do realize today is Saturday," he said.

"Sorry about that, but I bet a hotshot banker like you can get this done today or first thing Monday."

"Safe bet," Ted said. "Any particular denominations?"

"Not really," I said. "Twenties or fifties will be fine. Whatever's convenient."

"Where are you?" Ted asked.

"Singer Island, Florida," I said. "Find a bank in North Palm Beach or Juno."

"Will do," he said. "I'll call as soon as I work this out and tell you where. If I don't get you, I'll leave a message and my cell-phone number in case you have any questions."

"Thanks, Ted."

"Don, I'm curious. Have you found out anything about Walter Crane?"

"Not yet, Ted. I'm going to dig into that when I get back."

"Well, I hope it wasn't foul play," Ted said. "That would be awful."

"It certainly would," I said.

◆ ◆ ◆ ◆

I was doing sixty-five in a sixty-miles-per-hour zone. If Mary were driving, she would have been going eighty. A few minutes later, I made a call to Billy. His voice mail kicked in, and I left a message.

"I'm in Florida with Mary working a case," I said. "I should be back in a few days. I'll call you in the morning."

I knew he wouldn't call back. Billy was patient. He'd wait for my morning call.

I called Roy Husky.

"Hey, gumshoe," he said. "I hear you're out of town. Gretchen was a little vague about where."

Gretchen never volunteered information unless specifically told by me to do so.

"Singer," I said.

"Sweet," Roy said. "Mary's with you, I hope."

"She is."

"Are you working something?"

"Yes," I said. "I'll tell you about it when I get back."

"Try not to get shot or beat up," Roy said.

"Mary's with me," I said. "She won't let that happen."

"You're in good hands," Roy said. "That's one woman I wouldn't want to mess with. Call me when you get back. And email T. Elbert. He's bitchin' about not hearing from you."

◆ ◆ ◆ ◆

We met at a seafood restaurant on Main Street. We were supposed to be there at noon, but Mary and I arrived early and scoped out the place. We got a corner booth and waited. The place was retro. I wondered how long it had been around.

By the time I read the comprehensive menu from top to bottom, our guests arrived. I recognized Regina Capelli from the picture Carlo Vincente had given me. I stood, smiled, and motioned them to our table. Regina was short, curvy, and had curly, dark hair. She did not return my smile. Freddie fit the description Regina's roommate had given Mary. He was not quite as tall as me, and definitely not as good-looking, but still handsome in a boyish kind of way. He was, however, younger. Well, as Meat Loaf said, "Two Out of Three Ain't Bad."

"Mr. Youngblood," Regina said. "I'm Regina Capelli, and this is Freddie Destruge."

"Fernando," he said, shaking my hand. "Freddie is my American nickname."

His English was good, but he spoke with a definite accent that I bet the ladies found charming. If he wanted to be a gigolo, he had all the tools.

"This is Mary, my wife. Please sit down. Lunch is on me."

I saw them exchange looks and smiles. I bet their funds were limited.

"That is very kind of you," Freddie said.

After we got comfortable, the waitress came and took our order. I asked for the fried oyster special. Everyone else ordered fried shrimp. I wondered if they knew something I didn't. We exchanged small talk. I didn't want to ruin lunch by talking about what an idiot Freddie was. Mary was great about carrying the conversation. She asked good questions—ones that required more than single-sentence answers. Regina and Freddie seemed to relax.

The food arrived, and conversation took a backseat. The oysters were terrific, and I heard no complaints about the shrimp. I swapped an oyster for a shrimp with Mary. We both ate our trades and nodded approval. When our plates were cleared, we all ordered coffee. I seldom drank coffee at midday, but I didn't want to fall asleep at the wheel on our return trip.

"I can fix your problem," I said to Freddie as we waited on the coffee. "But I have some conditions."

Freddie held up a hand, signaling me to stop talking. "I want to say something first," he said, looking from Mary to me. "I was an idiot. I don't know what I was thinking. The betting was exciting. At first, I won. I thought, *This is easy*. Then I started losing. Then I started betting more, trying to get even. And then I promised I would make one more big bet and then I would pay. I lost. I didn't have the money. The stress was killing me, and I was scared. So I ran, and Regina ran with me."

Freddie's little speech sounded rehearsed. Whether or not it was sincere, I couldn't tell. I looked at Regina. She seemed uncomfortable.

"He really is a good person," she said. "He just did a dumb thing."

I believed her. Or at least I believed that she believed it. Whether or not it was true, time would tell. I had no way of knowing if Freddie had learned his lesson or if he was a habitual gambler.

Freddie looked at me with puppy-dog eyes. "I don't deserve her," he said.

"No," Regina said, "I don't deserve you."

Mary and I exchanged a look. *Young love*, I thought. *God help us.*

"You finished?" I asked.

"Yes," he said.

"Okay, here's the deal. First, I'll meet with your collector and pay off your debt. The money has already been arranged."

Freddie, hand up again, interrupted. "We'll pay it all back. I don't care how long it takes."

"We will," Regina said.

"That's up to you," I said. "It's not part of the deal." I looked at Regina and then back to Freddie before continuing. "Second, no more gambling as long as you and Regina are together."

"We will always be together," Freddie said. "I love Regina. And I am through gambling. The thought of it now makes me sick."

"Next, you go to three Gamblers Anonymous meetings. There's one in North Palm Beach on Northlake Boulevard. Here's the address and phone number." I handed him a folded slip of paper. "If you do more than three meetings, that's up to you."

"I will gladly do this," he said.

"I'll go with you," Regina said.

I looked at Regina. "Finally, you return to school immediately."

"What?" Regina said, anger in her voice.

Freddie put his hand on hers and said, "Please, Regina. It is best for you. I know you do not like to be told what to do, but please, do it for me."

The anger vanished. "Agreed," she said, looking at me.

"Then we're done," I said, standing to leave.

"How will you know if we keep our part of the bargain?" Regina asked. "Will you be watching our every move?"

A parting shot from an obstinate child. Freddie had his hands full.

"We're going back where we came from," I said. "I trust you two will do what you said you'll do."

"We will keep our part of the bargain," Freddie said. "You have my word."

I nodded, and Mary got up. Regina and Freddie remained seated.

"Mr. Youngblood," Regina said as I turned to go, "where did the money come from?"

"You know where," I said.

We turned and left.

"Well played," Mary said.

◆ ◆ ◆ ◆

We headed back to Singer Island. Something about the Regina-Fernando scenario nagged me, but I couldn't quite put my finger on it. I was missing something and couldn't figure out what. I let it slip away.

I wanted to makes some calls, but my Bluetooth needed recharging. I wasn't sure about Florida law, so I let Mary drive. When I checked my cell phone, I found I had a message. I dialed voice mail, entered my code, and listened.

"Don, it's Ted Booth. The money will be at Bank Atlantic in North Palm Beach, 600 North U.S. Highway 1. Ask for Paul Wescott. He'll expect you at ten o'clock Monday morning. I'll also send this information to your email address, in case you've lost your cell phone. Have a safe trip."

I had to smile. My cell phone and I were notorious for being separated. I disconnected from voice mail and called Carlo Vincente. He answered on the second ring.

"Yes, Mr. Youngblood."

"The meeting went well," I said. "They agreed to all our conditions."

"Very good," he said. "How was my granddaughter?"

"Somewhat annoyed that she had to agree to go back to school immediately," I said.

Carlo laughed. "Yes, that would be her. She hates to be told what to do. It's always a battle. But if she agreed, then she'll do it. Honor is very important to Regina."

"Honor seems to be important to Freddie also," I said, trying to cast him in a positive light. "He gave me his word that they'll keep their part of the bargain."

"Do you think they're a couple with a future?" Carlo asked.

"Hard to tell at their age," I said. "But if I was a betting man, I'd bet they are."

"Watch out," Carlo said. "Betting can get you in trouble."

I laughed. "It certainly can."

"Call me tomorrow after your meeting."

"I will," I said. "Goodbye, Mr. Vincente."

"Until tomorrow, Mr. Youngblood," Carlo Vincente said, and he was gone.

"Oh, crap," Mary said, glancing in the rearview mirror.

I looked over my shoulder. A Florida state trooper was coming up fast, lights flashing. Mary slowed and pulled over. I resisted the urge to say, "I told you so," not wanting to sleep on the couch. I was about to see if professional courtesy would prevail in the blue fraternity.

Mary slid the driver's side window down before the trooper reached our car.

"Ma'am, do you know how fast you were going?" the trooper asked.

"I do," Mary said.

"I'll need to see your driver's license and proof of insurance."

Mary flipped open the leather carrier that housed not only her driver's license but her detective's shield as well.

"You're a police detective," he said flatly, as if disappointed he wasn't going to write a ticket. "What's the big rush?"

"I'm in a hurry to get my prisoner back to Singer Island," Mary said.

He leaned down and looked at me. "Your prisoner isn't cuffed," he said.

"He doesn't need to be," Mary said. "We're married."

The trooper laughed. "Yeah, I heard that." He handed Mary her license and shield back. "Promise to keep it on sixty-five and I'll let this slide," he said.

"I'll do better than that," Mary said, pointing toward me. "I'll let him drive. He loves going sixty-five."

We switched places, and I drove the rest of the route to Singer Island, biting my tongue all the way.

14

Early the next morning, with Mary still sound asleep, I took my laptop and a mug of coffee to the balcony and watched the sun come up. The day was perfect—gentle breeze, temperature in the low seventies, low humidity. The sun sporadically peeked between clouds as it rose to attend another day. I checked my email and forwarded a few to Gretchen that needed to be attended to. I wrote T. Elbert an epistle that would hold him for a few days. I checked the Street—nothing interesting going on there, although the market was making a slow, steady rise toward twelve thousand.

I shut down the laptop and called Billy.

"Hey, Blood," he answered. "How is Florida?"

"Mary is with me," I said. "We're alone. It's as good as it gets."

Billy laughed. "I understand that."

"How's the campaign going?"

"Very well," Billy said. "I think Charlie will win easily."

"Good to hear," I said.

"We're going to have a little party at our place on election Tuesday. I hope you and Mary can come that night. Lacy, too, if she wants."

"We'll be there," I said. "I'm sure Lacy will come if she doesn't have a game, and I don't think she does."

"She doesn't," Billy said. "I already checked. They start the week after. If she had a game, I'd be there and not here."

Lacy and Billy had developed a special connection from the time they first met. Billy, Mary, and I had seen almost every game Lacy played. At least one of us was at every game.

"What's going on in Cherokee, Chief?"

"Nothing much," Billy said. "I'm investigating some petty theft. Looks like an inside job. I set up cameras after hours a couple of days ago. Other than that, things are quiet."

Billy had taken classes months ago on setting up surveillance cameras and hidden microphones and installing security systems. He said it made sense for Cherokee Investigations to have that expertise. I had never thought about it. Even if I had, I wouldn't have been interested. Too boring. But Billy was patient and detail oriented.

"How are Maggie and Little D?"

"Everyone is fine, Blood," Billy said. "Is Florida business or pleasure?"

"Some of both," I said. I told him what I was working on.

"Why would you help Carlo Vincente?" Billy asked.

I didn't have a good answer for that.

"Job experience," I said.

"No," Billy said. "You're curious, and you like living on the edge, and you're getting worse. I worry about you sometimes."

Once a mother hen, always a mother hen, I thought. But I heard an element of truth in what he said.

"Relax," I said. "This will be over tomorrow, and then I'll get back to the Crane case."

"Watch your back," Billy said.

"Mary's got that covered."

As I signed off, I heard the sliding glass door open. Mary came out with a steaming mug of black coffee, looking spectacular.

"Did I hear my name?" she asked.

"I was on with Billy," I said. "He thinks I'm getting out of control. He thinks I like living on the edge."

"You do," Mary said, sitting and taking a drink from her mug. "But I understand, and on some level I find it appealing."

"Because you're the same way," I said.

"Somewhat. But when I flirt with danger, I usually have no choice. You, on the other hand, do."

"But you chose to be a cop," I said.

"Yes. Or it chose me. I'm not sure which."

I could see how Mary, being a cop's daughter, felt that way. "And you like it," I said.

"I do."

"Sometimes, I don't choose danger," I said. "It just seems to find me."

"Yes, you do have a knack."

"And you married me anyway."

"I married the whole package," Mary said. "I wouldn't have you any other way."

I was silent for a while.

"I told Billy you have my back," I said.

Mary smiled. "And then some."

15

"Would you like to count it?" he asked. "It's been counted and recounted three times already."

It was Monday morning, and I was sitting in front of Paul Wescott's desk with a black leather briefcase in my lap that was supposed to contain fifteen thousand dollars. Paul was on the other side looking every bit the Florida banker. He was about my age and had a good tan, blond hair, and blues eyes. He was maybe six feet tall and looked in shape.

"No," I said. "I'll trust your count."

I released the latches simultaneously, raised the top of the briefcase, and stared at the fifteen grand in bundles of twenties. The blue-and-white bands around the bills read, "Twenties—$1000." I had never seen that much money in cash. The sight of it made me uneasy, like I had a bull's-eye on my back.

"You can take the briefcase," Wescott said. "Bring it back when you're finished."

I lowered the top and snapped it shut. I stood, and we shook hands.

"Pleasure doing business with you," I said.

"The pleasure is all mine," he said. "Ted Booth spoke highly of you."

"Ted speaks highly of everyone," I said. "That's just the way he is."

Paul Wescott smiled at my self-effacement.

"I'll bring this back later today," I added.

I turned and walked out of his office, through the lobby, and out the front door. Mary was waiting in the Navigator with the motor running. I got in the passenger side and closed the door.

"Want to see what fifteen grand looks like?" I asked.

"You bet," Mary said.

I showed her.

"Forget Alexandria," she said. "Let's go shopping."

Silly girl.

◆ ◆ ◆ ◆

We found a Dunkin' Donuts close by and got coffee and toasted bagels with cream cheese. Mary drove back to the mall and parked in the same spot we had used a few days earlier.

"I could get used to being chauffeured."

"Don't," Mary said.

We drank coffee, ate bagels, and waited.

◆ ◆ ◆ ◆

At eleven o'clock sharp, the silver BMW arrived. Morgan got out and gave a little waggle of his index finger.

"I guess they want the money," I said.

"So get it over with," Mary said. "We're wasting beach time."

I got out of the Navigator with briefcase in hand and strolled toward the BMW. "Nice day," I said as I got within speaking distance of Morgan.

"It is that," Morgan said as he opened the back driver's side door.

I climbed in.

"Nice to see you again, Mr. Youngblood," Alexandria said, smiling.

"I don't doubt it," I said, "especially since I come bearing fifteen thousand dollars."

"Yes," she said. "That could influence me a bit."

She paused, and her demeanor changed. "I wish you had told me you were working for Carlo Vincente."

"I never divulge who I work for," I said. "Client confidentiality and all that."

"Nevertheless, it would have made things easier."

I popped the latches and opened the briefcase. "Let's get this over with," I said.

Alexandria lifted a briefcase that had been sitting at her feet, placed it in her lap, and opened it. Hers was empty. "Ten thousand dollars will square us," she said.

"Ten?"

"Yes."

"Change of heart?"

"You could say that."

Carlo Vincente's reach was longer than I thought. I counted out ten stacks of bills and handed them to her one by one. When I was finished, I closed the briefcase and snapped it shut.

"Freddie Destruge is safe?" I asked.

"He is," Alexandria said. "And he will find it impossible to place a bet with a South Florida bookie."

"That's good," I said. "We're done, then."

"Did your wife drive you today?" Alexandria asked.

I looked toward the Navigator. Because of the glare on the windshield, it was impossible to tell who was inside.

"Yes," I said.

"What's it like to be married to a police officer?"

She was trying to impress me with how much she knew about me. I didn't bite.

"Exciting," I said.

"I'll bet you are pretty exciting yourself," she said. "You shoot first and ask questions later, I hear."

"When necessary," I said, reaching for the door handle.

"That Victor Vargas thing was most impressive," she said.

"Old news," I said. "I have to go now."

"Perhaps in the future I will find a need for a private detective."

I was feeling claustrophobic. "I'll bet plenty of good private detectives are in South Florida," I said as I got out.

I closed the door before she could get off a parting shot, nodded to Morgan, walked swiftly back to the Navigator, and got in.

"All done?" Mary asked.

"Yes," I said. "And there's still five grand in the briefcase."

"Oh, goody," she said. "We can go shopping after all."

16

The day after returning from Florida, I called Jessica Crane and scheduled a visit. Then I made an appointment with Allan Wilton, vice president of the Blue Ridge National Bank.

The BRNB corporate headquarters were in Morristown in a modern three-story building facing Highway 11-W. My dad had told me stories about "Bloody 11-W," as it was called back in the 1970s. Before I-81 was finished, the two-lane Highway 11-W from Kingsport to Nashville was the scene of horrific crashes that claimed numerous lives. Now, it was a four-lane highway with only local traffic.

Allan Wilton's office was on the third floor at the front of the building. The receptionist said he was expecting me. I took the elevator, and Allan Wilton was standing there when the doors opened. He introduced himself and led me to his office.

"What can I do for you?" he asked, from behind his desk after we were seated.

"I want to know about Walter Crane," I said.

"What do you want to know about Walter?"

"Anything that Jessica Crane doesn't know," I said.

"Ah," he said. "I'm not sure I know anything she doesn't. And if I did, telling you might get me in trouble."

"Anything you tell me that might get you in trouble stays between us." I'm not sure he bought it, but it was the best I could do. "Did you report directly to him?" I asked.

"Yes," Allan Wilton said.

"Anyone else report to him?"

"No," he said. "The office managers and branch managers report to me, and I reported to Walter."

"Was he a good boss?"

"Yes, he was," Allan Wilton said. "But he was all business. Not unfriendly, but not overly friendly either." He paused. "I just cannot believe he had a heart attack. He seemed so healthy. I mean, he worked out, played tennis, wasn't overweight."

I nodded. "Notice anything different in the last few weeks? Did he seem stressed or distracted?"

He thought for a moment. "Walter always seemed a little distant," he said. "Like there was something on his mind. But he was that way ever since I met him. You were never quite sure if he heard everything you were saying, but he always seemed to. Do you know what I mean?"

"Yes," I said. "I've known people like that. They listen to you while thinking about something else, but they're able to process both things."

"Exactly," he said.

"Think he might have been having an affair?"

"Not that I know of," Allan Wilton said. "Walter was a straight arrow. He seemed happy with his marriage."

"Did Mrs. Crane visit Walter here often?" I asked.

"Hardly ever," he said. "Office Christmas party and maybe one or two other times during the year. They talked on the phone. Why all the questions?"

"I'm trying to figure out why Walter had a heart attack," I said. "I want to learn of any unusual behavior on his part."

"None that I noticed," he said. "He could have been a little more distracted than usual lately, but I'm not sure. I'd have to think about it."

I questioned him awhile longer, but it yielded little. I did find out they shared a secretary, Miss Martin.

I handed him my card. "If anything else comes to mind, call me."

"I'll do that," Allan Wilton said.

Allan introduced me to Nora Martin, who occupied a cubicle outside his office. I sat and talked with her a few minutes. Nora Martin was a matronly woman who had been with the bank as long as Allan Wilton could remember. She wasn't a candidate for an affair. I spoke with her and soon realized that if she knew anything about Walter Crane, it would go with her to her grave.

◆ ◆ ◆ ◆

I drove to the Crane Mansion thinking about my visit to Blue Ridge National. It had not been a total waste. I had learned a few things about Walter Crane. He was an introvert who kept a social distance between himself and his employees. He was not excitable and seemed to be the last person likely to have a heart attack. That alone aroused my curiosity.

The Crane Mansion was a big, old, two-and-a-half-story white house with a porch that wrapped around all four sides. It looked well cared for. The small third floor was centered on the second—maybe a storage room or attic. It had two windows and sat perched like a top hat on the house. I imagined some fair maiden locked away in that high room by an evil land baron, waiting to be rescued by the dashing young detective. *Well, maybe not so young,* I thought.

Jessica Crane wore slacks and a fitted top that showed off more of her figure than when she had visited my office. She was not an unpleasant sight. She led me to a large room with a bar, a snooker table, and a dartboard on the wall. Comfortable chairs and small tables were scattered about. A game room, I supposed. A bottle of white wine glistened on a tray on the bar, accompanied by two wineglasses. Jessica Crane poured herself an ample glass.

"Would you care for something to drink, Mr. Youngblood?" she asked.

"Club soda," I said.

She opened a small refrigerator, removed a bottle of club soda, took ice from a nearby bucket, put a few cubes in a tumbler, and poured. The fizz was noticeable.

"Lime?"

"Please."

She placed the drink in front of me and sat on one of the barstools.

"I haven't seen a snooker table in many years," I said.

"Not many people would even know that's a snooker table," she said. "Walter loved to play. He said it was much more challenging than pool."

"Walter was right."

"Sit, please," she said.

I sat and took a drink. It was cold and clean.

"You dress nicer than I would expect for a private detective," she said.

I guessed it was intended as a compliment, but it didn't come out that way. I resisted the urge to tell her about my stint on Wall Street and my New York tailor.

"Thank you," I said.

"Do you not drink alcohol, Mr. Youngblood?"

"I do, quite often," I said. "At home, after work."

She smiled. "Are you married, Mr. Youngblood?"

I wasn't sure, but I thought maybe I was being flirted with. Her manner was much more casual than in my office. Mary said I was naïve about these things.

"I am," I said.

"How long?"

"A little over a year."

"Goodness," she said. "You're a newlywed."

"I suppose so," I said.

"A second or third marriage?" Jessica Crane asked.

"First."

"My, my," she said. "You held out a long time."

"To my benefit," I said.

She smiled again and took an ample drink of wine. "Does your wife work?" she asked.

"My wife is a police officer," I said, taking another drink of my club soda.

I thought I saw Jessica Crane tense a bit.

"Well," she said, her demeanor subtly changing. "A private detective and a police officer. That must be interesting."

"It makes for unusual dinner conversation," I said. "Is this an interview? I thought I had already been hired."

She laughed. I sensed the wine was having an effect.

"Sorry," she said. "With Walter gone, I haven't had anyone to talk with recently. We used to have drinks around this time and talk about our day."

I immediately regretted making the interview crack.

"Mary and I do that, too," I said. "It's my favorite part of the day."

"Mine also," Jessica Crane said. "Or it used to be. So, did you find out anything useful at the bank?"

"At this point, it's hard to tell," I said. "Allan Wilton seemed to think Walter might have been a little distracted, but he wasn't sure. Did you get that impression?"

She thought for a moment. "Walter often seemed distracted," she said. "We would be talking, and he would seem to be listening, but I got the impression his mind was focused on something else. I didn't notice anything different the week before his death. I would ask him from time to time if anything was wrong, and he would say there wasn't, but I think something was bothering him. He was always a little sad."

"Any idea what it might have been?"

"None," she said. "It was more a feeling I had than anything definitive."

She took another drink of wine. Although she was going slowly, I noticed she was making headway on the bottle.

I nodded and drained my glass. "What I'd like now is to see Walter's office."

"Certainly," she said. "Follow me. I'm afraid we'll have to climb some stairs."

17

The half-story third floor did not serve as a prison cell or an attic. It was in fact a large, tastefully decorated office. The desk had a good view of the only doorway and the windows. I looked around the room and saw the things I would have expected: filing cabinets, bookshelves, a worktable, and a small conference table with six chairs. Also in the office were a coffeemaker, a microwave, and a small refrigerator. Walter obviously didn't want to go down two flights of stairs to the kitchen. So, much like me, he had a quasi-kitchen in his office. On the walls were personal pictures, a few limited-edition prints, a diploma from the Harvard School of Business, some plaques, and various awards and certificates.

"Feel free to look at anything," Jessica Crane said. "And if you find something you think I shouldn't know about, get rid of it."

I gave her a questioning look.

"Well," she said, "I think I knew Walter pretty well. But one can never know anyone completely. We had a good marriage, and as far as I know we did not keep secrets. But Walter's gone now, and all I want to remember are the good things."

"If Walter was murdered, I might find out some things you don't want to know," I said. "Am I to keep those to myself?"

"Yes," Jessica Crane said, surprising me. "Unless you feel I need to know." She was indeed a woman conflicted. "If he was murdered, I want to find his killer and get justice. The details don't much matter to me."

Well, I thought, *that's pretty much the way I operate. Damn the details. Results are all.* Most people I worked for wanted to know every little detail. Sometimes, it got to be annoying. Working for someone who didn't want to know everything would be refreshing.

"I'll leave you alone," she said. "Take all the time you want."

She turned and left, and I heard gentle footfalls on the stairs. I looked at my watch. I could stay an hour and still get home in time for drinks with Mary.

I started with the filing cabinets. I found what I might have expected—insurance folders, car lease folders, tax files, warranties, and Blue Ridge National Bank files, but no clues. Some of the files were twenty years old.

I walked over and took a good look at the personal photos on the wall opposite Walter's desk. Most were 8½-by-11 shots in simple frames. A good many were of Jessica and Walter; I noticed that Walter didn't smile much. Also some pictures of older people—parents, I supposed. I didn't see any clues in the photos.

I sat in the chair at Walter's desk and started going through the drawers. I found more files like the ones in the cabinets, only more current. I found printer paper, ink cartridges, blank folders, and unused CDs. When I finished the drawers on either side, I tried the middle drawer, which proved to be locked. When someone locks a desk drawer on the third floor of his own home, something is probably in it he doesn't want anyone—even his wife—to see.

I went back down the stairs to the game room. Jessica Crane was watching CNN. A half-empty wineglass was on the table beside her. The bottle on the bar was three-quarters gone.

"Do you know where Walter kept the key to his desk?" I asked. "The middle drawer is locked."

She looked surprised. "Locked?"

I nodded.

"I didn't know Walter locked his desk drawers," she said. "I rarely went up to his office, and I never tried opening his desk drawers."

"Only the middle drawer is locked," I said.

"I have no idea where the key is."

I thought for a moment. I didn't relish the thought of tossing Walter Crane's office looking for the key, and I didn't like the idea of breaking into his desk.

"Do you have Walter's car keys?"

"Yes," she said. "I'll get them."

She left me at the bar for a minute or so and returned with the keys. I counted seven. One, I felt as I sorted through them, had possibilities.

I climbed the two flights back to Walter's office. The key that I thought might fit the desk drawer slipped easily into the lock and turned. I pulled the drawer open. Inside were a checkbook, a small pistol, a few deeds and other papers, and, at the bottom, an old envelope addressed to Walter. It had been opened. I removed a single sheet of paper, unfolded it, and stared at the cryptic one-line message in the middle of the page:

Seven die one by one and no one knows when their time will come.

A clue or a curse? I wondered. I examined the envelope. It was postmarked Durham, North Carolina. The postmark date was faded, but the year was legible: 1991. I reread the note. It sounded like a warning, but 1991 was a long time ago. I wondered why Walter had kept it. A thought flashed into my mind like a prairie dog popping out of its hole: *Was Walter part of a death list of seven? If so, why? Who else was on the list, and what was their connection to Walter?* I had lots of questions and no answers.

I put the note back into the envelope and slipped it inside my jacket pocket, then went back down the stairs to the game room. Jessica Crane was right where I had left her, half-empty glass in hand.

"I'm leaving," I said. "I'll be in touch."

"Did you find anything helpful?" she asked.

"Maybe."

"Anything that will upset me?" she asked.

"Maybe," I said. "Maybe not."

"Should you tell me about it?"

I thought about that for a moment. I didn't want to upset her, but she might know something useful.

"Probably," I said.

I stole a quick look at the bar and noticed the wine bottle was empty. If I shared the note, I hoped she'd be sober enough to grasp the significance.

Like a lot of smart women, she was a mind reader. "It takes more than one bottle of white wine to impair my judgment," she said, smiling. "Tell me how I can help."

I removed the envelope from my jacket and handed it to her, then sat in the chair next to her as she removed the note, unfolded it, and stared at it for a lot longer that it took to read. A frown formed on her face. She looked at me.

"You think this means Walter was murdered?"

"I don't know what to think," I said. "But I don't like coincidences. Walter dies, and I find a mysterious note in an envelope postmarked 1991 in a locked desk drawer. It might suggest something sinister, or it might be nothing."

Jessica Crane stared at the envelope. "Nineteen ninety-one was before we were married," she said. "I didn't know Walter then. I wonder why he kept this."

"Maybe so it would be found," I said. "Did Walter know anyone in Durham, North Carolina?"

"I cannot think of anyone," she said. "I'll look in my address books and see what I can come up with."

"That would be good," I said. "It will probably lead nowhere, but it's a start."

She nodded and then started to sob. I looked around for a box of tissues and mercifully saw one on the bar. I quickly retrieved the box, ripped out a couple of tissues, and handed them to Jessica Crane. She took them but held them in her lap with her head down while she continued sobbing. I waited. *I'd rather have a root canal than be here right now*, I thought.

A minute later, Jessica Crane dried her eyes and took a deep breath. "Sorry," she said. "It just hit me. Thinking your husband might have been murdered, then finding something that might substantiate it is a little more than I can handle right now."

We sat silently. She drank a little more wine and seemed to calm down.

"I need to go," I said. "Are you going to be okay?"

"I'll be fine," Jessica Crane said firmly. "You go and find out who killed my husband."

18

The next morning, the Mountain Center Diner was at full buzz by the time I arrived. The table in the back that Doris Black usually kept open for me was empty. I took my seat and had a good view of the door and the windows looking into the street. I ordered the French toast, made with the diner's thick, homemade sourdough wheat, along with a side order of sausage patties.

As soon as Doris left with my order, I spied the Mountain Center chief of police coming across the street. Big Bob had parked in a No Parking zone—one of the privileges of law enforcement.

As always, the buzz dropped a few decibels as the big man entered. He headed straight for my table, speaking and nodding to various customers along the way. Big Bob tracked me down about once a week for breakfast. It was never planned. It just happened. He was wearing his uniform and the cowboy hat I had given him a few years back. It had become his wardrobe's signature item. He tossed the hat on a chair and sat.

From nowhere, Doris Black materialized at our table. "What can I get you, chief?"

"Two scrambled, rye toast, bacon, home fries, and coffee," Big Bob said.

"You got it," Doris said before hurrying away.

"What's new?" Big Bob said.

"Nothing much. A potential disability fraud and a heart-attack victim who may or may not be a heart-attack victim."

"Is that something I should know about?" Big Bob asked. "I could use a little excitement."

Doris was back with Big Bob's coffee.

"No," I said. "It's not in your jurisdiction. It happened down Morristown way."

"Want to tell me about it?" Big Bob asked, taking a drink of coffee.

I spun my tale as our breakfast arrived. I left out names but gave him the gist of it. He nodded and grunted a few times, but mostly he ate, finishing before I did.

"Are you looking for a smoking gun where there is none?" the big man asked.

"I was pretty sure of that until yesterday," I said. "Then I found the note. Now, I'm not so sure."

"The note in the locked drawer is interesting," he said. "I'd call that a loose end."

"Me, too," I said, finishing the final bite of my French toast.

"But the note is twenty years old."

"Might not be connected," I said.

"What are you going to do?"

"Damned if I know," I said. "Any ideas?"

"Let me ask you a question," the big man said. "Does it feel like murder to you?"

"More today than yesterday," I said.

"Then go back to the house and snoop around some more. Dig into his past. If someone killed this guy, you'll find a motive somewhere."

"Not a bad thought," I said. "You're pretty smart for a chief of police."

Big Bob stood, threw money on the table, and picked up his hat. "And tough," he said. "Don't forget tough."

As he walked away from the table and out of the diner, more than a few customers watched him go.

19

We sat on the lower deck at the lake house early Saturday morning drinking from insulated mugs with lids on to keep the coffee warm. Lacy and her best friend, Hannah, who usually spent Friday nights, were still asleep. A cool mist sat like a blanket on the lake, which was dead calm. Occasionally, we heard the splash of an ambitious fish picking bugs off the top of the water. By midmorning, the sun would rise high enough to burn off the mist, awaken the lake, and bring out the Saturday crowd to fish, swim, boat, and enjoy the fall day. Portable radios would broadcast various college football games, and a few crazies would get drunk and have to be escorted off the lake by the sheriff's patrol.

"It's going to be a beautiful day," Mary said.

"It is," I said.

"Can you believe we've been married over a year?"

"Time flies," I said.

"That's original. You're supposed to say something romantic."

"It's been the best over a year of my life," I said.

"Much better."

We were silent as we drank coffee and enjoyed the early morning. A hummingbird came by for breakfast at our feeder. Then another zoomed in to shoo away the interloper, and then another buzzed by, and all of a sudden we were once again observing what I called "the hummingbird wars." They dove and darted like miniature F-16s trying to gun each other down.

"I'm glad you finally have a case that interests you," Mary said. "It's been awhile."

"I needed a break," I said. "The Three Devils took their toll."

"I hope you don't stir up a hornet's nest," Mary said. "You seem to be good at doing that."

"I'm not sure there's anything to stir up," I said. "But I'd sure like to know what that note means."

"When are you going to see Jessica Crane again?"

"Monday," I said. "I've been invited to lunch at the mansion."

"Lunch," Mary said, slightly annoyed. "Is the mourning period over?"

"Hard to say," I said. "She might miss the routine more that her mate."

That might be true for a lot of people, I thought, *but never for me.*

◆ ◆ ◆ ◆

Lacy and Hannah made an appearance around ten o'clock, anxious to go out on the lake. An hour later, I pulled the barge away from the dock, sorely outnumbered by three females. Well, at least the two dogs were males. The sky was a low-humidity blue, the air fresh, and the breeze light and cool. We fished for a while with no luck, then went for a swim. The water was downright cold. No one seemed to notice but me. We ate lunch. We fished some more and caught a few black bass, which we released before we headed back. We docked around four o'clock.

Hannah's parents arrived at five. We cooked out—boneless chicken, hamburgers, hot dogs, and pineapple on the grill, accompanied by Gorgonzola potato salad and barbecue baked beans. I ate like a starving man. A day on the lake always put my appetite into overdrive.

"I'm beat," I said.

Lacy, Hannah, and her parents had been gone for only a few minutes. Mary and I, now in jackets, sat on the lower deck and enjoyed the end of the day.

"How beat?"

"Not that beat," I said.

Mary laughed that laugh I loved to hear. "You're never *that* beat," she said.

20

We sat on the screened-in porch at the back of the mansion. The day was clear and mild, the temperature predicted to reach the mid-seventies. Some mature maple trees kept the sun off the porch. An overhead fan stirred the air. Our table was white wicker with a glass top. The chairs matched the table. I felt like I was in an F. Scott Fitzgerald novel.

It must have been salad day at the Crane Mansion. We had an elaborate tossed green salad, accompanied by chicken salad, potato salad, dinner rolls, and sweet tea. I was glad I had skipped breakfast. I took ample portions of everything. We talked as we ate.

"How much do you know about Walter's life before you were married?" I asked.

"Quite a bit, I think," Jessica Crane answered. "But I never pushed him about his past."

"Tell me about him," I said.

"He was an army brat," she said. "He didn't talk much about his early days. His family moved around a lot, and his mother got tired of it and divorced his father. Walter was close to his father. That's probably why he enlisted as soon as he graduated high school. He was part of Desert Storm, but he didn't like to talk about it. When his tour was up, he went to college."

"How did he get into Harvard?" I asked.

Jessica Crane looked surprised. "How did you know?"

"I saw his diploma on the wall in his office."

"Of course," she said. "Walter was smart. He took the SAT and scored very high. His father had connections. Harvard was only too happy to accept a smart GI from Desert Storm."

I nodded and took a drink of sweet tea. I had almost cleaned my plate. Jessica Crane had only nibbled.

"Are any of Walter's things stored somewhere other than his office?" I asked.

"Some are probably in the basement," Jessica Crane said. "Walter had an old steamer trunk that was in his family for years."

"After we finish, I'd like to see it," I said.

"Certainly."

She picked up a small bell on the table and gave it a jingle. The maid appeared seconds later. "*Anna*," Jessica Crane said, "*please hook up the portable vacuum cleaner and clean off the old trunk in the basement. Mr. Youngblood will be down shortly*."

I was surprised she spoke to Anna in Spanish. "Your Spanish is very good," I said.

"Do you speak Spanish?" she asked, surprised.

"I do," I said. "I learned from a friend in college."

"I also speak French," she said rather proudly. "Do you speak any other languages, Mr. Youngblood?"

"No," I said. "Two are plenty."

◆ ◆ ◆ ◆

The basement was clean and well lit and had a concrete floor, but it still had the moldy smell of an old house. Anna had finished dusting the trunk and was unplugging the vacuum when I came down the basement steps.

"*Gracias*," I said.

Anna smiled.

"*Do you live here or somewhere else*?" I asked in Spanish.

I could tell my Spanish surprised her.

"*I live in Sevierville*," Anna said cautiously, avoiding eye contact.

"*Do you work every day?*"

"*I work for the Cranes five days a week*," Anna said. "*I do shopping and cooking and also cleaning*."

I could tell Anna was uncomfortable with the conversation. I also noticed she had an unusual accent.

"*I have to go back upstairs now*," she said.

She picked up the vacuum cleaner and went up the stairs as if an immigration agent were pursuing her. I would have bet a hundred dollars she didn't have a green card. But I also felt something else I couldn't quite conjure up. The feeling passed, and I turned my attention to the steamer trunk.

The kind that used to appear in old movies, it stood upright and was latched in the center. When unlatched, it opened to reveal two separate compartments. The right side was intended for hanging clothes; the left side was like a miniature chest of drawers. The clothes side was empty. I pulled open the top drawer. It was full of old tax returns, each year in a dark blue folder. I went through the folders quickly and found nothing of interest.

The second drawer contained many small boxes of mementos. As I opened them, I found cuff links, old watches, and a few rings. One jewelry-type box contained a Silver Star. Not many servicemen were awarded the Silver Star. I wondered what Walter had done to get it.

The bottom drawer contained old photo albums and half a dozen envelopes with loose pictures. I took the albums and the envelopes to a workbench and began going through them. Some of the photo albums were old. They had obviously been passed down to Walter. In a manila envelope was a large black-and-white glossy print of seven servicemen in dress uniforms, wearing berets. Walter was in the middle of the group. The men looked serious; no one was smiling. Walter was staring past the camera, not looking directly at it. Something in his expression bothered me. I turned the picture over. Handwritten on the back were the words, "The Southside Seven." I put the envelope aside and looked at numerous photos from various times in Walter's life but found nothing else that piqued my interest. I returned everything except the envelope to the bottom drawer.

I carried the envelope upstairs in search of Jessica Crane. I found her where I had left her, on the porch. She was working on a laptop computer. She looked up and smiled as I approached.

"Did you find anything helpful?" she asked.

"You never know," I said. "I do have a question." I removed the picture from the envelope and placed it on the table in front of her. "Have you seen this before?"

A puzzled look crossed her face. "No, I have not. Walter never showed this to me. As I said, he didn't like to talk about his time in the army."

"Do you recognize anyone in the picture?"

She studied the photo and shook her head. "Well, Walter, of course, but no one else."

"Does the name Southside Seven mean anything to you?"

"No," she said.

I turned the picture over so she could see the back. "Is this Walter's handwriting?"

"No," she said. "It's not."

"Okay," I said. "I'd like to take this with me."

"Certainly," Jessica Crane said. "Take whatever you need. Do you think the picture is a clue of some sort?"

"I have no idea," I said.

I slipped it into the soft leather valise I had carried with me and stood to leave. I took the photo not so much because I thought it was a clue as because I'd found nothing else to pursue on this case.

"One other thing," I said. "What was Walter's middle name?"

"Robert," she said. "Walter Robert Crane."

I nodded. "Thank you for lunch. Tell Anna it was very good. I'll be in touch."

I looked for Anna on the way out to tell her myself, but as I suspected, she was nowhere in sight.

◆ ◆ ◆ ◆

"Where have you been?" Gretchen asked, pretending to be annoyed that I hadn't checked in. Well, maybe she really was annoyed.

"I had a hot lunch date," I said.

"At the Crane Mansion," Gretchen said.

"You called Mary."

"I did," Gretchen said, smiling. "I *tried* to call you."

My cell phone was probably dead. I was famous for that. It drove Mary, Lacy, Gretchen, and most of my friends crazy.

"Good thing I didn't have a hot date," I said.

"It is," Gretchen said. "We women have to stick together."

I shook my head, retreated to my office, and tossed my valise on a vacant chair. Gretchen followed me in with return call notes.

"Oscar was here this morning, just like you told him to be," she said, handing me a pink slip of paper.

"Sorry," I said sheepishly. "I forgot all about that."

"James West called and wanted an update," Gretchen said, handing me another pink slip. "Mary called to talk to you about dinner." She handed me a third pink slip.

"Call Oscar and ask him to come by in the morning to give me an update on the West thing," I said. "Tell him I'm sorry about this morning."

"You should tell him yourself," Gretchen said. Then she put up her hand, realizing she might have gone too far. "Sorry. I sometimes forget I work for you."

"I sometimes forget that myself."

"I shouldn't," she said.

"Okay, you call Oscar, and I'll take care of Mary."

"I'll bet you will," Gretchen said, laughing as she went back to her desk.

I called Mary.

"You called," I said.

"Take me out to dinner tonight."

"My pleasure," I said. "Where do you want to go?"

"How about the country club?"

"It's a date," I said. "I'm going to the gym first, but I should be home before you. I'll see you at the condo."

◆ ◆ ◆ ◆

I left the office early and went to Moto's Gym. Maintaining my weight in my post-bachelorhood life was a challenge. Mary was a good cook when she cooked, which was mostly on weekends. When she didn't cook, we went out or ordered in. We always ate well. We enjoyed good wine. Mary bought the good stuff because she said I could afford it. Lacy ate at Hannah's a couple of times a week. Sometimes, Hannah ate with us, but not as often. Hannah's mother, Suzanne, explained to Mary that it was her way of supporting Mountain Center law enforcement. God bless Hannah's mother.

I was usually able to get to Moto's about three times a week. Today, he greeted me with his usual disinterest. If Mary had been with me, he would have been highly interested.

I went right to work—a half-hour on the computerized rowing machine, then my usual weight routine. I punched the speed bag for five minutes to finish up.

An hour and a half after entering Moto's, I walked rubber- legged to my Pathfinder.

◆ ◆ ◆ ◆

As soon as I reached the condo, I took the dogs for a walk. Junior was in a big hurry. Jake, older now and more settled, was content to move at a slower pace. He looked at Junior as if to say, *Settle down, kid.* Once they took care of business, I let them run around the tennis court until Jake got tired.

Back in the condo, I gave each one a treat, filled their food dishes, and refreshed their water bowls. I grabbed a beer, went upstairs to the master bedroom, stripped, and got into the shower. The warm water from the dual showerheads was soothing. I took my time. I shampooed and drank some beer. I rinsed and shampooed again and drank some more beer. I used conditioner, which I did only occasionally. I shaved and finished the beer.

Once the beer was gone, I couldn't think of a good reason to stay in the shower any longer. I towel-dried, then brushed my hair and checked myself in the mirror. *Not too bad for forty-plus,* I thought.

I wrapped the towel around me and opened the bathroom door. Mary was standing there smiling at me, completely naked, hands on hips, legs slightly spread, glorious.

"We'll be late for dinner," I said.

She jerked the towel from me and tossed it back into the bathroom. "The hell with dinner," she said.

Dinner, much later at the club, was anticlimactic.

21

"This little camcorder is pretty cool," Oscar said. His English seemingly improved every time I saw him. "I got some good stuff. Also, some good long-range stills."

Oscar handed me the camera and the camcorder.

"Tell me about it," I said.

"I followed Jerry and a bunch of guys to Elizabethton," Oscar said. "And guess what? They went to play in an all-day softball tournament. I got a nice shot of him sliding across home plate in one game and making a diving catch in another. He's a pretty good softball player. It didn't look as if his back was bothering him much. In fact, it didn't look as if it was bothering him at all."

"That's good work, O-man," I said. "Send Gretchen an email with the hours you put in on this, and she'll cut you a check."

"One more thing," Oscar said. "He's cheating on his wife. I followed him to a cheap motel in Newport, where he hooked up with a pretty good-looking blonde. I got Jerry going in, then the blonde going in, then the blonde coming out, then Jerry coming out. They were in there about an hour and a half."

"So his back must have held up pretty well," I said.

"Unless she was on top," Oscar said, grinning.

◆ ◆ ◆ ◆

After Oscar left, I connected the camcorder to my desktop computer, downloaded the contents, and watched everything Oscar had recorded. The quality was good. There was no doubt it was Jerry Block. *He should change his last name to Blockhead*, I thought. One clip began with the *Elizabethton Star*, the date clearly visible. The camera then panned to the field and zoomed in on Jerry. *Very nice, Oscar*, I thought.

The blonde at the motel *was* good looking—a little heavy, but with curves in all the right places. Although I didn't recognize her, I'd bet a hundred dollars she worked at National Distributing Corporation.

I connected the digital camera to a USB port on my desktop and viewed the stills. They were even better than the videos—especially the shots of the blonde. I almost envied Jerry Block. Then I thought about Mary, and the blonde didn't seem so special.

I burned the videos and the stills to DVDs to give to James West, then buzzed Gretchen on the intercom.

"Yes?"

"Call James West and tell him we have what he needs. Set up a time for him to come over. After lunch or in the morning is okay."

"Will do."

I took what remained of the morning and looked over some investment notes Gretchen had left. Gretchen was handling some accounts on her own—accounts she had brought in. She also assisted me with my longstanding accounts. She was learning fast but didn't want the responsibility of the final decisions. I made notations for her and put them in my out box.

I retrieved the photo of Walter and the six other soldiers and studied it closely. Seven soldiers, all in dress uniform, wearing berets, standing at a slightly odd angle. *Why these seven?* I wondered.

I took out a magnifying glass and studied the uniforms. Then I saw the insignia high on their left shoulders—the Army Ranger tab. At that point, I knew the berets were black and not green. I looked at their decorations. They all had one thing in common—the Silver Star. Silver Stars were awarded for bravery above and beyond the call of duty. They were not given out on a whim. I knew that because my grandfather had been presented one in World War II. I had heard the story from my father, but I could never get my grandfather to talk about it. He feigned a bad memory whenever I brought it up. He died when I was fourteen. Whatever the guys in the picture had done, it was big.

It's curious how one thing will resurrect an ancient memory of another thing. I hadn't thought about my grandfather in years. He was a kind, soft-spoken, gentle man who lived near us on the lake. He loved to take me fishing. He told great stories about growing up in East Tennessee. I was slipping into nostalgia when Gretchen's voice came over the intercom.

"James West will be here at three," she said.

Returning to the here and now, I put down the magnifying glass and took another look at the picture. And then I got it. They had been posed specifically so the photographer could capture the Ranger tab and Silver Star on each man.

The picture was enough of a mystery to keep me interested in Walter Crane. I slipped it into my top right desk drawer, then went online to check the odds for Saturday's college football games.

◆ ◆ ◆ ◆

"What have you got, Mr. Youngblood?"

James W. West sat impatiently—a man in a hurry with a business to run. I came around the desk with my laptop and sat in the chair next to him. I placed the laptop on the desk facing us.

"A little sports short for you entertainment pleasure," I said.

I played the softball video.

"That little son of a bitch," James West said. "I'll nail his nuts to a tree with this."

It was a metaphor I didn't wish to dwell on.

"Good work," he said. "My compliments to your investigator."

"Thank you," I said. "In case Jerry tries to wiggle out of this, I have more."

"More?"

"He's cheating on his wife."

I played the motel video, which I had put on a separate DVD.

"Aw, crap," James West said. "That's our receptionist."

"Not against the law," I said. "Is she married?"

"Divorced, I think," he said.

"That's all I have," I said.

"It's plenty."

I gave him both DVDs. They were marked "Softball" and "Motel" in black magic marker.

He handed the "Motel" DVD back to me. "Keep this in your file," he said. "If Jerry decides not to go quietly, I might have to show it to him. I'd prefer not to."

"I think you'd better take it," I said. "I have a feeling Jerry may be trouble. Anyone that sneaky has a backup plan."

"You're probably right," he said.

I handed the DVD back to him. He took it, stood, and shook hands with me.

"I hope never to see you again," he said. "Professionally, that is."

"I completely understand," I said.

◆ ◆ ◆ ◆

Later, after Gretchen left, the office got quiet. The outer door was locked, the Closed sign clearly visible through the glass from the hall. I made one last call before I shut down.

Scott Glass, a.k.a. "Professor," was the special agent in charge of the Salt Lake City FBI office. I had met Scott at the University of Connecticut the day before I met Billy. Scott, Billy, and I were on the basketball team. They were on scholarship, and I was a walk-on. I later got cut, and they went on to be stars.

Except for being six-five, Scott looked nothing like a basketball player. He had a geeky, lanky, awkward, studious look that belied the fact that he was one of the best three-point shooters ever to wear the UConn blue and white. Scott's dark, curly hair and glasses earned him his nickname. Over the years, a few of my cases had crossed paths with his. From time to time, we had helped each other get the bad guys.

"Hey, Professor, got snow yet?" I said when Scott picked up his private line.

"Blood," Scott said. It had been awhile since we talked. "No snow yet, but soon. How's married life?"

"Married life is good," I said. "How about you? Still the confirmed bachelor?"

"So far," Scott said. "I'm taking a page from your book. I'm dating a cop. She's a detective for the Salt Lake City Police. I met her on the Three Devils case."

"Tell me all," I said.

"Married, divorced, no kids," Scott said. "Good looking, of course. No bullshit. Great in bed. Understands my job, and I understand hers. We get along."

"That's great, Professor," I said. "I hope it works out long term."

"Me, too," Scott said. "But you didn't call to check on my love life. I have a feeling something's up."

"Maybe, maybe not."

"It's been awhile since you found trouble," Scott said. "What is it this time?"

"I need some background on a Walter Robert Crane. He was in the army in Desert Storm. Army Ranger. Silver Star recipient."

"Army Ranger and a Silver Star," Scott said. "Impressive. What's this all about?"

"Walter's dead," I said. "His widow thinks maybe he was murdered. He died of an apparent heart attack, but the autopsy came up negative for cause of death."

"And you're looking into it," Scott said.

"It's something to do," I said.

"Let's hope it turns out to be nothing," Scott said.

"Might be interesting if it doesn't," I said. "See what you can find out—his outfit, commanding officer, stuff like that. Anything that might be useful."

"I'll get back to you, Blood," he said.

22

Scott called the next morning at eight o'clock—which meant six o'clock his time.

"You're up early," I said.

"Always am," Scott said. "I don't think I've ever gotten off Eastern Standard Time."

"You have something already?"

"Wasn't hard," Scott said.

"Tell me."

"I confirmed Walter Crane was an Army Ranger, and he did win the Silver Star," Scott said. "Good record, honorable discharge, did one tour in Desert Storm. He was in the First Ranger Battalion, B Company."

"Who was his company commander?"

"Captain Bradley Culpepper," Scott said. "He's now a lieutenant colonel working at the Pentagon under the secretary of the army."

"I'd like to talk to him," I said. "Can you get me a phone number?"

"I'll see what I can do," Scott said. "I'll send you an email as soon as I find out something."

"Thanks, Professor."

"No problem," he said. "That was an easy one. Let me know if this goes anywhere."

"Will do," I said.

◆ ◆ ◆ ◆

When I checked my email that afternoon, a direct-line phone number for Lieutenant Colonel Bradley Culpepper was waiting for me. *Way to go, Professor*, I thought.

I was more than a little apprehensive as I dialed the number that would ring a phone in what was generally regarded as the world's largest office building. I had done some research. A whopping twenty-three thousand men and women populated the Pentagon.

I heard five rings, then a click, and then a very military voice: "This is Bradley Culpepper. I'll be out of the office today. If you wish, please leave a message."

I left a cryptic message about Walter Crane, along with my phone number. I hoped I would spark his curiosity enough for a callback.

23

When I reached the office early the next morning, I had a message on my voice mail to call the lieutenant colonel. The message had come in fifteen minutes earlier.

I popped the lid on my Dunkin' Donuts coffee and returned the call.

"Culpepper," the voice said.

"Lieutenant colonel, my name is Donald Youngblood," I said.

"Yes, Mr. Youngblood," Culpepper said. "You're the Tennessee private investigator who worked that Three Devils case last year."

"That's correct," I said. "You did your homework."

"Yes, I did," he said good-naturedly. "Just showing off a little. What can I do for you?"

"I'm investigating the death of Walter Crane," I said. "Do you remember him?"

"Of course I remember him," Culpepper said. "I was his commanding officer. Good man, Walter. What happened?"

"I'd rather talk to you about it in person."

"I see," he said. "Have you ever been to the Pentagon, Mr. Youngblood?"

"No," I said.

"Well, having a guest is a hell of a lot harder that it was before 9/11," Culpepper said. "Can't we do this over the phone?"

"I'd rather not," I said. "It's been my experience that I find out much more face to face. Things just seem to come out."

He paused as if thinking it over. "I'll have to go through some red tape, do a background check. You ever had a government job?"

I laughed. "No, but I worked with the FBI on the Three Devils case. Maybe they ran a background check."

"What's your Social Security number?"

"I don't give out my Social Security number," I said.

"A little paranoid, aren't you?"

"More and more," I said.

"Okay, full name and date of birth," he said.

I gave them to him. In the background, I heard the faint clicks of a keyboard.

"FBI consultant," he said. "That will definitely make it easier, but I'll still have to do some paperwork. When can you come?"

"Anytime," I said. "The sooner, the better."

"I'll get back to you with the date so you can make flight reservations," Culpepper said. "I assume you're flying."

"Yes," I said. "Private jet." Now, I was showing off.

"The private investigator business must be pretty good."

"It does have its perks," I said.

"I'll send you a VIP pass via UPS and have a limo pick you up at the airport," he said. "It will get you in a lot faster than picking up a rental and using a parking pass. The VIP pass will be date-specific, so you'll have to come that day. I'll request Monday, but it could be later in the week. Can you risk giving me your email address?"

I laughed again. I was beginning to like this guy. "As long as your phone isn't tapped," I said.

"Hellfire, Youngblood, this is the Pentagon," Culpepper said. "All the phones are tapped."

I gave it to him anyway.

"I'll email the date as soon as it's confirmed," he said. "I look forward to meeting you, Mr. Youngblood."

"Likewise," I said. "And thanks for having me picked up."

"Thank the FBI," Culpepper said. "Your consultant status rates a pickup."

The American tax dollar at work, I thought.

◆ ◆ ◆ ◆

It was still early, and all I had put in my stomach that morning was one cup of coffee. Well, it was Dunkin' Donuts coffee, but nonetheless . . .

I walked to the Mountain Center Diner. When I arrived, my table was occupied. The occupier spotted me coming toward him and smiled. Few people had the pull to sit at my Mountain Center Diner table. This particular interloper was one of them.

"Haven't seen you in a while," I said, sitting down.

At least he wasn't sitting in my chair. I noticed an empty plate in front of him.

"I would have come by last week, but you were in Florida," he said.

Doris arrived and took my order. "More coffee, Mr. Husky?" she asked as she picked up his plate.

"Sure," Roy said, sliding his cup toward her.

Doris scurried away.

"Nice to see I'm not the only one she calls mister," I said.

"She calls me Roy when you're not around," he said.

"You're kidding."

"No, I'm not."

"I'd sure like to get inside her head and understand the logic to that."

"Forget it," Roy said. "You can't go through life trying to get explanations for everything, gumshoe. Some things need to remain a mystery. Now, tell me about your trip."

I told him.

"Carlo Vincente," Roy said. "Now, there's a blast from the past. How are Gino and Frankie?"

"Frankie's good," I said. "He picked me up at the airport. Gino is working somewhere in the city. According to Frankie, Gino is still pissed at me for breaking his nose."

"I'll bet," Roy said as my food arrived. "It hurt me just to look at it."

I dug into my breakfast.

"What's going on with the heart attack case?" Roy asked.

"The Crane case," I said. I told him the latest.

"The Pentagon. I may need your autographed picture now."

"Be quiet and drink your coffee," I said. "And find out if I can take one of the jets."

◆ ◆ ◆ ◆

My day was almost over, but I had one more phone call to make. I figured if I waited long enough, James W. West might be gone from the office, and I could leave a message. No such luck. I was regaled with the story of the crack private investigator (actually, Oscar) who got the goods on the dastardly miscreant who was trying to defraud National Distributing Corporation. He had called Jerry Block into his office and "lowered the boom"—West's euphemism for showing the softball video.

"How did he react?" I asked.

"Oh, he was clever," James West said. "Like you predicted, he had a backup plan. Seems Jerry was just testing the back, you see. Figured if he could play softball, then he could come back to work."

"Obviously, he didn't come back to work."

"No, he didn't," James West said. "It seems the back was sore the Monday morning after the softball weekend. Naturally, the test went badly. He threatened to call a lawyer if I fired him."

"Let me guess," I said. "You showed him the second video."

"I did."

"I'll bet that was fun."

"Oh, it was," James West said. "It was priceless. I thought we might have to call the company doctor."

"Were you alone?"

"Not a chance," he said. "Our human resources manager was with us."

"So Jerry said he'd resign if you keep quiet about the second video?"

"He did indeed," James West said. "At that point, he was a whipped puppy."

I didn't ask him about the receptionist. Frankly, I didn't want to know.

24

Saturday morning, I sat at the table with an umbrella on the lower deck at the lake house and thought about recent events.

First, I wondered why I had helped Carlo Vincente. I should have told him no thanks and left it at that, but I didn't. Was it curiosity or the need to walk close to the flame? Was I a danger junkie? It sure looked that way, judging by the last few years. Or did I just want to help a young girl not responsible for who her family was? I hoped so.

Then I wondered if Walter Crane's death was really a murder. But if it was murder, what was the motive? I didn't have a clue. Did I want to see a murder where it didn't exist because I hadn't worked a big case in a while? I wasn't sure. Big Bob was right about the note being a loose end. But the note was sent years ago, which didn't make sense. And then the picture, which might be an important piece of the puzzle; I had no idea how it connected.

I heard the storm door onto the upper deck open and close. I looked over my shoulder and saw Lacy. Every now and then, she surprised me and got up early on Saturday morning. She was carrying a cup of black coffee, which seemed unusual for a girl her age. Most would have been drinking Coke or Mountain Dew. Was she trying to emulate Mary?

"You're up early," I said. *Youngblood, master of the obvious*, I thought.

"I went to bed right after you guys," she said. "I was really tired. Basketball practice is wearing me out."

"How's the team look?"

"Good," Lacy said. "I think we'll win twenty."

It was unusually warm for a late-October morning. We sat in silence and enjoyed the day. The lake was calm. Every now and again, we heard the splash of a fish breaking the surface in search of breakfast.

"Don," Lacy said, a serious edge to her voice, "why did you adopt me?"

I was caught off guard by the question and had no idea where it was leading. "Mary and I both adopted you," I said, stalling.

"I know," she said. "But you didn't have to. I could have lived with you anyway."

"It's complicated, Lacy," I said, struggling for the right words. "Mary and I became fond of you, and when we decided to get married, adopting you just seemed logical. Together, we legally became a family. Why are you just now asking me this?"

"I've been wondering about it for a long time," she said. "I guess I was afraid it wouldn't work out. I just wanted to thank you for all you've done for me."

"No," I said. "I want to thank you for coming into my life and becoming my daughter."

A tear rolled down her cheek as she came toward me. I stood and held her tight. The tears came freely. We stood that way for a while.

"I love you, Don," she said, disengaging.

"I love you, too, Lacy."

"Sorry about that," she said.

"No need to be," I said.

"I guess I was just feeling guilty."

"Why?"

"I'm so lucky to have you and Mary," she said. "I have everything I need. A lot of kids don't. I'm real conflicted."

"Hannah has great parents and everything she needs," I said. "You think she feels guilty?"

"No. It's always been that way for her. It hasn't always been that way for me. Things in my world weren't good for a long time. Now, they're the best they could possibly be, and I'm terrified it won't last."

"Look," I said. "For now, just enjoy what you have and forget feeling guilty."

She was quiet for a minute. "You're right. I'm overreacting. Someday, I'm going to help someone like you've helped me, I swear."

"I don't doubt that one bit," I said.

She took a drink. "Yuk," she said. "My coffee's cold. Want me to get you a fresh cup?"

"Sure," I said.

She took our cups up the stairs to the upper deck and into the house. A few minutes later, I heard the door open and close again. A few seconds after that, I had a hot, fresh cup of coffee in front of me.

"Lacy got a phone call," Mary said.

"Thanks for the delivery," I said.

Mary got comfortable with her own cup of coffee where Lacy had been sitting.

"Did you have a little father-daughter talk?" she asked.

"We did."

"Everything okay?"

"It is."

"Good daddy," Mary said.

Why did I have the feeling Mary knew exactly what Lacy and I had talked about?

25

"The Pentagon," Jim Doak said as I boarded Fleet Industries jet number one. "What's next, the White House?"

I had dressed as if I were entertaining a big Wall Street client. I wore a dark Armani suit with the slightest hint of gray pinstripes and a red-and-black-striped silk power tie.

"I certainly hope not," I said. "Try not to violate the Pentagon's air space. Being shot down by my own government is not the way I want to go."

"I think I can handle that," Jim said.

I had being flying off and on with Jim Doak on the same Fleet jet for about four years. I was thoroughly spoiled. Before, I had never liked flying commercial. Now, I hated it.

After we were airborne and leveled off, I reviewed my file on Walter Crane and made a list of questions to ask Lieutenant Colonel Culpepper. I looked at the VIP pass he had sent me on Friday. It was very official, complete with a hologram and a silver clip to attach it to my clothing. I hoped I could keep it as a souvenir.

◆ ◆ ◆ ◆

An hour and a half later, we were on the ground in D.C. As promised, the lieutenant colonel had made arrangements for me to be picked up at the airport. A black limo was waiting as we taxied to a private hangar. Say what you want about our government, it does know how to go first-class.

The limo driver was a young second lieutenant. Jim Doak, ever the tease, insisted on carrying my briefcase.

"Welcome to Washington, sir," the young lieutenant said as we approached. He opened the rear passenger's side door.

"Your briefcase, sir," Jim said, handing it to me as we reached the limo.

"Thank you, James," I said. "I'll be back in a couple of hours."

"I'll be waiting, sir," Jim said with a slight bow.

When we reached the Pentagon, we went through a gate with a checkpoint that had a sign reading, "Authorized Personnel Only."

"Hand me your badge, please, sir," the young lieutenant said.

The guard checked my VIP pass and the lieutenant's ID and passed us through. Once the limo was safely in the underground parking garage, I was escorted to an elevator. We got off on the fourth floor. I followed the lieutenant through a maze of turns to Lieutenant Colonel Bradley Culpepper's office.

We entered an outer office and were greeted by a sergeant who was older that the lieutenant—no doubt a career man.

"Please inform Lieutenant Colonel Culpepper that Mr. Youngblood is here," the lieutenant said.

"Yes, sir," the sergeant said, rising.

The sergeant tapped on the inner office door and disappeared.

"When it's time for you to go, I'll take you back to the airport, sir," the lieutenant said. He then left the office.

Seconds later, the sergeant reappeared. "Lieutenant Colonel Culpepper will see you now," he said, holding the inner office door open.

Lieutenant Colonel Culpepper rose, came from behind his desk, and extended his hand. "Welcome to the Pentagon." His handshake was firm but not aggressive. "Please, sit down," he said, returning to his desk.

The lieutenant colonel was a stout man maybe five-foot-ten with a short haircut. Whether his hair was red or light brown was hard to tell. He had an intelligent face and looked directly at me with gray-blue eyes that I guessed missed nothing. I liked him immediately.

"Thanks for arranging the pickup at the airport and getting me past the red tape," I said.

"Happy to do it," he said. "I know you've worked with the FBI, and I know you're close to Joseph Fleet. Mr. Fleet is well known in military circles. Any friend of Joseph Fleet is a friend of ours."

I learned another thing about Joseph Fleet I had never known. *I'll have to talk to Roy about this*, I thought.

"Now, Mr. Youngblood, how can I help you?"

"How well did you know Walter Crane?"

"To be honest, not well at all," Culpepper said. "When he was recommended for the Silver Star, I pulled his record. Excellent soldier, of course—all Rangers are the best of the best. Spotless record, well decorated. But I didn't have any kind of personal relationship with my men. It's important to keep your distance. I was sorry to hear of his death."

"Why was he recommended for the Silver Star?" I asked.

He tapped a pencil on a notepad on his desk as he pondered my question. "What I'm about to share is confidential," he said.

I nodded. "I understand."

"He was chosen for a black ops assignment in Desert Storm. A handful of Rangers were chosen, and he was the only one from my company. I didn't know any of the others. The assignment was dangerous and classified. I knew little about it except that the men were told that some of them might not get back alive. Luckily, they all did. And all of them—seven, as it turned out—were recommended for and awarded the Silver Star. Walter was the team leader."

"Was it unusual for a black ops team to be chosen from different units?" I asked.

"No," he said. "You can see the logic. Pull them from different units, train them for the mission, and send them back after it's over. That way, they can't discuss the mission among themselves, and they have orders not to discuss it with anyone else."

I pulled the picture from my briefcase and handed it to him.

He looked at it and nodded. "That's Walter in the middle, of course, I don't know the others."

"Any chance of finding out?" I asked.

"Maybe, but I need to know what's going on."

I told him about Jessica Crane's suspicions. I didn't tell him about the note, I didn't know if the note had anything to do with Walter's death or not. I'd know more if I could talk to some of the guys in the picture.

"So," Culpepper said, "it might be something, and it might be nothing."

"Exactly."

"Well, not being able to determine the cause of death is something," he said.

"It is."

He stroked his chin like a man trying to make a decision. "What would you like for me to find out?" he asked.

"Names and last known addresses of the men in that picture," I said. "And if you can, check and see if any of them are still in the army. Also, find out if any are buried in Arlington National Cemetery or any other national cemetery for the military."

Culpepper made notes. "Okay," he said, standing and offering his hand. "I'll see what I can do. Might take a few days."

"I appreciate it," I said, shaking his hand.

He pressed his intercom button. "Sergeant, Mr. Youngblood is ready to leave now."

26

I had not seen T. Elbert in weeks and felt guilty about it. I knew Roy took up some of the slack, and I was grateful for that, but I knew T. Elbert was closer to me than anyone else. He had no family. I was his family, Roy and Billy, too, to a lesser degree.

I came up the walk that Tuesday morning carrying coffee, muffins, and bagels from you-know-where. October had cooled off considerably in the last couple of days. A chill was in the air and not a cloud in the sky.

"About damn time," T. Elbert barked as I climbed the few stairs to his front porch.

I noticed the overhead heaters were on. The temperature on the porch was comfortable.

"Sorry," I said as I set down our breakfast. "No excuses."

"Hell," he said. "Don't listen to me. You have your own life. I understand you're busy."

"I'd like to come more often," I said, handing him a cup of coffee. "Things are just complicated right now." *Listen to yourself, Youngblood*, I thought. *You're making excuses.* "I'll do better."

I passed T. Elbert a blueberry muffin.

"Donald," T. Elbert said, "I was just pulling your chain. Come when you can, and I'll be happy to see you."

I nodded, took a bite of poppy seed bagel with cream cheese, and washed it down with coffee. "You know that if you need anything, all you have to do is call and I'll come running," I said. "Roy and Billy, too."

"Jesus Christ," T. Elbert said. "Remind me not to kid you anymore."

I smiled. I knew he had let me off the hook.

"How are Mary and Lacy?"

"Both fine," I said.

"You adjusting to married life?"

T. Elbert asked me this every time I saw him. I couldn't figure out whether he was worried I wouldn't stay married or was just making conversation.

"Every now and then, I have a panic attack," I said. "But overall, I wouldn't have it any other way."

"That's good," he said. "Mary is one hell of a woman." He took a big bite out of his muffin and drank some coffee.

"So you've said. Many times."

"Tell me what you've been up to," he said, wiping his mouth.

I took a long time telling him about Carlo Vincente's granddaughter. T. Elbert was a stickler for details. I described Alexandria right down to her shoes.

"I'll bet Mary loved her," T. Elbert said.

I ignored him and kept going. I talked long enough to finish my first cup of coffee and the poppy seed bagel. T. Elbert shook his head a few times but made no other comments.

"You don't have a lick of sense," T. Elbert said when I finished.

"I've heard that before."

"I'll bet," T. Elbert said.

"Well, it came out okay. I sent Carlo a big bill."

"Like you need the money."

"Well, at least I'll get some of his," I said. "I'll donate it to your favorite charity."

"Fine," T. Elbert said. "You get paid yet?"

"Gretchen just sent out the bill," I said.

"Well, if you do get paid, give it to the Mountain Center Boys' Club."

"Agreed," I said.

"Tell me what's going on with the Crane case."

I told him about my visits to the Crane Mansion and my trip to the Pentagon.

"You went to the Pentagon and didn't tell me?"

"I'm telling you now," I said.

"About time," T. Elbert said, smiling. He just couldn't help jerking me around.

I told him the details of the Crane case.

"What do you think?" I asked when I finished.

"I think you're onto something," T. Elbert said. "You know what to do. When you find out who the guys in the photo are, start working through the list with face-to-face interviews. Look for reactions, body language. Sometimes, you can learn more by watching than listening. If there's something to find, I know you'll find it."

"Or it will find me," I said.

27

Nothing happened for a few days, which was fine with me. I bought and sold some stocks, went online and read everything I could find about Army Rangers, and went to the gym and ran four miles a day.

Friday after the UPS man made his deliveries, Gretchen walked into my office with an envelope marked for Donald A. Youngblood, Special Consultant, FBI, in care of Cherokee Investigations.

"The Pentagon," she said. "Impressive. And that new job title. I may need a raise."

"You just got one," I said. "Beat it."

"Yes, sir, Mr. Special Consultant."

She made an about-face and returned to the outer office as I opened the envelope. Either Lieutenant Colonel Culpepper had a sense of humor or he was covering his butt for sending me the information I requested. The list was complete—six names, six last known addresses. A notation said, "None of these men stayed in the Army when their tours were up, and none are buried at Arlington National or any other cemetery for the military."

I spent some time after lunch with a map, thinking maybe I could plan a driving trip to interview each man. I hoped I could locate them and that they were still above ground. Whether they were dead or alive, I wanted some answers. And the only way to get them was to go to the sources.

My father taught me that when I had a list of things to do that required driving, to start with the farthest and work my way back. I looked at the list to see if it made sense to drive. Farmington, New Mexico, was farthest away, straight out I-40 for about a million miles, then northwest on I-25 and a couple of state highways—too far to drive. Memphis, Tennessee, I could drive, but it was still an overnight trip—or a day trip on the Fleet jet. Lexington, Kentucky, and Orangeburg, South Carolina, could be day trips in the Pathfinder. Gretna, Louisiana, was a day trip in the air. The last stop was north—Stamford, Connecticut.

I studied the list and made my decision—two driving trips, four flying trips, and no nights sleeping alone. *This whole case is probably a wild-goose chase anyway*, I thought.

◆ ◆ ◆ ◆

Before leaving the office, I called Billy. I hadn't talked to him since returning from the Pentagon. We were talking less and less, but it didn't diminish our friendship.

"Nice of you to call, Blood," Billy said. I couldn't tell if he was teasing me or not. Billy, like T. Elbert, loved to get me going.

"Phone works both ways, Chief," I said.

"It does," Billy said. "I should have beat you to it, but things here have been a little crazy."

"Getting close to Election Day," I said.

"Very close," Billy said.

"How does it look?"

"It still looks like we're going to win."

"I can see where this is heading," I said.

"Where?" Billy said.

"You'll get into this deputy thing, and it's going to lead to a full-time job," I said. "Someday, maybe even sheriff."

"Think so?"

The fact that he didn't deny it made me think he'd considered it.

"I do," I said. "And that's okay."

"I'd feel guilty about leaving Cherokee Investigations," Billy said.

"Don't. It's been fun, but all good things come to an end. I'm not going to be a private investigator forever."

"I don't believe you," Billy said. "You're just trying to give me an out if I need one."

"Maybe," I said. "But you need to follow your own dreams, not mine."

"Don't worry about that," Billy said. "Knowing you support me makes it easier."

I hadn't meant for the conversation to go this route, but some things must be said, and I was glad they had been.

"How's my namesake?"

"He's great," Billy said. "It's hard to explain, Blood. I never thought I'd be a father. Life is good."

"If you don't shut up, I'm going to start crying."

Billy laughed. "It is getting a little deep, isn't it?" he said. "Tell me what you've been working on."

I told him about the Pentagon trip and the list of names.

"So you're going to track down all these guys?"

"It's all I've got, Chief," I said.

"And if this list is a dead end, then what?"

"I'll tell the widow I gave it my best shot and close the file," I said.

"I have a feeling you'll turn up something," Billy said.

"Why?" I asked.

"Because, Blood, you always do," Billy said.

28

Monday, I was airborne and headed for Farmington, New Mexico, the rising sun in hot pursuit.

Jim Doak had called the night before to let me know the jet was available. We met early at Tri-Cities Airport.

"Want to sit in the copilot's seat?" Jim asked as we boarded.

"Sure," I said. "As long as you give me a flying lesson."

"Why not?" Jim said. "Then I can take a nap."

"Only if you don't want to wake up," I said.

We squeezed into the cockpit, Jim taking the left seat, then me bumbling into the right. I felt slightly claustrophobic. Jim talked me through his preflight routine. I listened intently, though I soon forgot most of what he said. The instrument panel was intimidating. If my Pathfinder's dashboard was third-grade math, this was Einstein's Theory of Relativity.

As we roared down the runway, Jim explained about achieving takeoff speed. "That's probably enough," he said as he pulled back on the wheel.

We gently lifted off the tarmac, and I saw the ground fall away.

Twenty minutes later, we were cruising at thirty-eight thousand feet and I was bugging Jim with questions.

"The most important thing to remember is minimum air speed—or stall speed, as it's sometimes called," Jim said. "It's different for each aircraft. If you don't maintain minimum air speed, you fall like a rock."

"That's a comforting image," I said.

"Not to worry," Jim said. "Probably won't happen."

I knew he was trying to rattle me, so I ignored him. "What's the minimum air speed for this jet?"

"About a hundred miles an hour," Jim said.

"How fast will it go?"

"The book says we can cruise at five-fifty. I would guess with a good tailwind, we might do six hundred or better."

"What's our range with a full tank?" I asked.

"Around twenty-seven hundred miles," Jim said. "We have plenty of fuel to get us to Farmington without stopping."

I eventually ran out of questions, and Jim seemed to appreciate that. I was also cramped and desperate to stretch my legs.

"Okay if I go back in the cabin and do some work on my laptop?"

"Go ahead," he said. "Try not to break anything getting out. When it's time, I'll call you and let you do your first landing."

I laughed. "I'll pass on that."

I squeezed out of the copilot's seat and slipped from the cockpit, glad Jim had given me the opportunity to see what it was all about but not yearning for another lesson.

◆ ◆ ◆ ◆

Hertz at Four Corners Airport in Farmington had a limited selection of SUVs. The best I could get was a Nissan Xterra. It would be fine for a day.

I exited the airport and followed the directions from my Garmin GPS, which Mary had insisted I buy. I had programmed it during the flight out after escaping the cockpit. The demanding female voice—which I had nicknamed Hilda, as in Broom-Hilda, as in witch—recited a litany of rights, lefts, and distances that led me toward the last known address of one Roderick Random Butler. *Fancy name*, I thought. *Maybe he descended from Rhett.* I occasionally talked back to Hilda, but she never responded, remaining aloof with her rights and lefts.

The last right led me to the driveway of the Butler house, which was located in a cul-de-sac of an upscale neighborhood on the outskirts of Farmington. I knew it was the Butler house because a small, tasteful sign beneath the mailbox told me so. All the houses looked relatively new—built probably in the last twenty years.

I parked, got out of the SUV with briefcase in hand, and went up the walk to the front door. I rang the bell and waited.

A small, attractive-looking woman with short gray hair, neatly dressed in slacks and a sweater, opened the door and smiled at me. "Can I help you?"

"I'm looking for Roderick Butler," I said. "Does he still live here?"

Her face clouded. "You mean Randy," she said. "We called him Randy. His middle name was Random. It's an old family name." She had the distant look of someone trying to bring back a memory.

"Yes, ma'am," I said. "I guess I do mean Randy."

"Randy's been gone for quite some time," she said absent-mindedly. "I'm his mother."

"Gone?"

"Oh," she said. "He was killed in a motorcycle accident a year after he got out of the army. He was a Ranger, you know."

"Yes, ma'am, I did know that. I'm sorry for your loss."

"He won the Silver Star," she said. "Did you know that?"

"Yes, ma'am, I did."

"Why are you looking for Randy?"

"I'm doing some research on Silver Star recipients," I said. "I wanted to interview your son."

"You would have wasted your time. He wouldn't talk about winning the Silver Star," she said. "Every time I asked, he just got annoyed with me and said it was classified and that he couldn't talk about it."

"I understand," I said. "Did Randy ever mention a group of army buddies who called themselves the Southside Seven?"

"No," she said. "He never talked about being in the army."

I intended to show her the picture of the seven Silver Star recipients but changed my mind at the last minute. The fewer people who knew about the picture, the better. I had the list of names. I didn't need to go flashing the picture.

By the look on her face, I could tell that talking about her son brought back painful memories. At that moment, all I wanted to do was escape to the privacy of my Hertz rental.

"Would you like to come in for coffee?" she asked.

"No, thank you," I said. "I'm on a tight schedule. I really must be going. Thank you for your time."

I turned and made a hasty—and slightly guilty—retreat to my ride.

◆ ◆ ◆ ◆

"Okay, Hilda," I said. "Time to do your stuff."

Preparing for the worst, I had programmed the local sheriff's office into the GPS, hoping I wouldn't need it.

Ten minutes later, I walked through the front door. A young deputy looked up from his desk. He was slight of build, clean cut, fresh faced, and eager.

"May I help you, sir?" he asked.

"I'm investigating an accident that happened here back in the nineties," I said, showing him my ID. "I'm wondering if you have a file on it I can look at. A man named Randy Butler was killed on a motorcycle. I don't know the exact date."

"Hang on," he said. He stroked his computer keyboard—*peck, peck, enter, peck, peck, enter, click*. "Got it," he said. "Not much here. Victim ran off the road. No other vehicles involved. Late at night, alcohol suspected. Reported by a motorist the next day. Happened near the Arizona border in the middle of nowhere."

"Anybody around who might remember it?" I asked.

"Not me, that's for sure," he said. "Let me ask the sarge."

The young deputy disappeared to the back of the office and a minute later reappeared with an older, stouter man showing gray at the temples.

"I'm Sergeant Conner," he said, offering a hand. "How can I help you?"

"Donald Youngblood," I said. "I was asking the deputy here about the Randy Butler accident and if anyone was around who remembered it."

"Come back to my office and we'll talk," Conner said.

He was a little shorter than I was and probably a few years older. I followed him to an office big enough for only his desk, a chair, and a couple of filing cabinets. In all fairness, his desk was large and ornate, which made the office look smaller.

He caught me looking. "It ain't much," he said, "but it's home."

"Nice desk."

"My father's. Figured I might as well get some use out of it."

I nodded.

"Randy Butler, huh?"

I nodded again.

"Why are you asking about Randy so long after the accident?"

"Long story," I said.

"I love long stories."

"Cop curiosity," I said.

"Exactly."

I told him most of it. I didn't tell him about the note. I wanted it to sound like the whim of a grieving widow.

"So you're just helping her find some closure," he said.

"Something like that."

"But you don't like the fact that he died and no one can tell you why," he said.

"That, too," I said.

"I don't blame you. I hate loose ends." He grew silent, digesting all I had told him.

"Did you know Randy was awarded the Silver Star?" I asked.

"Oh, sure," he said. "That was a big deal around here. They wanted to throw Randy a parade, but he wouldn't hear of it."

"Did you know him well?"

"No better than most," he said. "We're not that big a town. I know lots of people well enough to say hello and chat. I knew Randy's parents."

I didn't mention that I had talked to Randy's mother. He might think I should have come to him first, and I wanted him as cooperative as possible.

"Ever have a problem with Randy?"

"Never," he said.

"Tell me about the accident."

"Well, Doug said he read you the report," Conner said. "Not much else to tell."

"What did you see at the scene?" I asked.

"Nothing to make me think it was foul play, if that's what you're asking," he said.

He wasn't telling me something. I could hear it in his voice.

"What didn't you see?" I asked.

He stared hard at me across his desk. "You're pretty good," he said.

"Tell me," I said.

"It looked as if Randy failed to make a turn and went off an embankment," Conner said. "From the distance of the body from the road, he was going flat out."

"What else?"

"Randy knew those roads like the back of his hand," he said. "I didn't see any signs he tried to make that curve. Just tire tracks in the dirt leading straight off the road."

"Think he did it on purpose?"

"I don't know why he would," he said. "He was a local hero, had everything to live for."

Apparently not, I thought.

"Anyone I can talk to who knew him well?"

Sergeant Conner thought for a moment. "Woman named Abigail down at the local brewpub. They were an item before Randy left for the army."

He gave me the address. I thanked him and left.

29

By the time I got to the Main Street Brewpub and Grill, lunch hour was over and the place was empty. A woman with dark blond hair in a single pigtail, wearing a light blue T-shirt and cream-colored cargo pants, was wiping down tabletops. She was probably forty but looked younger, thanks to a trim figure and a killer rear end.

"Sit anywhere," she said.

I took a booth in the back and waited as she brought a menu and placed it in front of me.

"Do you know what you want, or do you need a minute?" she asked. Her voice was deeper that I expected—sexy without trying to be.

You're married, Youngblood.

"Are you Abigail?" I asked.

"Yeah," she said. "Abby. Nobody calls me Abigail anymore."

"Got a minute to talk?"

"Sure," she said, sliding into the other side of the booth. "What's up?"

I showed her my ID.

"Private investigator," she said. "From Tennessee. You're a long way from home."

"I am," I said. "The sergeant at the sheriff's office told me you knew Randy Butler pretty well."

"Randy, yeah, you could say that," she said, a touch of bitterness in her voice. "But he wasn't the same guy after the Rangers fucked him up, pardon my language. What's this about?"

"A guy he knew in the Rangers died recently, and I was asked to track down some of his old service buddies."

"Well, I guess you know Randy was killed on his motorcycle," Abby said. "A long time ago. Nineteen ninety-four."

"Yes, I learned that today. What can you tell me about his accident?"

She rested her left elbow on the table, put her chin in her hand, and stared into space with much the same look I had seen that morning in the face of Randy's mother.

"He was in here that night," she said, raising her head, eyes shifting back to me. "He had a couple of beers, and we talked some, and the next morning he was dead."

I waited, knowing more would come.

"You knew he was a Ranger, but did you know he won the Silver Star?" Abby asked.

"I did," I said. "The guy who just died also was awarded the Silver Star."

"Really?" she said. "Randy never talked about it. Said it was classified. I think that was bullshit."

"Why?"

"I don't know," she said slowly. "But I think something terrible happened over there and it haunted Randy."

"You were close?"

"Before he went off to be a Ranger, yeah, we were close," she said. "We might have even gotten married, but Desert Storm changed him. He wasn't the same person when he came back. But we stayed friends."

"Any idea what happened the night he died?" I asked.

"Whatever was bothering Randy," she said, "He got rid of it that night."

A chill passed through me. "You don't think it was an accident?"

"Hell no," she said. "He knew what he was doing. I didn't know it then, but I knew it later."

"How?"

"He said goodbye to me," Abby said, her voice quavering. "He kissed me and said, 'Goodbye, Abby.' He never said that. I was too damn busy to notice. When I thought about it later, I realized he was saying goodbye for good." She brushed away a tear.

I was starting to feel uncomfortable. "Sorry," I said.

"Me, too."

We were silent awhile.

"This guy who died," she said. "How did he die?"

"Nobody seems to know," I said. "Apparently, his heart just stopped."

"That's weird."

"It is," I said.

She looked around. "I've got to get back to work," she said, regaining her composure. "Want anything to eat?"

"What's good?"

"I like the Monte Cristo," she said, sliding out of the booth.

"All right," I said. "Sounds good."

"Fries?"

"Half an order."

"We'll charge for a full order."

"I don't care," I said. "I have a bad habit of eating what's in front of me. It it's not there, I won't eat it."

"Smart," she said. "Drink?"

"Do you have an amber ale?"

"We do."

"A pint," I said. I'd probably fall asleep on the plane, but that was okay.

"You got it," she said, giving a smile that showed off her nice, straight, white teeth. She turned and went back past the bar and into the kitchen, her backside receiving my undivided attention all the way.

Ten minutes later, I had my food, my beer, and Abby again sitting across from me.

"I've got a fifteen-minute break," she said. "Okay if I join you?"

"Sure," I said as I bit into the Monte Cristo.

"That guy you told me about," she said. "Did he win the Silver Star for the same thing Randy did?"

"Same mission," I said. "Seven of them. They were all awarded the Silver Star."

"Do you think this other guy's death could have been suicide?"

"I don't see how," I said. "But it's a thought."

She was silent as I ate my Monte Cristo and fries and drank my beer. I realized how hungry I was.

"You staying long?"

"I'm leaving for the airport right after I finish eating," I said.

"You married, Donald?" she asked.

Observant, I thought. *She actually read my ID. But not so observant that she noticed my wedding band. Or did she?*

"Don," I said, raising my left hand to show her.

"Long?"

"A little over a year," I said.

"First?" she asked.

I nodded.

"Must be one hell of a woman to get you off the market," she said, smiling.

I might have blushed a little. "She is that," I said.

30

On Thursday morning, Jim Doak flew me to Gretna, Louisiana. He didn't invite me into the cockpit, nor did I ask to sit there. Being a pilot was not in my future, and training me was evidently not in his.

I was in search of the second name on my list.

We flew into Louis Armstrong International Airport. I rented an SUV from Hertz. The selection in New Orleans wasn't any better than in Farmington. I ended up with another Nissan Xterra.

I drove from the airport through New Orleans and across the bridge to Gretna. I had programmed Hilda with the last known address of Armand Coltran Priloux. He was one of the two dark-skinned men in the picture—Creole, maybe.

Forty-five minutes after leaving the Hertz lot, I parked in front of a weatherworn, dirty-white two-story house in a less-than-desirable neighborhood in Gretna. I clipped my Ruger to my belt and exited my rental. Better safe than sorry.

The house had a chain-link fence around it. I spied a doghouse in the side yard. The grass there was well worn. A sign on the fence read, "Beware of Satan." I hoped that was some kind of religious message, but I had my doubts.

I raised the latch on the gate. It squeaked. Suddenly, a large, black, powerful dog exploded from the doghouse and charged the gate. I put the latch back down and slid my hand to the Ruger and took a few steps backward. The dog, a male Rottweiler, just about made it to the gate when his chain ran out. He created enough of a racket to let his owner know a visitor was on the property, and then he quieted. I waited a safe distance from the gate to see it anyone would come to the door. No one did. The dog sat and stared at me like I was a porkchop and maintained a low, menacing growl.

A minute later, a rather large black woman who didn't look any friendlier that the Rottweiler stepped onto the front porch of the house next door. She looked at the dog, then at me.

"Satan," she snapped. "Go lie down."

The dog rose obediently, turned, and trotted back to his doghouse.

Satan, I thought. *Not a bad name for a watchdog. Certainly got my attention.*

"Can I help you?" the woman asked as I walked toward her porch.

"Maybe," I said. "I'm looking for an ex–Army Ranger by the name of Armand Coltran Priloux. That house is his last known address."

"Never heard of anybody by that name," she said. "Must have moved before we got here." Her manner belied her looks. She was pleasant and self-assured, almost friendly.

"Who lives there now?" I asked.

"My son," she said. "James Cobb. I'm Louise Cobb. James is at work."

"Scary dog," I said, looking back toward her son's house.

"Satan's a good dog," she said. "Real sweet, just protective."

"Has anybody on the block lived here longer that you?" I asked.

"Yes, sir," she said. "The Tuckers, in the blue house, and the Smiths, in the gray house." She pointed across the street. "They been here a long time."

"Thanks."

"You a cop?"

"No," I said.

"You're carrying a gun." She didn't seem alarmed by that.

"Private detective," I said as I turned to leave. "Thanks again for your help."

I walked across the street and visited the Tucker house. Mrs. Tucker had lived in the neighborhood for fifteen years but hadn't heard of Armand Coltran Priloux. She told me the Smiths had moved in two years after her and her husband. She knew of no one else who had been there longer.

I didn't bother going to the Smith house.

I walked back across the street toward the Xterra. Louise Cobb was sitting on her porch in a rocking chair drinking what looked to be a glass of iced tea.

"Any luck?" she asked.

I went up the walk to her steps. "No," I said. "Mrs. Tucker never heard of him, and she said she's been here longer than the Smiths."

"That a fact?" she said. "I didn't know that."

I thought Louise Cobb and Mrs. Tucker were telling me the truth, but I couldn't be positive.

I took out a business card, climbed the steps to the porch, and handed it to Louise Cobb. "If you hear anything about Armand, get in touch with me," I said. "I'll pay one hundred dollars for good information."

She looked at the card. "Donald Youngblood," she said. "Nice name. I'll ask around. I could use the money. Want a glass of iced tea, Mr. Youngblood?"

My first thought was to say no, but for some reason I heard myself saying yes.

For the next half-hour, I sat on Louise Cobb's porch drinking iced tea and listening to stories about her childhood, her son, and the decline of the neighborhood. I left her sitting in her rocking chair enjoying the day. By the time I left, I was positive she had never heard of Armand Coltran Priloux.

◆ ◆ ◆ ◆

Before leaving for New Orleans, I had called Liam McSwain, the Knoxville chief of police and Mary's former boss, to ask him if Bud Hoffman, former Knoxville police officer, was still on the New Orleans police force. He had called back to say that Bud was not only still with the NOPD but had been promoted to detective.

I had met Bud Hoffman while tracking down leads on the Fairchild case. More importantly, a short time before that, I had met Mary. She was subsequently wounded in the line of duty trying to stop a bank robbery. Mary killed one of the perpetrators, but two escaped. Liam McSwain, fearful of payback, asked me to be Mary's bodyguard while the police pursued the suspects. I reluctantly said yes and later wondered why. One thing led to another, and, as they say, the rest was history.

Now, Bud was only too happy to meet me when I offered to buy him lunch. We sat at an out-of-the-way table in the Court of the Two Sisters restaurant enjoying the jazz brunch buffet. Bud's plate was loaded. Mine had a nice sampling of Creole jambalaya, duck à l'orange, and shrimp étouffée. We had exchanged pleasantries but not much else. The food was excellent and had Bud's full attention. He looked as if he had put on a few pounds since I last saw him but didn't appear out of shape. He was about five-ten with a dark complexion and a look that would make anyone think twice about messing with him.

"Congratulations on your promotion," I said.

"Thanks," Hoffman said as he deftly peeled a pile of crayfish, then popped one into his mouth. "This is great. I can't afford to eat here on my salary. I appreciate the invitation, but I'm sure it comes with a price. So what's going on, Youngblood? What brings you to New Orleans?"

I told him a little about the Crane case—that I was tracking down some service buddies of Walter Crane and that Armand Coltran Priloux was on the list. I told him about my morning excursion to Gretna and my talk with Louise Cobb.

"You got lucky there," Hoffman said. "Most black folks in that part of Gretna wouldn't give a white detective air if he was in a jug."

I shrugged. "What about Priloux?"

"Never heard of him," Hoffman said, working on a pork rib.

"Maybe you could do a little research," I said. "For Gretna and New Orleans. See if you can come up with an address."

"Yeah, I could do that. I know a few cops in Gretna." He licked his fingers and wiped them on his napkin. "Let's get dessert."

Hoffman picked the bananas Foster, and I chose the bread pudding. We both ordered coffee. I'd need it to stay awake for my drive back to the airport. I rarely ate so much for lunch.

"Man, that was good," Hoffman said when he finished his dessert. "Thanks, Youngblood."

"My pleasure," I said. "When do you think you can get back to me on Priloux?"

"Couple of days."

We were silent as we drank coffee and took in the clientele.

"You've changed, Youngblood," Hoffman said.

"What do you mean?"

"Last time I saw you, you were an amateur. Now, you're a pro. You've got that hard look."

I didn't respond, not knowing how to take what he said. Killing three people could change a guy—even if they were bad people and it was more or less self-defense.

"That was a compliment," Hoffman said.

"I thought it might be," I said. "I'm just not sure I like the change."

"Goes with the territory."

I finished my coffee. When the waiter came to refill my cup, I waved him away.

"Whatever happened to Mary Sanders?" Hoffman asked.

"You mean Mary Youngblood?" I said.

It took a few seconds for it to register. "You married her?"

"I did."

"Youngblood," Hoffman said, "you are one hellacious lucky guy."

Can't argue with that, I thought.

◆ ◆ ◆ ◆

By the time I drove back to the airport, turned in the rental, and boarded the Learjet, I was feeling the full effects of lunch at the Court of the Two Sisters. Jim went to work preparing for takeoff, and I went to the bar and fixed a club soda with lime, hoping to settle my stomach and stay awake. I settled into one of the leather seats, fastened my seat belt, and took a long, refreshing drink.

"Ready to taxi, Don," Jim said over the intercom. "Buckle up."

Fifteen minutes later, we were airborne, New Orleans looking cleaner and neater as we gained altitude. When we leveled off, I fixed another drink and returned to my seat to think.

I knew some things about three of the men in the picture. Walter Crane was dead. Maybe he was murdered, or maybe he took his own life, or maybe he just died. I hadn't considered suicide before Abby suggested it. Walter had been in the Middle East. Maybe he had acquired some exotic poison there. I didn't think so, but it was possible. Randy Butler was dead, maybe by accident or maybe by suicide. It certainly didn't look like murder. But if it was, it was cleverly done. And Armand Coltran Priloux was missing—maybe dead, maybe alive. I hoped Bud Hoffman could tell me.

I was surprised Bud hadn't known Mary and I were married. Apparently, Bud had brushed the dust of the Knoxville PD off himself and moved on without looking back. Liam McSwain had been at our wedding, along with a few others on the force who Mary had been close to, so I was sure the word had made the rounds among Knoxville's finest. Apparently, Bud Hoffman was not a man staying in touch.

My mind wandered back to the wedding over a year ago. It didn't seem possible—Donald Youngblood married, and with an adopted daughter, no less. Yet none of my close friends seemed surprised.

"You're a romantic and a sucker," Big Bob had said. "And you're a lucky bastard. Mary is one hell of a woman." Leave it to Big Bob to get right to the heart of it.

The wedding took place on the lower deck at the lake house on a beautiful day in early October. All the usual suspects were in attendance, including out-of-towners Bruiser Bracken, Sister Sarah Agnes Woods, and Raul Rivera, who put the full-court press on Wanda Jones and couldn't figure out why she didn't faint at his feet. Wanda seemed more interested in Bruiser, whom she had met a few Thanksgivings ago at Joseph Fleet's.

A local Methodist minister—a female Mary had met while investigating a church break-in—performed the ceremony. Reverend Jane insisted on a pre-marriage counseling session, and Mary had practically dragged me to the church in handcuffs. I hadn't been to church since my parents' funeral. But the building remained standing, and I felt an odd sense of belonging the entire time I was there.

When I took a deep breath and said, "I do," I realized life as I knew it was over. But I was sure life in the future would be even better, shared with the woman I loved.

Those were my last thoughts before the drone of the jet's engines and the elaborate French Quarter lunch put me to sleep.

31

The next morning, we were in the bathroom together. Lacy had already left for school. Mary was in front of one sink putting on her makeup, and I was in front of the other lathering up for a shave. We rarely shared the bathroom. I was usually up early and out of the condo before either female got out of bed.

Mary was wearing Victoria's Secret black bikini panties and matching bra. She had her hair pulled back in a ponytail, a look I liked. I had just come out of our walk-in shower wearing a plush white towel around my waist. I began shaving while sneaking admiring peeks at Mary.

"I'm getting fat," Mary said, turning this way and that, surveying her gorgeous body in the mirror that spanned the entire wall in front of us.

"You're not fat," I said. "You're sexy and curvy, and I love it."

Mary had put on a few pounds since we married, but they had gone to all the right places. I noticed the tiny scar where she had taken the bank robber's bullet. Even that was sexy.

"You think?" Mary said.

"I think," I said, working on the left side of my face.

"You know why I love you, Mr. Youngblood?"

"I haven't a clue, Mrs. Youngblood," I said, working under my nose.

"Because you always say the right thing at the right time," she said.

"It's a gift." I wiped off the excess shaving cream with a hand towel. My eyes widened as Mary unhooked her bra and dropped it to the floor.

"Speaking of gifts," Mary said as she ripped my towel off. "I think you're about to get one."

And it wasn't even my birthday!

◆ ◆ ◆ ◆

I arrived at the office wearing a smile that piqued Gretchen's curiosity.

"You're later than usual," she said, as if she knew why.

"Overslept," I said. I tried not to smile but couldn't help myself.

"What's so funny?"

"Nothing," I said. "What's up?"

"Bud Hoffman from the New Orleans Police Department called. He wouldn't tell me what it was about." She handed me a pink slip with a telephone number as I headed toward my office. "Were you a bad boy in New Orleans?"

"Bud's a detective," I said, ignoring her jab. "He probably has some information regarding the Crane case."

"How's that going?" she asked, turning serious.

I paused in my doorway and turned toward her. "I'm not really sure. One person I tried to talk to is dead, and another is in parts unknown. Hold my calls."

I shut the door behind me and went to my desk. I settled in, picked up the phone, and dialed the number.

"Hoffman," the voice said.

"It's Youngblood."

"Okay," Hoffman said, getting straight to it. "Here's what I did. First, I checked our database. Your guy's not in there. Then I called a friend on the Gretna PD, and he checked their database. He's not in there either, so no criminal record."

"I didn't think there would be, but thanks for checking," I said.

"I'm not through," Hoffman said. He was working hard for the Court of the Two Sisters lunch. "I went to a source at the motor vehicle department and gave him the name. He got a hit. Your guy's last known address was in the Ninth Ward."

"He was living there when Katrina hit?"

"He was," Hoffman said.

"He's dead?"

"Don't know," he said. "He's not on any list, either dead or missing. From what I hear, almost one hundred bodies in the morgue were never identified. And the missing list totals almost twenty-three hundred."

"Good God."

"You said your guy was a vet, so I'm sure he's not one of the unidentified from the morgue," Hoffman said. "They pulled prints and ran them through all the available databases, including military."

"So, unofficially, he's missing," I said.

"Guess so," Hoffman said. "He could be among the missing dead, or he could have beaten the storm and relocated somewhere else. It's impossible to know."

"Okay," I said. "Thanks for checking."

"Not a problem," he said. "I really enjoyed that lunch."

"You come up with anything else and I'll buy you another one."

"You got a deal," Hoffman said.

◆ ◆ ◆ ◆

Gretchen left at four o'clock. The office was quiet. I leaned back in my black leather chair, put my feet on my desk, and thought about things some more. Orangeburg, South Carolina, would be my next stop. There, I hoped to track down the next name on my list, Robert Henry McMullen. I hoped to find him alive. I hoped he would talk to me.

Hoffman was right about one thing he said in New Orleans. I was lucky Louise Cobb had talked to me. I had never thought much about it, but I guessed a private investigator could scare some people—make them forgetful, shy, and withdrawn. I needed an alternate persona.

I considered that for a while and then made a phone call.

"Amos," I said when he answered, "it's Donald Youngblood. I need a favor."

"Tell me," Amos said.

I told him.

"This should be fun," he said. "I'll get back to you."

32

I always smiled to myself when I thought about fictional detectives working a big case. The story was usually about only that case, which had few or no interruptions. Even with my first big case, I had gotten sidetracked. And now that I'd been an active private investigator for over five years, and my business had grown, I got sidetracked more and more.

Friday night, I was sitting at the kitchen bar with Lacy, eating takeout Chinese food. Mary was having dinner with Wanda. Spread before us were Kung Pao chicken, sesame shrimp, house-fried rice, and egg rolls. Lacy had grown to five-foot-ten, and it appeared her growth spurt was over. We talked basketball. She could play the three position—small forward—or the two—shooting guard—with equal skill.

"Coach wants me to shoot more," Lacy said, biting down on a sesame shrimp.

"That would be music to my ears," I said, forking in a mouthful of house-fried rice.

In high school, I hadn't been shy about shooting the ball. When I got an open shot, I let it fly, a tendency encouraged by Big Bob, who often rebounded my stray shots and deposited them into the basket. I told him often that if it weren't for me, he would never have led the team in scoring or rebounding.

"You know me," Lacy said. "I'd rather play defense, rebound, and pass the ball."

"You're a good shooter," I said. "Especially from three-point range. You should do what your team needs you to do."

"I guess so." Lacy didn't seem enthusiastic.

I finished my egg roll and ate some of the hot and spicy Kung Pao chicken with peanuts and water chestnuts.

"I have something else I want to talk to you about," Lacy said.

I knew I was about to be sidetracked. "Okay," I said. "What?"

"Bullying."

My ears perked up. "Somebody bullying you?"

Lacy smiled. "Of course not, Don. I'm Lacy Youngblood, daughter of the famous Mountain Center private detective who shoots first and asks questions later. And my mother is a Mountain Center cop. And in case you haven't noticed, I take crap from no one."

I heard pride in her voice. I relaxed and tried not to smile. Our girl had attitude. I liked that.

"Hannah?"

"No," Lacy said. "Hannah falls under the same umbrella as I do because she's my best friend."

"Who, then?"

"A kid named Alfred Lucas. They call him 'the Brain.'"

"With a name like Alfred, what should he expect?"

"Don!" Lacy gave me the stare she had learned from Mary.

"Okay," I said. "Tell me about it."

I started to work on another egg roll. Alfred was a total nerd, Lacy said. If he wasn't the smartest kid in school, he was definitely in the top three. He was average in height, skinny, quiet, and wore glasses. A kid named Doolin—Lacy didn't know his first name—picked on Alfred constantly, pushing him around and generally making his life at school miserable. Lacy wasn't the only one who was getting tired of it. But Doolin was a mean kid, and nobody wanted to rat him out to the school office.

"It would make it worse," Lacy said. "I need to figure out a way to handle it without involving the school."

"I could have him whacked," I said.

"Believe me," Lacy said, "a part of me is not totally against that idea."

While we finished the Chinese in silence, it came to me that what Alfred needed was a bodyguard.

"Who's the toughest kid in school?" I asked.

Lacy thought about it. "Probably Biker McBride. Leather jacket, Harley. Not bad looking, now that I think about it. Why?"

"I might make it worth his while to look out for Alfred," I said. "Ask around. Tell me where he hangs out when he's not in school."

Lacy smiled. "That would be something," she said. "No way Doolin would want any part of Biker."

33

I had just sat in the back corner booth at the Bloody Duck, a combination blue-collar and redneck biker bar and grill with six pool tables. The Duck, as Roy called it, was a few miles out of town on the highway to Johnson City. I had discovered it while working a case and found out that Roy was a frequent visitor. It was four o'clock on a Monday. Rocky, the owner and a friend of Roy's, came walking toward me.

"Haven't seen you in a while, Don," he said. "What's happening?"

"Business as usual," I said. "Give me a draft."

"Amber Bock?"

"Right," I said.

Rocky strolled back toward the bar. The place was quiet. A few teenagers shooting pool and a couple of guys at the bar were the extent of it. When I walked in, I had noticed an old, mint-condition Harley parked out front. One of the teenagers wore a leather jacket with a Harley emblem.

Rocky returned and placed a coaster, napkins, some peanuts, and the Amber Bock on my table.

"Thanks," I said. "Got time to sit a minute?"

Rocky smiled and sat. "Didn't think you were out here just to have one of my drafts," he said.

"The kid wearing the Harley jacket," I said. "Is he Biker McBride?"

"Yeah," Rocky said. "He do something?"

"Not that I know of. Tell me about him."

"Comes in here most days after school to shoot pool," Rocky said. "He's quiet, polite, and doesn't cause any trouble."

"Tough kid?"

"Must be," Rocky said. "The other kids walk soft around him. You know the type. They just seem to give off a silent alarm that says, 'Don't mess with me.' "

I nodded and took a long drink. "Ask him to come over when he's done with his game," I said. "Whatever he's drinking, I'm buying."

Ten minutes later, Biker came to my booth carrying what looked like a Coke in a beer mug filled with ice. He was solidly built, dark, about my height, and, as Lacy said, not bad looking. He appeared calm and casual.

"You want to see me?"

I nodded. "You know who I am?"

"Yeah, you're Lacy Youngblood's father, the private detective," he said.

"Right," I said, extending my hand. "Donald Youngblood. Pleased to meet you."

He stared at me for a second or two, then shook hands. "What's this about?"

"Please," I said. "Sit down."

He sat.

"I need a favor," I said.

"A favor," he said, as if he was having trouble processing my response. He took a drink of his soda, staring at me over the mug. "What is it?" he asked, setting the mug on the table.

"Know a kid named Alfred Lucas?" I asked.

"Yeah," Biker said. "The Brain."

"Well, Alfred is being bullied by a kid name Doolin," I said.

Biker smiled. "Yeah, Doolin is a bully. Never picks on anyone who could be a threat."

"So he wouldn't pick on you?"

He smiled again. "Not in a million years."

"So here's the favor," I said. "I want you to be Alfred's unofficial bodyguard. Put a stop to the bullying."

"Why me?"

"Lacy said you're probably the toughest kid in school."

"She did? I didn't think she knew I exist."

"I guess you have a reputation."

Biker laughed. "A reputation built on one fight."

"Sometimes, that's all it takes," I said.

"I guess so," Biker said.

We stared at each other as I took a drink of my beer and he sipped his Coke.

"So why would I do this?" Biker asked.

"I'd owe you a favor," I said.

"Like writing a college recommendation letter."

That surprised me. I was thinking more along the lines of bailing him out of jail, but I kept that to myself.

"Sure," I said. "Like that."

"And when my friends ask me why I'm all of a sudden protecting this geek, I say what?"

I had already thought about that, so I was ready for the question. "How are your grades?" I asked.

He looked down at the table. "They could be better."

"And you want to go to college?"

He nodded.

"I'll bet if you ask Alfred to tutor you in some of your courses in exchange for getting Doolin off his back, he'd jump at the chance."

He took another drink of his Coke as he silently processed the idea.

"That your Harley out front?" I asked, relieving the awkward moment.

"Yeah," he said. "It's really my dad's. It's a 1990 Fat Boy Grey Ghost, a real sweet bike. He doesn't ride much anymore, so I've taken it over."

"Nice ride," I said.

"You know Harleys?" Biker asked.

"I do," I said. "My partner has one, a 1984 FLT."

"Billy Two-Feathers," Biker said. "I've seen him around. I love that turquoise trim. I'd love to take that bike for a spin."

"I might be able to make that happen," I said.

"That'd be great."

"Biker, you're up!" a voice from the front of the Duck shouted.

Biker slid out of the booth and picked up his drink. "Nice meeting you," he said. He drained the mug and set it on the table. "I'll think about the favor."

He turned and walked back toward the pool tables.

34

Election night, Mary, Lacy, and I went to Billy's place to await the results of the sheriff's race. From all indications, it was going to be a victory celebration. All of the men and some of the women were in Billy's studio, where a light buffet was set up. Billy and Maggie were nonconsumers of alcohol, so wine and beer were out and coffee, iced tea, and soft drinks were in. Maggie, Mary, Lacy, and a few other women were in the main house ogling seven-month-old Donald Roy Youngblood. I hoped Mary didn't come back with any ideas.

Several men in the group were current deputies hoping to catch on with the new regime. The women were mostly wives and girlfriends and one potential new deputy. A few of the men were on cell phones getting updates on the results. I made the rounds meeting people and engaging in casual conversation.

Across the room, I spotted Billy's candidate, Charlie Running Horse. I had met Charlie briefly when we arrived. He was talking on his cell. When we made eye contact, he held up one finger. A few seconds later, he closed his phone and headed my way. He was a little taller than me and had a slender, wiry build like Roy.

"What's the latest?" I asked as he approached.

"Looks good," he said. "We should have it wrapped up in a few hours."

"Good to hear," I said.

"I want to thank you for supporting my campaign."

"No offense, but I was really supporting Billy."

"None taken," he said. "Let me rephrase. Thanks for supporting Billy."

"My pleasure," I said.

I took a drink from my big glass of sweet tea with lemon.

"How long have you known Billy?" he asked.

"Long time," I said. "We met in college."

"Interesting man," Charlie said.

"He has an unusual background for a Cherokee Indian," I said.

"That he does," Charlie said. "He's going to make one hell of a deputy."

"No doubt about that."

"Tell me about Cherokee Investigations," he said.

"Long story short, it started as a hobby and turned into a full-time job," I said. "The job turned dangerous somewhere along the way. At least three people have tried to kill me, and I've been in the hospital three times."

"I hear you've had to use deadly force," Charlie said.

"You did some homework."

"I did," he said. "In case you haven't noticed, Billy doesn't talk much." Charlie had a soft, soothing voice with a slight rasp.

"I've noticed," I said. "The first year I knew him, I don't think he said a dozen words."

Charlie laughed, took a drink from the bottle of local spring water he carried, and looked around the room. I could tell he didn't miss much.

"What can you tell me about Billy?" Charlie asked, refocusing on me.

"If I had a choice of one person to go to war with or to cover my back, it would be Billy Two-Feathers," I said. "If you want to know more than that, ask Maggie."

Charlie Running Horse smiled. "I think you about said it all."

"What do you have in mind for Billy?" I asked.

"Well, of course, I want him to do our forensic photography. I hear he's good."

"He is," I said.

"And I want him to be our liaison with the Safe Trails Task Force in Asheville, North Carolina."

Charlie went on to explain that the Safe Trails Task Force was a joint operation of federal, state, local, and tribal law enforcement working together to reduce crime in Indian territory. Eighteen Safe Trails Task Forces were presently scattered across the United States from North Carolina to the state of Washington.

"With his background, education, and experience as a private investigator, he'll be the perfect man for the job," he said.

"Can't argue with that," I said.

◆ ◆ ◆ ◆

The official word of Charlie's victory came around ten o'clock. The group started thinning out after that.

We were back at the condo by midnight. Mary and I were in bed reading, trying to wind down.

"Little D is so cute," she said for maybe the tenth time that night. "He looks like a miniature Billy."

"Sure does," I said, my nose buried in the latest Robert B. Parker novel.

"Don't worry," Mary said. "I'm done birthing babies."

"That's a relief."

We read. Every now and then, Mary would make a comment or ask me a question. I would give the shortest response possible and go back to reading.

"What's your next step in the Crane case?" she asked.

"I'll try to track down another name on the list," I said.

"So you have this picture of seven Silver Star winners, and three of them are dead," Mary said a few minutes later.

"Two dead, one missing."

She put her book on her nightstand and looked at me. "Doesn't sound promising."

"No, it doesn't."

I marked and closed my book. I knew reading was hopeless. Mary was wired.

"You have much easier ways of tracking down the list than visiting each last known address," she said.

"I know that."

"But you want the element of surprise, should you find one alive."

I looked at her and smiled. "Precisely," I said, making severe eye contact.

She moved closer and kissed me, her hand sliding underneath my pajamas.

"It's pretty late," I said, trying to act uninterested.

"Apparently not," Mary said, reaching her target.

35

A few days later, I was at my regular table in the Mountain Center Diner finishing breakfast. The ancient digital clock on the wall flipped to 9:02. The morning crowd was thinning, most heading to work. The ones who remained snuck curious glances at my guest, Amos "Teaberry" Smith. Amos was black. He was a lean, mid-forties man less than six feet tall. An Ivy League graduate, he looked the part in light gray slacks, a white shirt with a button-down collar, and a black cashmere sweater vest. Flecks of gray showed in his closely cropped hair.

Amos was a retired master forger. The government had started the retirement process by putting Amos in prison. Every now and then, he came out of retirement. He had helped me on a couple of occasions when I was working cases, and I had repaid him with financial advice. He was now heavily into the Internet, providing all sorts of information to those who were willing to pay.

Doris hurried over to refill our coffee cups and clear our plates. "Was everything okay?" she asked.

"Breakfast was great," Amos said in that slow, sophisticated voice of his. "I can see why Mr. Youngblood frequents your establishment."

Doris beamed and hurried away.

I turned my attention to Amos. "You didn't have to come all this way to bring the stuff. You could have mailed it."

"Not a problem," Amos said, looking at me through his John Lennon–style glasses. "I need to get out more, see how the other half lives. Nice little town you have here."

"Yes, it is," I said. We were running out of small talk.

Amos took a drink of coffee and removed a folder and a small rectangular box from his briefcase. He slid the box over to me. I removed the lid. Inside were business cards. I maneuvered a card free and took a look.

D. Alexander Youngblood
National News Network
Freelance Journalist
Email: youngbloodNNN@cryx.net

I smiled and nodded. "This will work. What if someone sends me an email?"

"I'll route it to your Cherokee Investigations email address," Amos said.

He reached back into his briefcase and handed me a laminated card slightly larger than a credit card with a clip that would attach to a pocket or lapel. It read, "PRESS ACCESS." The card showed my picture in color and said I was a member of the media working for the National News Network. Underneath the picture was a series of letters and numbers. A faint, official-looking seal was in the background in the center of the card. The seal was also in color.

"Nice work," I said. "Looks authentic."

"Thanks," Amos said. "I had fun with that. It might fool country bumpkins, but I wouldn't try getting into a presidential press conference with it."

"What is the National News Network?" I asked.

"As far as I know, it doesn't exist," Amos said. "But it does have a nice ring to it, like something you think you've heard before."

"You're right. It sounds real."

"You also have a website, in case anyone gets curious and checks you out," Amos said. "I wrote a few articles for it myself. Pretty damn good, if I do say so. If you Google Alexander Youngblood, it will show a link to your website."

"I'll take a look later," I said. "What do I owe you?"

"On the house," Amos said. "I made a killing on that last stock tip you gave me. I've even started doing some day-trading."

"Be careful with that," I said.

Amos laughed. "I hear you. Day-trading is not for the faint of heart."

◆ ◆ ◆ ◆

That night, Mary fixed crabmeat-stuffed tilapia with wild rice and baked broccoli. We took no prisoners; the only thing left was dirty dishes. After dinner, we sat at the kitchen bar eating rice pudding for dessert and finishing the last of our drinks. Mary got up and carried some dishes to the sink.

"That problem we discussed last week looks like it's working itself out," Lacy said, leaning in toward me.

"Good," I said equally quietly. It didn't work.

Mary spun and looked at me, then Lacy, then back to me. "What problem?"

Elephant ears!

"Nothing you should know about, Wonder Woman," I said, trying to lighten the moment.

That didn't work either. "Lacy," Mary said sharply.

"He's right," Lacy said. "It's better you don't know. You've got to trust us on that. We'll tell you later. Right now, it's too soon."

"Bending the rules again?" Mary said, looking at me.

"In a good way," I said.

She let it pass, which surprised me. Mary was naturally curious. Like all good cops, she wanted to get to the bottom of everything.

Lacy cleared the rest of the dishes, and they both came back and sat at the bar.

I changed the subject. "I'm going to get a new Pathfinder. I ordered it today."

"It's about time," Mary said. "It's not like you can't afford it."

"Want a new truck? We can trade yours in."

"Nope, I like my truck just fine," Mary said.

Mary had purchased a used Ford F-150 just before we were married. I wanted to buy her a new one, but she had flat refused. I got even by giving her a new, loaded F-150 on our first anniversary. When I offered her the keys, she had given me the cop stare, then smiled, grabbed them, and took the truck for a spin.

Mary looked at Lacy, then at me. "What are you going to do with the old Pathfinder? It's in great condition."

"I don't know," I said absent-mindedly. "What do you think?"

"What about giving it to Lacy?" Mary asked, on cue.

We had already discussed the matter and agreed Lacy could handle the responsibility. She held earned a learner's permit at fifteen and graduated to an intermediate restricted driver's license soon after her sixteenth birthday. She could now drive alone with one other person in the car, unless a licensed driver above age twenty-one was present.

"There's a thought," I said, looking at Lacy. "Want it?"

"You're kidding, right?" she said. "Of course I want it!"

"Okay, then," I said. "It's yours."

"Yes!" Lacy said with a fist pump.

"You'll have to wait until my new one comes in," I said.

"Not a problem," Lacy said. "I can wait." She paused. "When is it coming in?"

Mary laughed.

Women!

36

The next day was crisp and bright—a perfect driving day. I spent the morning heading to Orangeburg, a small South Carolina town of about fifteen thousand located forty miles southeast of Columbia. I went south out of Mountain Center through some beautiful back country and picked up I-40 East. Near Asheville, North Carolina, I transitioned to 1-26 South. I crossed into South Carolina around ten o'clock and was in Orangeburg by noon. I followed Hilda's directions to a generally well-kept middle-class neighborhood on the outskirts of town and parked on the street in front of the house. I headed up the concrete walk carrying my attaché case, climbed the few steps to the front porch, and rang the doorbell. A few seconds later, a round, little woman with a pleasant face answered the door. She had short, curly hair garishly colored jet black and dark eyes hiding behind black-framed glasses.

"Yes," she said through the screen door. "May I help you?"

"I'm looking for Robert Henry McMullen," I said.

Her face clouded. "Bobby's been dead for several years," she said. "Are you a friend of his?"

Dead, I thought. *Why am I not surprised?*

"No, ma'am," I said. "I'm a reporter doing a story on Silver Star recipients, and I wanted to interview Bobby. Are you his mother?"

"Yes," she said vacantly.

A tall man with a full face and salt-and-pepper close-cropped hair appeared behind Mrs. McMullen. "Edith, who is it?" he asked.

Mrs. McMullen repeated my cover story.

"Well, invite the young man in," he said. "He can talk to us."

Edith unlatched the screen door, and I followed the couple into the living room. I was disappointed they hadn't even asked for my ID.

"This is my husband, Arthur," Mrs. McMullen said. "I'm Edith."

"Alexander Youngblood," I said, shaking Arthur's hand.

The house was chilly. Both Edith and Arthur were wearing sweaters. I kept my leather jacket on. The forest-green carpet was clean but showing wear, as was the dated furniture. I sat in a comfortable chair facing the McMullens, together on the couch. The house was old but in good condition. A fireplace with a large mantel was on my left. Wood, kindling, and paper awaited a match. Given the coolness of the day, I guessed that by evening it would be burning warmly.

I opened my attaché case, took out a spiral notebook, and set the case on the floor facing them. My press pass, clipped to the inside of the case, was clearly visible. I handed each of them a business card. They looked and nodded approval. I unclipped my pen, flipped open the notebook, and launched the first question.

"When did your son die?" I asked.

"Almost five years ago," Edith McMullen said.

"How?"

She glanced at her husband and then looked back at me.

"Complications from pneumonia," Arthur McMullen said. "He got a bad case of the flu and then a mean strain of pneumonia."

"Not the flu," I wrote in my notebook.

"I'm sorry," I said. "I would have liked to have met him."

They both nodded solemn approval.

"What did Bobby think about receiving the Silver Star?" I asked.

"He didn't like to talk about it," Arthur said.

A recurring theme, I thought.

"He said he didn't deserve it," Edith added. "We didn't even know he had it until I found it one day while cleaning."

"What did the town think about it?" I asked.

"Hard to say," Edith said. "Bobby didn't want us to talk about it, but you know how parents are. We couldn't help it. We told a few friends, and then word got around. The local newspaper came to interview Bobby, but he told the reporter he couldn't tell about the mission that led to the medal. The paper did a general story on him called, 'The Humble Hero.' Then things got back to normal, and the Silver Star was never mentioned again."

"Did Bobby ever mention a group of army buddies who called themselves the Southside Seven?"

"No," Edith said. "I don't think so."

Arthur shook his head.

"What did Bobby do for a living when he got back?" I continued.

"Odd jobs," Arthur said. "He was good with his hands. He had lots of work. People liked him. After the newspaper story, he had more work than he could handle."

I nodded and wrote in my notebook.

"Did Bobby have a military funeral?" I asked, already knowing the answer.

"No," Arthur said, tight-faced. "He was cremated."

"That was his wish?"

"Yes," Arthur said nervously.

I made a note: "Lying about the cremation?" I knew I had struck a nerve. Edith, too, was starting to look nervous. Lying to the press did that to people.

I looked at the urn I had noticed earlier on the mantel. It was surrounded by pictures. The mantel was a Bobby McMullen memorial.

"Bobby's ashes?"

"Yes," they said together.

I flipped my notebook closed. "I'm sorry for your loss. I won't take any more of your time."

They stood quickly, seemingly pleased that the interview was over. Arthur went to the door and opened it for me. I nodded at Edith and exited onto the porch.

"By the way," I said, "what was the name of Bobby's doctor?"

I could tell I had caught Arthur off guard. Later, I would realize that was the question that had stirred the pot.

"Some emergency-room doctor," he said. "I don't remember his name. I think he left town awhile back."

Another lie, I thought. I didn't push. I thanked him again, returned to my Pathfinder, and drove downtown.

◆ ◆ ◆ ◆

I chose a local restaurant, The Four Moons, located an out-of-the-way table, ordered a club sandwich and a beer, and thought about my conversation with the McMullens. They had been glad to talk to me until the conversation came around to how Bobby died. The more I asked, the more nervous they were. I knew there was more to know.

I had finished my sandwich and beer when I noticed a man approaching my table. He reminded me a little of Roy Husky—not as lean but rugged looking, some gray in his short-cut hair, a serious look on his face. He wore khaki slacks and a blue denim shirt with "Orangeburg, SC" embroidered over the left pocket. I knew from the badge clipped to his brown belt that he might be trouble.

"Mr. Youngblood," he said as he approached.

I stood. "Yes?"

"Tyler Davis," he said, extending his hand. "Chief of police."

"Am I double-parked or something, chief?" I asked, shaking his hand.

He laughed. "No, you're fine. May I sit?"

"Sure," I said.

The waitress came over. "Want something, chief?" she asked.

"Sweet tea, Molly," Chief Davis said. "Thanks."

Molly went away.

"I hear you're a reporter," he said.

"News travels fast."

Faster than it should, I thought.

"Small town," Tyler Davis said.

Not that small, I thought.

"I guess the McMullens called you," I said.

He nodded. "You upset them a bit; brought up some bad memories."

"They seemed okay until I started asking how Bobby died," I said. "After that, they couldn't wait to get rid of me."

"I need you not to write about Bobby McMullen," Chief Davis said.

"Why?"

"Let's just say for the good of the community."

"Tell me the whole story, and I guarantee nothing will ever be written about it," I said.

"Can't," he said.

I knew I had a better chance of getting him to talk if he didn't think I was the press. I took out my private investigator ID and showed it to him.

"I'm not surprised," he said flatly. "You don't act much like a reporter. What's this about?"

"I'm working a case that could be connected to Bobby McMullen. I figured if the McMullens knew I was a private investigator, they'd be less likely to talk with me," I said.

"You got that right," Chief Davis said. "They would have stroked out."

"The case I'm working on might be murder," I said. "Bobby knew the deceased, and I wanted to talk to him. I didn't know he was dead, although I'm not surprised. I need to know the circumstances of his death to see if or how it ties to my case."

"Tell me about it," he said. "All of it."

"It's a long story."

"Come with me," he said. "I have just the place for a long story."

37

We sat in the conference room of the Orangeburg Police Department as I told Tyler Davis most of what I knew about the Crane case. The more I talked, the more uneasy he looked.

"That's it," I said when I finished. "I'm tracking down six guys who were in a picture with Walter Crane. So far, two are dead, and one is missing and probably dead."

"Shit," he said, running his fingers through his hair.

"What?"

He shook his head. "How do I know I can trust you?"

"I promise that whatever you tell me goes no farther," I said. "My word's good."

"Maybe so," Chief Davis said. "But how do I know that?"

I opened my attaché case, took out the spiral notebook, flipped it open, wrote Big Bob's number on a blank page, ripped it out, and handed it to Tyler Davis.

"Call this number in Mountain Center, Tennessee, and ask for Chief Wilson," I said.

"Big Bob Wilson?"

"Yes."

"Hell, I met him once at a Tennessee–South Carolina football game in Columbia," Tyler Davis said. "He probably wouldn't remember me, but he's certainly not easy to forget."

"That'd be him," I said, wondering how Big Bob seemed to know every chief of police south of the Mason-Dixon Line.

Chief Davis called and got Big Bob on the phone and introduced himself. Whether he did or not, Big Bob said he remembered him. Tyler Davis put the call on speakerphone.

"I'm here with Donald Youngblood," Chief Davis said. "You know him?"

"Known him since he was in diapers," Big Bob said. "What's he done? Poking his nose where it isn't wanted?"

"Sort of," Tyler Davis said. "He wants some sensitive information. Can I trust him with it?"

"You best tell him what he wants to know," Big Bob said. "If you don't, he'll hang around and make a pest of himself. Then you'll get tired of it and lock him up. Then he'll call his friends at the FBI, and they'll come down and tear your town a new asshole. If Don says he'll keep it secret, you can bet on it."

Chief Davis was silent as he absorbed Big Bob's oratory.

"You still working the Crane case, Blood?" Big Bob asked.

"Yes," I said, loud enough for him to hear over the speakerphone. "And the more I work it, the more I don't like where it's leading."

"Call me when you get back," Big Bob said, his voice booming through the speaker. "Let's have breakfast."

"Will do," I said.

"Are we good, Chief Davis?" Big Bob asked.

"We're good, Chief Wilson. Thanks for your time." Chief Davis looked at his watch after he disconnected the call. "I got things to do," he said. "Hang around here for a while. We'll have an early dinner, and I'll tell you the whole story. We've got wireless, if you have a laptop."

◆ ◆ ◆ ◆

I spent what was left of the afternoon on my laptop getting caught up with the Street. The Dow was hanging around twelve thousand. I wasn't sure how. The economy continued to struggle, gas prices were outrageous, and unemployment was high. Still, signs were there that good things might be on the horizon. A lot of fat had been trimmed from a lot of businesses, and it was showing in the bottom line. I bought.

Chief Davis collected me at five, and we went back to The Four Moons. The dinner crowd had yet to arrive, so we had the place mostly to ourselves.

"I'm buying," I said.

"Trying to bribe a police officer?"

"Just a thank-you," I said. "For helping my investigation. Consider this a business dinner."

"My pleasure," he said.

We ordered beer and appetizers—firecracker shrimp for Chief Davis and fried calamari for me—from a rather attractive dark-haired waitress.

A minute after she left with our order, she was back with the beer. Chief Davis took a long drink and began telling me about the death of Robert Henry McMullen.

"I'm going to cut to the chase," he said. "Bobby McMullen died of anthrax, and we covered it up."

I stared at him in stunned silence. I knew about anthrax, and it scared me. Anthrax was a mean way to die. We both drank some beer.

"The doctor didn't know it was anthrax until it was too late. He kept quiet and called me to see how to handle it. I called the mayor. The mayor called a few other town leaders. We didn't want to start a panic, along with other reasons, so we cremated the body and let the records show the cause of death as pneumonia. We should have notified the CDC, but we didn't. Thank God no other cases showed up. Anthrax isn't contagious, so we weren't concerned about an epidemic."

Our appetizers arrived, and we began to nibble.

"How many people knew?" I asked.

"The town leaders; the powers that be, maybe five or six people, who all had a vested interest in keeping their mouths shut."

"Bobby's parents?"

"Yeah, they knew," he said. "We had to tell them so we could get permission to cremate the body."

"You said you had other reasons."

"We were in the running for an automobile plant," he said. "Lots of jobs, tax dollars—you get the picture. We figured an anthrax scare would pretty much rule us out."

I caught the waitress's eye and ordered another round of beer.

"Did you get the plant?"

Chief Davis swallowed a mouthful of shrimp and washed it down with the last of his first beer. "No," he said. "Go figure."

"Best-laid plans," I said.

He nodded.

"Would you handle it the same way if you had it to do over?" I asked.

"Hell no," he said. "We got lucky, and it worked out, but it was still the wrong thing to do."

Our second round of beer arrived with some hot bread. I ordered salmon with a whiskey glaze, and Tyler Davis ordered prime rib. The waitress disappeared toward the kitchen. We were silent as we worked on the bread.

"The doctor never could figure out how he might have gotten exposed to anthrax, either on purpose or accidentally," Chief Davis finally said. He looked like a man searching for a memory.

"Wouldn't be hard to expose someone if they didn't see it coming," I said.

"Apparently not." He paused. "Are you going to be good on your promise about keeping this to yourself?"

"No reason not to," I said. "It's over and done with. I might have to tell a few people who need to know, but I can't see it coming back to you."

"Good enough," he said. "If it was murder, who do you think did it?"

"I have no idea," I said.

38

The next morning, I sat with T. Elbert on his front porch drinking coffee, eating a toasted sesame seed bagel with cream cheese, and bringing him up to date on my adventures. I was hoping to get some insight. The overhead heaters held back the chill of a cold, damp day made worse by a nasty mist hanging over Mountain Center.

I did the talking, and T. Elbert listened. I told him about my trips to Farmington, Gretna, and Orangeburg. When I got to the anthrax, he whistled.

"That's scary stuff," he said.

"You have to keep that to yourself," I said. "It's ancient history, and I promised the chief I'd keep it that way."

"Whatever is said on this porch stays on this porch," T. Elbert said. "That's the rule. You know that."

"Never hurts to reaffirm the rule."

"If it makes you feel better," T. Elbert said, but I could tell he was annoyed. "So you got one apparent suicide, one missing, and one dead from anthrax. And you have nothing solid that any of them was murdered."

"Except coincidence," I said.

"Yeah," T. Elbert said. "There's that. I don't like that either. Maybe someone who's very clever is working from a hit list and taking their own sweet time about getting it done. Either that or you've uncovered a curse on Silver Star recipients."

"I guess I'll have to track down the other three," I said. "If they're all dead, that would be too big a coincidence."

"I agree," T. Elbert said as a black Lincoln Town Car pulled up in front of his house.

The driver got out and came up the walk.

"You're late," T. Elbert said, pretending to be irritated.

I was glad to see I wasn't his only victim.

"I'm a busy man," Roy said.

"I left coffee for you on the kitchen counter," T. Elbert said. "Put it in the micro and push the Easy Minute button."

As Roy disappeared inside, I rose to leave. "Got to go," I said. "I'm meeting Big Bob for breakfast."

Roy came back out with his coffee.

"Bring Roy up to date," I said to T. Elbert. "And remind him of the porch rule."

"I don't need to be reminded of the porch rule," I heard Roy say as I went down the walk.

◆ ◆ ◆ ◆

Big Bob and I sat in the back of the Mountain Center Diner at my usual table. It was the height of the breakfast rush, and the place was buzzing.

Dishes clattered, waitresses hustled to and fro, and the patrons were just a little bit louder that normal.

I ordered only scrambled eggs and an English muffin, which distressed Doris to no end until I explained about the bagel with cream cheese. Big Bob ordered the eggs Benedict with double home fries. In awed silence, I watched him eat.

"I'm hungry," he snarled. "I was out late last night and missed dinner."

"I love to see a man enjoy his food," I said. "Especially if I'm buying."

"And it tastes even better because you're buying," he said. "Eat your puny little breakfast and let me enjoy my manly one."

As I nibbled, I told him about my travels and what I had found. He listened, nodded, grunted, and ate.

"Damn, that was good," he said, pushing his plate to the side. "Sounds like you're making some progress."

"If that's what you call turning up dead people," I said.

Big Bob's only response was to drink his coffee.

"What would you have done about the anthrax?" I asked.

"Called the CDC," Big Bob said without hesitation. "You don't screw around with anthrax. They got lucky."

"Chief Davis did say that if he had it to do over, he'd choose differently," I said.

"Only one problem with that," Big Bob said. "In this job, you rarely get do-overs."

I took a drink of coffee and changed the subject. Big Bob was rarely in a benevolent mood when it came to law enforcement protocol.

"Do you know the Memphis chief of police?"

"Used to," he said. "But they've got a new guy now I haven't met."

"The next name on my list is a guy from Memphis," I said. "I figured I'd save myself a trip if I could get someone there to look into it. I'm tired of traveling."

"Good idea," he said, standing and putting on his cowboy hat. "Call Liam McSwain. I'll bet he knows someone on the Memphis police force."

He took a few steps toward the front door, stopped, and turned around. "Blood," he said, "thanks for breakfast."

◆ ◆ ◆ ◆

"Donald!" Liam McSwain said in that captivating Irish brogue of his. "Good to hear from you. How is the lovely Mary?"

Liam McSwain was the longtime Knoxville chief of police. If it hadn't been for Liam, Mary and I might never have gotten together and fallen in love. But that was another story.

"She's fine," I said.

"You're a lucky dog, Youngblood," McSwain said.

"I am that," I said. "Listen, Liam, I need a favor."

"If it can be done," he said, "I'll do it."

◆ ◆ ◆ ◆

McSwain was true to his word. Soon after lunch, the phone rang, and then my intercom buzzed.

"Detective Ross Dean, Memphis Police Department, for private investigator Donald Youngblood," Gretchen announced.

"Man, do I feel important," I said into the intercom.

"Get over it," Gretchen said, laughing. "Pick up line one."

I pushed the line-one button and then the Talk button on my portable phone. "This is Donald Youngblood."

"Mr. Youngblood, my name is Ross Dean, Memphis PD. I was told to give you a call and help you in any way I can."

"I appreciate that, Detective Dean," I said. "And please call me Don."

"If you'll call me Ross."

"Sure," I said. "Now that we're on a first-name basis, Ross, let me tell you what I need."

I told him I was looking for a Thomas Jefferson Barry, whose last known residence was in Memphis. I gave him the address.

"Sorry to bother you with this," I said. "It'll save me a trip. I've been traveling a lot lately. Everyone I've been trying to talk to on this case turns up dead."

"Not a problem," Ross said. "I was told the request to give you an assist came from the top. That means you have some juice, so I looked you up. You cracked that Three Devils case. That was good work. Besides, you're married to a cop. You're family."

"It seems my life is an open book," I said.

"In today's world," Ross said, "all our lives are open books. I'll get back to you."

◆ ◆ ◆ ◆

Late in the afternoon, the phone rang. Then it rang again, and a third time. I was so used to Gretchen answering that it didn't dawn on me she had left for the day.

"Youngblood," I said, pressing the Talk button.

"It's Ross."

"What have you got?"

"You're not going to like it," he said.

"Let me guess. He's dead."

"As a mackerel," Ross Dean said.

"How?"

"Murdered."

"Why?"

"Don't know," Ross said. "He was in a bad section of town at night and was shot with a .32. Could have been a drug deal gone wrong, or it could have been somebody with a grudge."

"How long ago?"

"Little over three years," he said.

"Who caught the case?"

"Guy I know," Ross said. "I talked to him about it. Then I pulled the file. No motive and no leads—dead-end case."

"Was Thomas Barry married?"

"Wife and two kids," he said. "According to the file, the wife said Barry got a phone call from an ex-military buddy. The wife couldn't remember the name. Barry told her not to wait up. Next day, she gets a knock on the door from one of MPD's finest with the bad news."

"Damn it," I said.

"My sentiments exactly," Ross said.

"Anything else?"

"Got the widow's address," he said, "in case you want to come out and interview her."

"Give it to me."

He did.

"Did you know that Barry was an Army Ranger who was awarded the Silver Star?"

"No," Ross said. "That's not in the file. A man who serves his country like that deserves some closure. This is still an open case. Anything you can do to help us close it will be much appreciated."

"If I can help with that, I will," I said. "Right now, I'm still trying to find someone to talk to. If I do come out, we'll have lunch."

"I'm always free for lunch," Ross said.

39

Two days later, I met Ross Dean for lunch at the Rendezvous on Second Street, an institution in downtown Memphis since 1948. He had promised to take me to see Thomas Barry's widow, and I had promised him lunch. Much to my dismay, both Fleet jets were in use, so I booked a direct flight from Tri-Cities to Memphis on Northwest Airlines and rented a brand-new Mitsubishi Endeavor SUV from Hertz.

Ross was a large black man in his mid-thirties with an easy demeanor and a round, boyish face. He probably weighed two-fifty or two seventy-five, but he didn't look fat, just huge. He wore black slacks with a white polo shirt. The sixteen-ounce mug of sweet tea looked like a shot glass in his hand. I imagined no one messed with Ross Dean.

We were working our way through our rib dinners and talking sports. Ross was a football and basketball fan, both college and pro. So far, we had established that we both were Tennessee Titans and Tennessee Volunteers fans in football.

"Of course, I'm a Grizzlies fan," Ross said. He shoveled in a mouthful of coleslaw.

"Me, too," I said, stripping another rib. In truth, I didn't follow the NBA much.

"And then I'm a Memphis Tigers fan, as far as college basketball is concerned."

"Connecticut Huskies," I said.

"Why in the world?"

"Went to school there," I said. "Tried out for the team as a walk-on and was cut after a couple of weeks."

"You play in high school?" he asked.

"I did."

"I played football," he said.

"I don't doubt it," I said.

◆ ◆ ◆ ◆

We took Ross's car and left my SUV downtown. Ross drove east on Poplar Avenue, going away from the Mississippi River. It was a pleasant day in the land of the Delta blues, near sixty degrees with scattered clouds. As we rode, Ross supplied a running commentary on places we passed—a good many of them dining establishments. While I listened, I looked over the file on Thomas Barry's murder. He was shot in the back of the head. His billfold was later found on the street, minus the cash and credit cards. None of the credit cards were ever used.

"Someone murdered him and made it look like a robbery," I said.

"How you figure?"

"They took the credit cards and never used them," I said. "If they were going to use them, it would have been soon after the murder."

"That'd be my guess, too," Ross said.

He honked at a squad car and waved. The driver waved back.

"I appreciate your taking the time to introduce me to Mrs. Barry," I said.

"Thought she might be more willing to talk if you were accompanied by a black detective from MPD," Ross said.

"Glad to have you along," I said.

Traffic was light, and we made good time. Ross took a right off Poplar and headed south.

"I was surprised at lunch that you didn't grill me on my case," I said. "Every other cop I've dealt with has."

He laughed. "Hell, this is Memphis. I've got a stack of cases to work, and I don't need yours clouding up my already overloaded brain."

"Fair enough."

"I know why you came," he said. "You're hoping a face-to-face with Mrs. Barry might shake loose a memory or a detail you can run with."

"I've got nothing to lose," I said. "Every lead I've followed has ended with someone dead or missing."

"Sounds like a lot of my cases," Ross Dean said.

"Did Thomas Barry have a record?" I asked.

"None," Ross said. "Not even a speeding ticket."

We drove past a stadium on our right.

"Liberty Bowl," Ross said. "Played some games there before I blew out my knee."

"The glory days," I said.

"Oh, yeah," he said. "You got that right."

Then Ross Dean grew quiet. I imagined he was reliving a few of those memories.

A few minutes later, we parked in front of a two-story house in a middle-class neighborhood. I followed Ross Dean up the walk to the front door. An attractive black woman in a nurse's uniform opened it. She was about five-foot-six and had delicate features and a slim figure.

"Detective Dean?" she asked.

"Yes, ma'am. And this is private investigator Donald Youngblood."

"Charlene Barry," she said, nodding to me. "Pleased to meet you."

"Pleased to meet you, too," I said. "Thanks for seeing us."

"I've got a few minutes before I have to go to work," she said. "Come into the kitchen. I made some coffee and pound cake."

We sat and enjoyed her offerings. I was glad I hadn't ordered dessert at the Rendezvous. I don't think Ross gave it a second thought.

"Great cake," Ross said.

He wasn't just being polite. The cake was excellent. But I hadn't come for that. I took a drink of coffee and looked at Ross. He got the message.

"As I said on the phone, Mrs. Barry, Mr. Youngblood is a well-known private detective working on a case that could involve your husband's murder," Ross Dean said. "He'd like to ask you some questions."

"That would be fine," she said, looking from Ross to me. "What is it you want to know, Mr. Youngblood? I'll help you any way I can."

I nodded. Even though I had read the file, I wanted to hear it from Charlene Barry.

"Tell me about the night your husband was killed," I said.

"Murdered," she said with some venom. "My Thomas was murdered." She shook her head as if trying to rid herself of something. "Sorry. I'll always be angry."

I nodded again. That seemed the safest thing to do. I resisted the urge to say I understood. No way did I understand. I might be able to imagine what it was like to lose a mate, but I didn't want to try. Losing your mate to a murder was unacceptable. It made *me* angry.

I waited.

"It was about nine o'clock that night," Charlene Barry said after taking a deep breath. "The phone rang, and Thomas answered. I'm sorry I wasn't paying more attention. He was on for maybe a minute or two and then hung up. Then he told me he was going out. I asked him why, and he said the call was from a bartender downtown, and an old army buddy he hadn't seen since Desert Storm was drunk in her bar and causing a ruckus and asking for Thomas. He said he had to go, that Rangers didn't turn their backs on other Rangers. He told me everything would be okay and not to wait up. That was the last time I saw him."

A tear rolled down her cheek. It is well documented that I don't do well with female tears. I felt like a kid in church who didn't understand the sermon. I wanted out of there.

"Sorry," she said.

"It's okay," Ross said in a voice so comforting any priest would have been jealous.

I pushed on. "Did he say the name of the old army buddy?"

"I think so, but I can't remember," she said. "I want so desperately to remember."

"Was it Randy Butler?" I asked, knowing it couldn't have been.

"No," she said, not hesitating.

"Bobby McMullen?" I asked, still testing.

"No," she said, appearing annoyed that I couldn't come up with it.

"Armand Priloux?"

She looked like she'd been stunned with a Taser. "Yes!" She slapped her hand hard on the kitchen table. I thought she was going to jump out of her chair. "That's the name! Now, why couldn't I remember that? They called him 'Army' because his first name was Armand. I remember now. Thank you so much, Mr. Youngblood. Is that helpful?"

"I honestly don't know, Mrs. Barry," I said.

"Charlene," she said.

"You said *her* bar. So it was a female who called?"

"That's what Thomas said," Charlene Barry said.

I gave Ross a look, and he made a note in his notebook.

"Did Thomas have any pictures taken when he was an Army Ranger?" I asked.

"No," she said. "Thomas said that was a time he would just as soon forget."

"You knew he was awarded the Silver Star," I said.

"Oh, yes. I was very proud."

"How did Thomas feel?"

"He didn't want to talk about it," Charlene Barry said.

"Did he have a military funeral?"

"No," she said. "He didn't want one. We talked about that soon after we got married, about what both of us wanted."

"Did Thomas ever mention the Southside Seven?" I asked.

"Not that I remember," she said. "What's that?"

"Doesn't matter," I said.

"How long were you two married?" Ross Dean asked. He had been so quiet I'd almost forgotten he was there.

"Thirteen years," Charlene Barry said, her voice quavering. "It went so fast. Now, I'm left with two kids and no husband. You have no idea what it's like. When Thomas was murdered, the Charlene I knew was murdered. What was left was a different person. If it weren't for the kids, I would have gone to a really dark place."

Her pain filled the room. I looked at Ross. He was motionless.

"How old are your kids?" I asked, trying to move her past the memory.

"My boy is six, and my girl is four," she said. She stood from her chair as she tried to recover her composure. "I'm sorry, but I have to go to work."

"Where do you work?" Ross asked.

"St. Jude," she said. "Those kids remind me every day of how blessed I am in other ways." She looked at me. "If you find out who killed my Thomas, please promise to ask him why. I want to know what was so important that they had to kill my man."

I held her gaze and nodded as I felt the anger building inside me.

"Thank you for coming, Mr. Youngblood," she said. "I think God sent you, I really do."

◆ ◆ ◆ ◆

We left Charlene Barry's house together and headed back downtown. We were silent for a while.

"I feel bad for that woman," Ross said.

"So do I," I said. "The whole thing makes me mad as hell."

"That was a good catch on the female bartender," Ross said. "The file didn't mention that. I'll check out bars with female bartenders."

"It's not that uncommon, but it's worth a shot," I said.

"You know who this Priloux is?" Ross Dean asked.

"Yeah, I do. Thomas Barry and six other guys were on a mission in Desert Storm that resulted in all of them being awarded the Silver Star. Armand Priloux was one of them. He's been missing since Hurricane Katrina."

"Missing," Ross said.

"Or dead," I said.

"So it could have been him."

"Or not," I said.

We drove in silence.

"Silver Star," Ross said. "Heavy duty."

"Very," I said.

"Seven guys," Ross said. "The Southside Seven."

"You catch on fast," I said.

"What's it mean?"

"Hell if I know," I said.

40

A case that started with an apparently paranoid wife had led me to three dead Silver Star recipients. And the jury was still out on the fourth. The deaths of Randy Butler and Bobby McMullen had not looked like murder, but they could have been. On the other hand, Thomas Barry's death was murder, pure and simple. Armand Priloux could be the murderer. Or someone in the shadows was making it appear as if he was. I had no definitive answers, but I had a gut feeling that Armand would never be found, whether he was the killer or not.

I had some smart friends, but the most analytical guy I knew was Scott Glass. On a cold November morning the day after I returned from Memphis, I called Scott's private number.

"Blood," he answered. "What's going on?"

"I'm seeking counsel, Professor," I said. "I need to bounce this case I'm working on off you."

"I thought you went to the nun in Connecticut for that," Scott said. "The one I met at the wedding. Sarah Agnes, right?"

"Sarah Agnes for the psychology of a case, yes. But this is different. I need a master analyst—statistics, probabilities, and all that jazz."

"My meat," Scott said. "Talk to me."

"Okay," I said. "I have this picture. In the picture are seven Army Rangers who were awarded the Silver Star for a black ops mission in Desert Storm. When I found the picture, I already knew one Ranger was dead from apparent natural causes, although two different medical examiners, including Wanda Jones, could not explain what the natural causes were. So far, I've managed to track down four more of the guys in the picture. Three are dead, and one is missing."

I laid it all out for him, hoping the FBI might want to get involved. When I finished, Scott was silent. I knew he was processing.

"So you have an unexplained death from apparent natural causes, an accidental death that could be a suicide, a missing person who could be dead, a death from anthrax that may or may not have been murder, and a real, honest-to-God murder," Scott said.

"And a partridge in a pear tree."

Scott laughed. "Don't let it drive you crazy. What else have you got?"

"Two more names on my list," I said.

"No apparent motive, no two deaths alike, and no suspects," Scott said.

"Maybe one suspect," I said. "Armand Priloux, if he's still alive. But I don't think so."

"Neither do I," Scott said.

"What are the odds that five guys in their forties—all Silver Star recipients, all survivors of Desert Storm, and all in this picture—are now dead?" I asked.

"About the same as me winning the Boston Marathon in my street shoes," Scott said.

"You couldn't win the Boston Marathon on a bicycle."

"Very funny," Scott said. "I was speaking metaphorically."

"Okay, smart guy, want to get involved?"

"No," Scott said. "It's weird for sure, but it could just be bad luck. And it's out of my jurisdiction. And you don't have enough hard evidence that the deaths are connected."

"Bullshit, Professor," I said. "I know something is going on here. I just don't know what."

"Look, Blood," Scott said. "I'll tell you what. Track down the last two on the list. If they're both dead, then I'll take it up the ladder."

"You've got a deal," I said.

I would have bet a million bucks the last two men on the list would turn up dead.

◆ ◆ ◆ ◆

For lunch, I had a turkey and Swiss sandwich and a bag of Doritos at my desk while I read *Rocky Top News*. The Tennessee football team was 4–6 with two games to play. They would be favored in their two remaining games. Win both and get a bowl bid. Lose and a black cloud would hang over the program until the start of next season. Most of the fan base was antsy but trying to be patient. Next year looked promising.

I was still reading when my intercom buzzed.

"Jessica Crane to see you," Gretchen said.

I hesitated. I should have called her. No way could I avoid seeing her.

"Send her in," I said.

I rose to greet Mrs. Crane as she came in and sat.

"I haven't heard from you. I was in town on business, so I thought I'd drop in," she said.

In town to see me, I thought, but I left it alone.

"I'm glad," I said. "I was going to call you with an update, but things have been hectic."

"Well," Jessica Crane said, "I'm glad I can save you a phone call." Her smile was not warm, nor her words sincere. Her meaning was not so hidden: I needed to stay in touch.

I told her the information I had found about the men in the picture.

"Somebody killed these men, including Walter," she said. "I want him, her, or them brought to justice."

"I'm working on it," I said. "I have a commitment from the FBI that if the last two men in the picture are dead, they'll get involved. Right now, all I have is circumstantial."

"Don't you feel it's an awfully big coincidence that all these men are dead?"

"I do," I said.

She thought about that, her eyes moving toward my window. She went far away for a moment, and then she was back.

"You've done well so far, Mr. Youngblood," she said. "I don't know if anyone else could have uncovered as much as you have. Please do keep digging, and please update me more often."

I nodded. "How are you doing personally, Mrs. Crane?"

She looked surprised by the question and seemed to soften a bit. "It's kind of you to ask," she said. "I miss Walter, but I realize I must move on. I'm participating in group therapy, and Anna is staying with me full-time. I'm a survivor. I'll be fine."

I didn't doubt it.

◆ ◆ ◆ ◆

I was ready to close the outer office door when the phone rang. I went back in and picked up the portable on Gretchen's desk.

"Cherokee Investigations," I said, tired and slightly annoyed.

"You sound like me at the end of the day," the voice said.

I recognized that voice, deep and melodic.

"Sorry," I said. "I was halfway out the door. You know how it is."

"I do," Ross Dean said. "I usually have to leave about three times."

"What's up?"

"I checked out female bartenders in the area where Thomas Barry was killed and didn't come up with anything. Bartenders, male and female, come and go, so whoever made the call may be long gone. I've got the word out, so I may turn something up. If I do, I'll give you a call."

"Thanks, Ross. I appreciate the effort."

"Let me know how this shakes out, Don," he said. "I'd be interested."

"I will," I promised.

41

That night, Mary and I went to the opening game of the season for the Mountain Center Lady Bears basketball team. Lacy was starting at the two-guard, a position she had won as a sophomore. Billy and Maggie came over from Cherokee. Little D, a bit too young to understand the game, stayed home with a babysitter. Unless the fates dealt him a cruel blow, he was destined to be tall and play basketball.

Billy and I sat with T. Elbert, who had not missed a game in Lacy's sophomore season and vowed not to miss one her junior year either. I noticed Biker McBride standing on the back row. I gave him a quick one-finger point, and he nodded. Mary and Maggie sat behind us with Wanda Jones. I sensed male eyes all over the gym looking in our direction.

"I'm your date," Wanda said to T. Elbert.

"Hot damn," T. Elbert said. "Want to sit in my lap?"

Wanda laughed. "Later."

The Lady Bears led by eight points at the half. By my calculations, Lacy had scored ten points and dished out five assists. In the third quarter, she quit shooting, and the team from Asheville closed the gap to one point. During the break before the fourth quarter, I noticed the coach having an intense one-way conversation with Lacy. She didn't say a word, but she sure nodded a lot.

Billy, who never missed anything, noticed it, too. "She's telling her to shoot, Blood."

"No doubt," I said.

The first time Lacy touched the ball in the fourth quarter, she came off a screen, squared up, and knocked down a three. She hit two more threes before the game ended. The Lady Bears won by ten.

"Nice game," I said to Lacy soon after the final buzzer.

"Thanks," she said. "But I hate looking like a ball hog."

"That's your job, Little Princess," Billy said. "Get used to it."

"If you say so, Chief," Lacy said, smiling over her shoulder as she walked toward the locker room.

I noticed Biker was still hanging around. In fact, he was leaning against the wall underneath one of the goals and staring straight at me.

"I'll be back in a minute," I said to Billy.

I walked over to where Biker was standing.

"Lacy played well, Mr. Youngblood," he said. "You should be proud."

"I am," I said.

"I took care of that little favor you asked," he said.

"I heard."

"And I figured out the favor I want to ask of you."

"Okay," I said. "Let's hear it."

"I want to date Lacy," he said.

I hadn't seen it coming, yet I was not surprised.

"That would be up to her," I said. "Within reason, we don't tell her who she can and cannot date."

"Within reason." Biker smiled. "I hope I fall within reason."

"Until you prove otherwise," I said.

"Don't worry, Mr. Youngblood," Biker said. "I hear you loud and clear."

◆ ◆ ◆ ◆

After the game, we went back to the condo—except for T. Elbert, who said he was going home, and Wanda, who didn't say where she was going. Mary, Maggie, Billy, and I were at the kitchen bar, and Lacy and Biker McBride were on the lower level in the den. Lacy had already gotten permission from Mary to ask Biker over after the game. The conspiracy had played out as usual. I was the last to know.

"Seems like a nice kid," Billy said. "Besides, he rides a Harley."

Biker and Billy had bonded immediately. Mary and Maggie thought he was cute. All three felt I was overly protective.

"What happened to Jonah?" I asked. "I just got used to him."

"That was never going to last," Mary said. "And this probably won't either, so you need to relax."

"Yeah, Blood," Billy said. "You need to relax."

"Quit picking on Don," Maggie said. "He's just being a good father."

"Thank you, Maggie," I said.

"If we had a girl," Maggie said, "she would never have a date because all the boys would be too afraid of Billy to ask her out."

"But we had a son," Billy said, grinning widely.

42

My new Pathfinder, in a color Nissan called "Silver Lightning," arrived sooner than expected. The local dealership had found an SUV in Cincinnati that met my exact specifications and a firm to take care of the after-factory request—one that freaked out my sales rep, Gina. My new vehicle also came equipped with a built-in navigation system. So when I turned my old Pathfinder over to Lacy, I gave her, with absolutely no regrets, Hilda.

"Don't trust her," I said to Lacy. "She lies sometimes."

Early on a cold November day, the Monday before Thanksgiving, I took my new wheels and headed to Richmond, Kentucky, a sleepy little town of around thirty thousand about twenty miles south of Lexington. Richmond was the last known residence of Franklin Lloyd McCurry, the fifth name on my list. I picked up I-81 South to I-40 West toward Knoxville. In Knoxville, I took I-75 North toward Lexington. I stopped at a Bojangles' and had a sausage and egg biscuit and coffee courtesy of Dunkin' Donuts from my own thermos. Not exactly the breakfast of champions, it was more like a guilty pleasure I indulged in every so often.

I arrived in Richmond before lunch and found Franklin's last known address, a middle-class three-story apartment building on the west side of town. I went through the first set of a pair of double doors and immediately saw the apartment directory—but no listing for McCurry. Beside each name was a three-digit number to be used when calling an apartment for access to the building. I dialed the manager.

"Yeah," a rather disinterested voice said.

"I want to ask about renting," I said. "Is anything available?"

"Hang on," the voice said. "I'll be right down."

I waited until a large man opened the door to the lobby. He was maybe twenty pounds overweight and had thinning black hair.

"Come on in," he said. "I'm Al Carbone."

We shook hands.

"Have a seat," he said, sizing me up.

I wore caramel-colored cords and a blue shirt with a button-down collar. My dark brown belt matched my boots and leather jacket. *Mr. GQ.*

In the lobby was a large coffee table surrounded by a couch and two armchairs. The furniture had seen better days. I sat in one of the chairs, my back to a wall. Al Carbone sat on the couch. He had on jeans and a gray work shirt with the sleeves turned up.

"I have a one-bedroom and a two-bedroom available," he said. "Would you like to see one or both?"

I didn't think my reporter cover would work for Al, so I flashed my private investigator ID.

"I'm not looking for an apartment," I said. "I'm trying to find someone who used to live here but apparently no longer does. I just need to ask him a few questions."

"Who?" He sounded like he didn't really want to know.

"Franklin McCurry," I said.

"Frank?" He snorted. "Good luck with that. Frank's been dead for about a year now."

Big surprise, I thought.

"How?"

"The big C," Al said.

"Cancer?"

"You know another big C?"

Car crash would have made more sense. But anyway, that was two big Cs, so I moved on.

"What can you tell me about Frank?"

"Nothing much," Al said. "He kept to himself, paid the rent on time, and didn't cause trouble."

"Anybody here know him well?"

"I think Larry did," he said. "Larry Jacobs. Third floor, apartment 4."

"Is he in?" I asked.

"He's at work," Al said. "Usually gets in around five."

I nodded and stood. "I'll be back," I said, doing a really good Arnold Schwarzenegger. It was totally lost on Al Carbone.

◆ ◆ ◆ ◆

At the last minute, I had packed an overnight bag, as I had something I wanted to do the next day—a promise I had to keep. I drove north on I-75 and got off at the South Hamburg exit. I checked into a Residence Inn, worked awhile on my computer, then changed into my running gear and went for a long run. Part of my route included Man o' War Boulevard.

As a kid, I was fascinated with racehorses; thanks to a horse-racing game my parents gave me when I was around ten. All the old greats were in the game—Seabiscuit, War Admiral, Citation, Whirlaway, and, of course, Man o' War, the horse with the really cool name, the horse I always chose. I took a toy horse to school one day for show and tell and pretended it was Man o' War. I told the class about the great racehorse, about how he raced twenty-one times and won twenty, about how in the only race he ever lost he finished second to a horse named Upset, a horse he had beaten in several other races.

I was so engrossed that the running seemed secondary. I clicked off the miles without noticing how heavy my legs had become. By the time

I returned to my room, I was totally spent. I took a long shower, dressed, and headed back to Richmond.

◆ ◆ ◆ ◆

Larry Jacobs was in his mid-forties. He was slim and of medium height and had light brown hair and a wisp of a goatee. He looked like a hippie college professor and sounded like a hill-country hick. When I told him I wanted some information on Frank McCurry, he invited me into his apartment for a beer, seemingly excited to meet a real-life private detective.

We sat at his kitchen table. Larry placed a jar of peanuts between us, after shaking a few out in his hand and popping them into his mouth. I had the feeling he didn't entertain much. The beer was Budweiser. *When in Richmond . . .*

"Were you and Frank McCurry close friends?" I asked.

"Frank didn't get close to anybody," Larry said. "I guess I was his best friend, but it was pretty much one-way. He did thank me for visiting him in the hospital, though."

"When did Frank die?"

"A little over a year ago," Larry said. "I can't remember the date. Is that important?"

"Probably not," I said. "The apartment manager said it was cancer."

"Yeah, the big C," he said. "Pancreatic cancer, nasty stuff."

The big C, I thought. *Must be a Richmond thing.*

"You knew he was an Army Ranger, right?" I asked, drinking a little beer.

"Hell yeah. Frank was a tough dude. Got the Silver Star."

"Did he ever talk about being in Desert Storm?" I asked.

"Once," Larry said. "We were both drunk."

"What did he say?"

"That it was bullshit. That the Silver Star was a curse. That they got it for fucking up a mission, and that he had bad dreams about what happened."

"What did happen?"

"He wouldn't tell me. Said if I knew, I'd have bad dreams, too. I let it drop. I don't need bad dreams."

Larry drank some beer and ate some peanuts. I took another swallow of beer and ignored the peanuts. Once I started on peanuts, I couldn't stop.

"Did Frank have a girlfriend?" I asked.

"Not that I know of," he said. "I think he did a hooker every now and then, but I'm not sure. Frank didn't volunteer a whole lot."

"Did he ever mention a group of guys called the Southside Seven?"

"No," Larry said. "I'd remember that."

"Okay," I said. "That's it. Thanks for the beer."

I walked into the living room toward the front door.

"What's this all about?" Larry asked from behind me.

Larry Jacobs was certainly not a person I wanted to share the Crane case with. He'd talk about it to anyone willing to listen.

"It's confidential," I said. "I'm working with the Department of Homeland Security. Don't talk to anyone about our conversation. DHS is real paranoid about that. You've probably heard stories."

Larry went a little pale. "Yeah, sure," he said softly. "No problem. I won't say a word, I promise."

I immediately felt bad that I had shaken him up, so I tried to do some damage control.

"It'll be okay. Just forget I was here."

"It's forgotten," he said. "You were never here."

43

The next morning, I got up early and drove to Louisville. I was about to keep a promise I had made to myself over a year ago.

The Maple Oaks Retirement Community was on the east side of the city a few minutes off I-64. I had been there last July to visit the father of a man I had killed, the head devil in the Three Devils case. Bret Sherman didn't know I killed his son. He hadn't heard from his son in many years.

Bret was over eighty and suffering from Alzheimer's. I had no idea what to expect now.

"I'm here to see Bret Sherman," I said to the receptionist at the main desk.

She nodded. "Go to building five and ask for Jane."

I remembered Jane from my previous visit. I saw her as I came through the entrance to building five. She was talking to a nurse at the front desk, a young, cute redhead I had also seen the last time I was here. Jane was a tall, athletic-looking woman probably past fifty. Her hair was shorter and had more gray than I remembered.

"Can I help you?" she asked.

"I'm here to see Bret Sherman," I said.

"Yes, I remember you," she said. "You were here last summer, I think."

"July," I said.

Jane turned to the red-headed nurse. "Nancy, do you think Mr. Sherman can have a visitor?"

"Sure," Nancy said. "I don't know how responsive he'll be, but we can give it a try."

◆ ◆ ◆ ◆

Bret Sherman was sitting at a table in the cafeteria and staring out the window. A cup of coffee was on the table in front of him. The coffee looked cold.

"You have a visitor, Mr. Sherman," the nurse said.

"Oh." He hesitated. "Oh, okay, thank you, nurse."

I sat in a chair next to him. He looked puzzled.

"Do I know you?" he asked. "I don't remember things very well these days."

"We've met only once," I said. "I visited you last year. My name is Don."

"Don," he said, studying me.

I waited for him to process. He seemed to go off somewhere and then struggle to return.

"I had a visitor last summer, and we sat in the shade by that bench down there," he said, looking out the window. "I think his name was Don. Was that you?"

"Yes, it was," I said. "Your memory is better than you think."

"Sometimes." He smiled absently. "It's cold today, isn't it?"

"Yes, it is," I said.

I spent an hour with Bret Sherman. We talked about things in his distant past, about food, about baseball, about the weather. He didn't mention his sons, Sammy, who had died young, and Matthew, the one I had killed saving a teenage girl. I was thankful they did not come up in the conversation.

When I thought I had stayed long enough, I stood. "I have to go now."

"Please come back," he said. He seemed childlike and needy.

"I'll try," I said. But I didn't make any promises to him or to myself. I doubted I would ever be back.

At the front desk, I wrote down my name and phone number for Jane. I saw no need for her to know I was a private detective. That would only arouse suspicion.

"If he needs anything, let me know," I said. "If he passes, let me know that, too."

"Are you related?" she asked.

"No," I said. "But I've been recently involved with the family."

"Okay," she said. "I'll put you in the computer as a friend of the family."

I went out the main entrance to building five, got in my new Pathfinder, and drove away vowing not to end up in a retirement home alone and without friends.

44

I was in the office early the next day, the Wednesday before Thanksgiving, trying to sort out what was going on with the Southside Seven. I had never worked on a case in which everyone I tried to interview turned up dead. It was unsettling. I was beginning to believe there was a curse on the seven. I was at a point in the investigation where that seemed more believable than murder. I had to find out what happened to the last soldier on the list. If he was dead—and I was sure he was—then I'd call Scott. My head hurt from thinking about it, so I did the only thing that would help. I locked up and went to the Mountain Center Diner for breakfast.

About half the time at the diner, I could expect to find someone at my table, or someone would join me before I finished breakfast. Roy Husky sat in his usual spot drinking coffee and reading the *Knoxville News Sentinel.*

"Hey, gumshoe," he said as I sat.

"Mr. Vice President," I said.

Roy smiled. He started to say something, but Doris appeared, poured coffee, took our order, and hurried away.

"I sure hope I have that kind of energy when I'm her age," I said.

"Me, too," Roy said. "And I *am* her age."

I laughed.

"Market's up again," he said. "Think it'll make thirteen thousand this year?"

"Probably," I said, at that moment not caring one damn bit about Wall Street.

Roy picked up on my mood. "What's going on? You seem distracted."

"This case I'm working on," I said. "Monday, I got one more piece of the puzzle, and all it did was muddy the water even more."

"T. Elbert filled me in, but take me through it from the beginning," Roy said. "We ex-cons have a nose for this kind of thing."

I told him all of it. While I talked, Doris brought breakfast. I ate and talked. Roy ate and listened. Not surprisingly, he finished breakfast before me.

"What do you think?" I asked. Half my food was still on my plate.

"I don't believe in curses," Roy said. "So it's either bad luck, or a clever killer is knocking them off, or it's a combination of both. It was a long time between Randy Butler's accident and Armand Priloux's disappearance. I don't think a killer working off a list would wait that long. And it's hard to give someone cancer. At this point, I'd vote for bad luck."

"Me, too," I said.

But I wasn't entirely committed to the idea.

◆ ◆ ◆ ◆

The final name on my list was John Francis Kelly, whose last known address was in Stamford, Connecticut. I had been to Stamford with Billy on a few occasions when we were in college. I knew I had to make the Stamford trip, but I did not want to miss the fourth annual Joseph Fleet Thanksgiving extravaganza. I could think about Stamford later. I wanted to enjoy the long holiday week.

I called Bruiser Bracken to find out what time his flight arrived at Tri-Cities. No answer. Bruiser would see that I called and call me back.

I needed a distraction. I went online to CBS Sports and got lost in college football stats.

Sometime later, the phone rang once, and then Gretchen's voice came over the intercom. "Bruiser Bracken, line one."

I had met Bruiser my senior year of college, before he became an NFL lineman. Then I lost track of him for years before running into him in Las Vegas while working on the Malone case.

"Bruiser," I said. "What time do you get in?"

"Six o'clock."

"I'll pick you up."

"No need," Bruiser said. "That's why I called. I have a ride."

Probably Roy, I thought.

"You staying at the mansion?" I asked.

"No," Bruiser said. "I'm staying with Wanda."

"Wanda?"

"Don't sound so surprised." Bruiser laughed. "Wanda says she has a spare room."

"Uh-huh," I mumbled. "I take it you and Wanda are more that just friends."

"It's beginning to look that way," he said.

"And you kept this a secret because?"

"I wanted to see where it was going before I said anything," Bruiser said. "You're really the first to know."

I'll bet Mary knows, I thought, but I kept that to myself.

"Well, you could do a hell of a lot worse that Wanda," I said. "I hope it works out."

"Me, too. I'll see you tomorrow, Don, okay?"

"Okay," I said, still trying to process Bruiser with Wanda. I never saw that coming. But upon further review, I wasn't surprised. They seemed to connect at our wedding.

I wanted to play it cool, but I couldn't help myself. I picked up the phone and called Wanda. I had to wait while her assistant tracked her down.

"Well, that didn't take long," she said when she answered. "When did Bruiser call?"

"Bruiser who?" I asked.

"I forget his last name. Big, good-looking guy who used to play football for UConn. That Bruiser."

"Oh, yeah," I said. "Him. He called a few minutes ago."

"I like him a lot, Don," Wanda said. "I know long-distance relationships are hard, but we'll see where it goes."

"I can see you two together," I said.

"Thanks," Wanda said. "I really can't talk now. I'm slammed. See you tomorrow?"

"You bet," I said. "But I want all the details."

Wanda laughed. "Not all," she said. "Most."

I didn't have much time to think about Bruiser Bracken and Wanda Jones before the phone rang. This time, it was someone I never expected to hear from.

"A woman on line one says she's Alexandria from West Palm Beach," Gretchen said. "She says you'll remember her, and she sounds *way* too sexy for my liking."

"I'll take it," I said. I knew I'd have to explain later. Gretchen was staunchly loyal to Mary and felt it her duty to protect me from a condition she perceived existed in all members of my gender—an inherent weakness to stray.

"Donald Youngblood," I answered.

"Mr. Youngblood, it's Alexandria," she said. "You remember me, of course."

"Of course," I said, trying to maintain the utmost professionalism. "What can I do for you?"

"I want to pass on some information and get your opinion," she said.

"I'm listening."

"Yesterday, Regina Capelli tried to place a two-thousand-dollar bet on professional football with one of my people," Alexandria said. "He refused to accept it, as per my instructions. She threw a fit and demanded to speak to his boss. I met with her and told her the same thing. She was furious and threatened to call her grandfather. I told her to go ahead, and if Carlo Vincente said to take the bet, then I would take it."

"Well played," I said. "I'm guessing she didn't make the call."

"You guess right," Alexandria said. "Then she turned on the tears and said her boyfriend was forcing her to place the bet, and that he would be very mad if she didn't."

"And you still said no."

"I did," Alexandria said.

"And she pouted and stomped off," I said.

Alexandria laughed. It was sexy as hell, and she wasn't even trying. "Were you hiding in my car?"

"No," I said, "but I can imagine."

"Will you share this information with Carlo Vincente?" she asked. "I'd like to know how to handle this."

"I think you're handling it just fine," I said. "Carlo has been billed, and the bill has been paid. My work for him is finished."

She was silent for a moment. "Then I'd like to hire you to find out what is really going on."

I'd like to know that myself, I thought. Freddie and Regina had made me a promise. I wanted to know why it wasn't being kept.

"I'm expensive," I said.

"How much?"

I told her. "Plus expenses," I added.

"Agreed," she said. "How soon?"

"Next week."

"We'll need to meet," she said.

"No," I said. "We've met. If we need to again, I'll let you know."

"Afraid?"

"With good reason," I said.

She laughed again. "Very well. Call me when you arrive and let me know you've started."

"I'll call as soon as I land," I said. "And one more thing. Was she asking for credit?"

"No," Alexandria said. "She had the cash."

45

The guest list for Thanksgiving at Joseph Fleet's mansion had grown every year. All the usual suspects were there, and then some. I counted thirty people, including a few I didn't know. With Roy's permission, Lacy had invited Hannah and Biker McBride. Hannah had invited Alfred Lucas, I was guessing at Biker's request.

The dinner had been moved from the dining room to the ballroom, where a long series of tables was set up end to end. A string quartet played softly in the background. The women were dressed up and gorgeous—especially Mary, who wore a string of pearls and a little black dress that showed off every curve. The men wore jackets, some with a shirt and tie, others with a turtleneck. I wore dark gray slacks, a light gray turtleneck, and a blue blazer. Mary said I looked dashing, especially with the gray flecks in my hair. I'm not sure why she had to mention the gray flecks.

The tables were set with place cards. I was at the foot of the table on the left side, far away from Joseph Fleet, who was at the head. Roy sat on my left, and Mary was across from me. Billy was on Mary's right, with Maggie next to him. On Roy's left was a woman who worked for Fleet Industries, an attractive redhead a few years younger than Roy. They conversed in low tones and seemed familiar with each other. I wondered.

Joseph Fleet said grace. Dinner was a catered affair, an elaborate buffet with so many choices that I had to be disciplined not to overeat. After dinner, the tables were torn down and hauled away, leaving the floor available for dancing. Mary and I took to the dance floor first, and others followed—Maggie and Billy, Bruiser and Wanda, even Biker and Lacy. The guests mingled between dances.

I caught up with Biker when Lacy and Hannah went off to the ladies' room.

"Having a good time?" I asked.

"A very good time," he said.

"You look comfortable in that shirt and tie."

Biker smiled. "My dad makes me dress up for church once a month. Thinks I should get used to it. Wants me to have a shirt-and-tie job someday, after I get out of college. That's what he calls it, 'a shirt-and-tie job.' He even taught me how to tie a Windsor knot."

"Fathers always want more for their kids," I said.

"I guess so."

"Where's the Brain?"

"With Mr. Johns, discussing computers," he said. "It's weird. Alfred and I have become pretty good friends. He's okay—funny without trying to be, and of course he's really smart."

"Interesting how circumstances lead to friendships," I said.

"It is," Biker said.

Lacy appeared out of nowhere and took Biker's arm.

"I want to show you around the Fleet Mansion," she said. "See you later, Don." And they were gone.

Across the room, I caught Joseph Fleet's eye. He tilted his head toward a far door. I knew what the signal was for—our annual Thanksgiving drinks in his study.

◆ ◆ ◆ ◆

Ten minutes later, we were in his study with after-dinner drinks. I had Baileys Irish Cream, and Joseph Fleet had an expensive Martell cognac. We sat in front of the fireplace.

"Does it seem just four years ago that we started doing this?" he asked.

"No," I said, "it doesn't. It seems like we've been doing it forever. I guess that's the trick time plays. Thanksgiving at the Fleet Mansion has become a tradition, and traditions seem like they've been around awhile."

"To many more," Joseph Fleet said, raising his glass.

"To many more," I said, duplicating his gesture.

We sat silently and enjoyed our drinks, mesmerized by the dancing flames in the fireplace.

"That first Thanksgiving we all got together probably saved my life," Joseph Fleet said. "I was in bad shape."

"As I recall, it was your idea."

"Roy's, really," he said. "I just went along."

"I think it was good for a lot of us," I said.

"I'll never really get over losing Sarah Ann," he said. "I'm dealing with it and doing okay, but I have some hard days."

"I know," I said. "I feel the same way about my parents."

"You've helped not only me," Joseph Fleet said. "You've helped Roy. He's changed since he met you. I want to thank you for that."

"Roy's friendship is all the thanks I need," I said.

The conversation was getting a little too serious for me. Fortunately, I was saved.

"I knew I'd find you here," Mary said, entering the study. "It's getting late, and Lacy has an early practice tomorrow."

We stood.

"Mary, you look lovely tonight," Joseph Fleet said. "I meant to tell you earlier. Don is one lucky man."

Mary smiled. "That's what I keep telling him."

◆ ◆ ◆ ◆

Late that night, Mary and I lay in our king-sized bed, the glow of a night-light from the bathroom the only illumination. I was exhausted but not sleepy.

"So when were you going to tell me about Wanda and Bruiser?" I asked.

"Bruiser wanted to tell you," Mary said. "I found out just last week."

"How long has it been going on?"

"Since last Thanksgiving," Mary said. "Neither one of them was at Fleet's, remember. Bruiser told you he was spending it with family, and Wanda told me the same thing. Bruiser flew Wanda to Vegas."

"Won't last," I said.

"Bet it does."

"I cannot see Wanda moving to Vegas," I said.

"Neither can I."

"And you think Bruiser is going to move to Tennessee?"

"Wanda says he likes it here," Mary said. "He's tired of Vegas."

"That I can understand," I said.

We were silent. Mary scooted closer to me.

"I'm making a quick trip to Florida next week," I said.

"Why?"

I told her about my phone call from Alexandria—all of it.

"That woman is trying to get you into her bed, Mr. Youngblood," Mary said.

"Really?" I asked. *Mr. Innocent.*

"Definitely. And you know it."

"Tempting," I said.

"If you have a death wish."

"You'd kill me?"

"Of course not," Mary said. "But I'd sure make you suffer."

"It's not going to happen," I said. "I'm not even going to see her."

"Better not," Mary said.

She rolled on her side against me. Her hand went under my T-shirt, stroking my stomach.

"Why are you even going?" Mary asked.

"I don't like being lied to," I said.

"We were both lied to."

"We were."

"So you'll represent both of us and find out why," she said.

"I will, unless you want to come along."

"I can't," Mary said. "Big Bob would have a fit."

"Guess I'll have to tough it out alone."

"Then you'll need a proper send-off."

"I will."

"Brace yourself," Mary whispered in my ear.

46

Jim Doak and I flew out of Tri-Cities early on the Monday following Thanksgiving. Rather, Jim flew and I sat comfortably in the center of the Learjet drinking coffee, eating a cheese Danish, and reading *USA Today*. I enjoyed the feel of a newspaper. Nooks and Kindles were all the rage. They were eco-friendly—buy a Nook, save a tree. The younger generation was losing sight of the printed word. Even some older folks were going over to the dark side. I wondered how many books would still be printed on real paper and bound in the traditional way in twenty-five years.

We landed at Palm Beach International Airport around ten o'clock. I took a shuttle bus to Hertz and picked up my rental, a white Cadillac Escalade. I was sure Alexandria would want me to go first-class.

"I'm on the ground," I said when I called her.

"Would you like to take a break and have dinner tonight?" she asked.

"I'm hoping to wrap this up today and send you a bill," I said.

"I may want to pay you in person."

"Mary takes care of collections."

"Smart lady," Alexandria said. "Let me know when you conclude our little venture."

"Tomorrow at the latest," I said, and closed my phone.

I was hoping to be done in a day so I could get back to Mountain Center and the Crane case. I drove to Palm Beach Atlantic University, to the same apartment building I had visited in October. I asked around for Regina Capelli. No luck. I asked for Angela Bennett. No luck there either. So I went to the only other place I could think of—the tennis courts at Carlin Park in Jupiter.

Freddie was on court one, hitting balls with the two young Hispanics I had questioned in October. For a few minutes, I watched in anonymity behind the tinted glass of the Escalade. Freddie was a good player. He moved well, hit with power, and was smooth on the court. The other two were not quite as good but still miles ahead of the average player.

When I got out of the SUV, I was surprised how warm the sun was. The sky was crystal blue without a cloud in sight. I walked to the fence. Freddie spotted me. He didn't seem surprised.

"I thought I might see you again," he said.

"We need to talk."

Freddie turned to his two playing companions. "*I will be back in a few minutes*," he said in Spanish. Then back to me. "Let us sit at the picnic table," he said. "We will have some shade there." His English was excellent and precise.

He came through the gate, and I followed, the whack of racket on ball behind us. We sat.

"Did you know Regina tried to place a bet recently?" I asked.

"Yes," Freddie said.

"But not for you."

"How did you know?" he asked.

"It didn't quite add up," I said. "A kid from Ecuador betting on pro football; soccer maybe, but not pro football. But a girl from Long Island, I could see that. You covered for her and took the heat."

"I was in love with her," he said. "I tried to help her. But I could not, so I ended our relationship."

"Still love her?"

"Love is hard to turn off and on," Freddie said.

I took that as a yes.

"Still want to help her?"

"If I knew how, of course," he said.

"Tell me about the betting," I said.

"I think she is an addict," Freddie said. "She bets football, baseball, dogs, and horses. I do not know how long it has been going on because I began to suspect only after she asked me to place bets on football. Then she ran out of money and could not afford to pay and begged me to run away with her until she could get more money. So we went to Sarasota.

You know the rest. She promised to quit if I would say it was me doing the betting."

"Where did she get the money to bet?"

"She has a trust fund," Freddie said. "But she can withdraw only so much a month. She told me that when she started betting she mostly won. Now, she cannot pick a winner, and she cannot force herself to stop."

"Know where we might find her?"

◆ ◆ ◆ ◆

Regina was in a Starbucks near the Florida Atlantic University campus. She sat at a corner table with a latte reading the *Sporting News*. When she saw us coming, she looked both surprised and frightened.

"What's he doing here?" she asked Freddie.

"Trying to get to the bottom of this," I said.

"Did my grandfather send you?" Regina asked, fear in her voice.

"No," I said.

"He is here to help," Freddie said.

"I don't need help," Regina said.

"You do," Freddie said. "You know it, and I know it."

Regina didn't argue. She looked off in the distance and seemed on the verge of tears.

"Let him help you," Freddie said. "I still love you. We can still have a life."

Regina was quiet. She drank her latte and stared at the tabletop. Finally, she turned her gaze on me. She looked calm and focused.

"Okay," she said. "I'm listening."

"I'll need to make some phone calls, but here's what I think I can arrange."

I laid out my plan. When I was finished, she sat silently.

"My father can't be involved," Regina said firmly. "He'll just say I'm weak, which I am, but I don't need to hear that right now. He won't support what you're suggesting."

"No father involvement," I said. "I'll make sure."

"How soon?" she asked.

"Tomorrow," I said.

"I'd have to leave in mid-semester?"

"School will still be here," I said. "You weren't in a hurry to go back the last time we met. No stalling. You need to put this problem behind you before it gets completely out of control."

"Please, Regina," Freddie said. "Let him help you."

She paused to gather her breath. I knew this was a big leap for her.

"Okay," she said.

"We'll go to your dorm, and you'll pack a bag," I said. "We'll stay at my condo tonight."

"Afraid I'll run?" Regina asked.

"You might be tempted," I said.

"Can Freddie stay with me tonight?"

"Sure," I said. "I have two extra bedrooms."

I caught the look that passed between them, but they made no comment.

◆ ◆ ◆ ◆

Freddie went with Regina to pack while I made my phone calls. The first was to Sister Sarah Agnes Woods, who ran a rehab addiction center named Silverthorn in the backwoods of Connecticut. I had known her a long time and supported Silverthorn with personal donations and investment counseling. I had no idea if she dealt with gambling addictions, but I aimed to find out.

"It's been awhile," she said when I finally got her on the phone. "How's married life?"

Why does everyone ask me about married life? I thought.

"So far, so good," I said. "But I didn't call to chat. I have someone who needs help."

"Explain," she said.

I explained.

"Over the years, we've treated only a few gambling addicts," she said. "And none as young as this girl."

"So?"

"So let me know when she'll be arriving," Sarah Agnes said. "We'll see if we can help her."

"Thanks."

"I don't need your thanks, Don," she said. "You're part of the Silverthorn family."

"Well, thanks anyway," I said.

"You're welcome," she said. "How is Roy?"

"Roy is fine," I said. "Whatever you did for him, it worked."

"He did it for himself," she said. "But I'm glad to hear it. Tell him to touch base sometime."

"I'll do that," I said.

◆ ◆ ◆ ◆

Cynthia Capelli listened without interruption—no mean feat when someone was explaining that her daughter had a gambling addiction. I had managed to call when Carlo Vincente was out. It afforded me a private conversation with his daughter.

"I know my father trusts you," she said. "Whatever you suggest, I'll agree to."

"Your husband cannot be involved," I said. "Regina was very specific about that."

"My husband has moved out," Cynthia said. "We're separating. I don't think Regina needs to know that right now."

"It's certainly not for me to tell her," I said. "Another thing: I think *you* should take her to Silverthorn. By yourself. I have some details to work out, but I plan on flying into MacArthur before lunch tomorrow."

“My father has to know,” she said.

“That’s up to you,” I said. “Give me your cell-phone number, and I’ll call when we’re in the air.”

She recited the number, and I keyed it into my cell.

“Thank you so much, Mr. Youngblood,” Cynthia said. “I’ll be waiting at the airport.”

“See you then,” I said, and flipped my cell phone closed.

Carlo Vincente is not going to be happy with me, I thought.

◆ ◆ ◆ ◆

After we settled into my Singer Island condo, I sent Regina and Freddie to Johnny Longboats to pick up dinner. While they were gone, I made some more calls.

The first was to Joseph Fleet to explain why I wanted to keep the jet in Florida.

He was supportive. “You keep it as long as you need to,” he said. “What you’re doing there is more important than anything Fleet Industries has going on.”

I called Jim Doak to give him the news.

“No problem,” he said. “I’ll sleep in the jet.”

Finally, I called Mary and explained what I was up to.

“Things like this are why you’re becoming such a good father,” she said. “I love you for it.”

I went to sleep marveling at how I managed to get myself into such predicaments.

47

We jetted out of Palm Beach International Airport around eight o'clock the next morning. We left clear skies and warm temperatures and flew into cloudy skies and cold temperatures. Two and a half hours later, we landed at MacArthur Airport and taxied to a private hangar.

The sight of Carlo Vincente's icy stare as I followed both Regina and Freddie off the Fleet Industries jet did nothing to warm my day. Two cars were waiting—a silver Lexus and the black Lincoln Town Car that Frankie had picked me up in when I visited in October. Carlo leaned against the Town Car—arms folded, expression unreadable—as Cynthia came to meet her daughter. I couldn't see into the Town Car because of the tinted windows, but I imagined Frankie was behind the wheel.

I grabbed Freddie's arm as Regina ran to her mother. He immediately understood. Both mother and daughter were crying as I walked past them and headed toward Carlo. It was time to face the music.

"I hate loose ends," I said by way of explanation as I stopped in front of him.

He paused just long enough to make me nervous. But I had read him right.

"As do I," Carlo said. "I should be mad at you for making an end run on me, but I find myself grateful that you cared enough about Regina to risk it."

He held out his hand, and we shook.

"I owe you more than I can repay," he said. "I hope someday you'll need a favor from me."

"You never know," I said.

"I see that Freddie has come also," Carlo said.

"Freddie cares for Regina," I said. "She's lucky to have him."

"It would seem so," he said.

"Take care of yourself, Mr. Vincente," I said, turning to leave.

"And you, Mr. Youngblood," he said.

As I walked back toward the jet, I stopped to say goodbye to Regina and her mother. Freddie had joined them.

"I'm leaving," I said. "Good luck."

Regina threw her arms around me, kissed me on the cheek, and hugged me fiercely. I hugged her back.

"Thank you," she whispered. "I feel like a huge weight has been lifted from me."

I slowly broke the embrace, held her by the shoulders, and looked straight into her eyes.

"Trust Sarah Agnes," I said. "If you do, you'll be fine."

"I will," she said. "I promise."

Addictions are powerful things. I prayed Regina had the will to overcome hers.

◆ ◆ ◆ ◆

We landed at Tri-Cities in midafternoon. We had left the clouds on the East Coast, but cold temperatures reached far into the Southern states.

Jim was still in the cockpit when I was ready to exit.

"Thanks for a smooth ride," I said.

"You're welcome. When will you need me again?"

"I'm going to rest up for a few days, then I'll need to go back east again, Connecticut this time. We should probably fly into White Plains. Maybe Monday, if you're free."

"Should be," he said. "I'll call you Friday."

"You and this plane might as well be married, as much time as you spend together."

"We are," Jim said. "Flew off to Mexico for a private ceremony."

"I'm sure you two will be very happy," I said over my shoulder as I walked down the stairs.

◆ ◆ ◆ ◆

By the time I reached the office, Gretchen had left for the day. I checked my messages, then went online to check my email. Nothing urgent in either case. I checked the Dow, which was vacillating in the mid-twelve-thousand range. I didn't buy or sell; I was in watching mode. I closed down and was about to leave when the phone rang.

"Cherokee Investigations," I answered.

"Mr. Youngblood, it's Jessica Crane. I'm sorry to bother you, but I just wondered if you have anything new to report."

I got straight to it. "I was told by a friend of the fifth man on my list that Frank McCurry died of pancreatic cancer," I said. "I'll get a confirmation on that, but it's probably true."

"That doesn't do much to support our murder theory," she said.

"No, it doesn't."

I heard her sigh over the phone.

"I've been flying all over the country trying to interview dead people," I said.

"Don't worry about the cost," Jessica Crane said. "Find out what happened to the last man, and then we'll talk."

◆ ◆ ◆ ◆

I drove slowly into the underground parking garage at the Mountain View condo complex and headed toward my assigned spot at the end. The lot was dimly lit. Suddenly, a figure dressed in black came out of the shadows. I saw the arm rise, heard the shots, saw the mushrooms form on my windshield. I gunned the engine and roared straight at the shooter, who dodged the Pathfinder and fired another shot into my driver's side window. I raced to the end of the parking garage, did a quick U-turn, turned on my high beams, and scanned the garage. Nothing. I stayed in the Pathfinder and waited a few seconds. No movement.

I quickly dialed Mary's cell.

"Hey, cowboy," she said. "Where are you?"

"Listen up," I said. "A shooter is in the parking garage. Fired three or four rounds at me. Might still be here, might not. Call it in. Send the elevator down, but don't be on it."

"Understood," Mary said, all business. "I'm on my way."

I cracked both windows so I could hear better and edged the Pathfinder forward. I heard the ding of the elevator. Then I heard two shots, then two more from a different gun. The figure in black darted across my path and into the outer parking lot, moving fast. I gunned the engine to pursue. Mary appeared on my right, and I slammed on the brakes. She was inside the Pathfinder in an instant.

"Go!" she shouted.

I burned rubber into the outer lot and turned left in time to see the shooter disappear through the gate to the tennis courts. I drove down the parking lot to the courts in seconds.

"No way out," I said. "We've got the bastard now. Be careful."

We were out of the Pathfinder and through the gate in an instant. My Ruger was in my hand. I went left and Mary right. The courts were dark, but we had enough light from the parking lot to see. In the distance, I heard sirens. I also heard the creak of the gate that led to the next court and saw a shadow move. I raced to the gate and went through low, Mary right behind me. Then I saw something I never expected. The shooter went up and over the tennis-court fence at the far end like Spiderman, in one fluid motion, then vanished into the darkness. I started toward the fence, but Mary grabbed my arm.

"No," she said. "He's gone. You'll never find him in those woods. He could lie in wait and shoot you dead. Let's wait for backup."

I knew she was right. "Damn it," I said.

◆ ◆ ◆ ◆

The parking lot pulsated with the red and blue lights of four Mountain Center police cars. Big Bob Wilson stood looking at my new Pathfinder and shaking his head.

"Bulletproof glass," he said to no one in particular. "Well, I'll be damned." He turned to face me. "Why in the world did you think to get bulletproof glass in your new SUV?"

"It was on special," I said.

"Try not being funny," the big man said. He meant to act annoyed but was suppressing a smile.

"I figured in my line of work, someone might take a shot at me sooner or later," I said. "I just didn't figure it would be this soon."

"Saved your ass," Big Bob said.

"Apparently so."

"Anybody out there you know of want to kill you?" the big man asked.

"Maybe a friend of Teddy Earl Elroy," I said. "Or maybe a friend of Victor Vargas. Or maybe I struck a nerve on the Crane case."

I knew I had struck a nerve on the Crane case. I just didn't know whose. I was narrowing in on something that someone didn't want me to get close to. I needed to get there in a hurry.

"I'm going to put somebody on you for a while," Big Bob said.

"Waste of time. The element of surprise is over. Whoever it was just barely escaped. I don't think he'll be back."

"Sean will pick you up in the morning and take you to your office," Big Bob said. "Don't argue."

Sean Wilson, Big Bob's brother, was within earshot. He looked my way.

"Don't argue," Sean said. "Big brother has spoken. What time?"

I knew they were concerned and just trying to help.

"Eight o'clock," I said.

48

The next morning when Billy heard the news of my attempted murder, he immediately drove over from Cherokee. The Mountain Center Police Department's crime-scene unit had already been over the area with the proverbial fine-toothed comb, but Billy wanted to look for himself. He nodded and grunted but said little.

"Not much here," Billy said as we left the parking garage.

"Let's see if we can pick up his trail on the other side of the tennis courts."

Sean Wilson was tagging along to protect me, on orders from Big Bob. He wouldn't be much help if someone was out there with a high-powered rifle with a scope. But I didn't think that was the case. Small towns have few secrets; it would be hard for a stranger to go unnoticed. The whole department was on high alert for anyone suspicious, any new faces in town, and any cars with out-of-state tags. I felt reasonably sure the shooter had taken his best shot, then left for parts unknown. At least I hoped so.

Big Bob had ordered the woods sealed off until Billy took a look. Billy had learned how to track by reading books on the subject and doing research online. When he moved to Mountain Center, he had spent time with experienced Cherokee trackers. With his book knowledge and research added to his personal experience, Billy was able to track almost anything. I was convinced it was genetic.

He picked up the shooter's trail, and Sean and I followed.

"He was moving fast," Billy said. "Knew where he was going. Came in the same way."

I looked at Sean, who shrugged as if to say, *Could have fooled me*. We followed Billy to the other side of the woods and came out on a quiet residential street. We stood in the cold morning sunlight and looked around.

"Probably parked close to here," Billy said to Sean. "You should canvass these houses and find out if anyone saw anything."

"You're talking like a cop," I said as Sean stepped away to make a call.

"Well, I am a deputy sheriff," Billy said. "I had to learn the lingo."

"How is that going?" I asked.

"Fine. I actually like it more than I thought I would. And I'm learning a lot about my people."

Sean walked back to us. "Big Bob is sending a unit," he said. "They'll go house to house. I need to get you to work, Don. They want me on patrol."

"You go ahead," I said. "Billy can drop me, and you can pick me up later. I'll cover for you with Big Bob, if he says anything."

"Since it's Billy, he won't," Sean said. "I'll call you around four."

Sean headed back into the woods. Billy and I stood there for a few minutes, looking around for clues and waiting for an epiphany.

No clues. No epiphany. We left.

◆ ◆ ◆ ◆

I spent the balance of the week being chauffeured to and from work by Sean Wilson and trying to convince myself the shooter had left the area. Billy, ever the mother hen, hung around in the shadows for two days, looking for anyone who didn't fit. When he slept—which was little—it was at the office. On the morning of the third day, he went back to Cherokee—disappointed, I think, that he couldn't put a knife in someone and end the suspense.

I had my new Pathfinder hauled off on a flatbed to Cincinnati to replace the glass. The sales rep that worked for the company supplying the bulletproof glass, proud of the fact the glass had saved my life, promised a fast turnaround. He seemed impressed that I was working a case dangerous enough to get me shot at. I refused to do a testimonial.

The house-to-house interviews on the street where we assumed the shooter had parked his car turned up a man walking his dog after dark. He had seen a gray Taurus with an out-of-state tag parked near where we presumed the shooter had come out of the woods. The man couldn't remember which state the tag was from.

Well, at least it wasn't someone local who tried to shoot me.

Doris Black called late in the week and wanted to know why I hadn't been to the diner. Rather than tell her someone was gunning for me and I wanted to keep a low profile, I simply said I was busy looking for hot stock tips. That seemed to satisfy her.

Friday night, the Youngblood gang went to Lacy's basketball game. I scanned the crowd for would-be assassins but didn't see any. The Lady Bears won and remained undefeated. Lacy had fifteen points, five assists, and four steals and created havoc on defense. She seemed totally unfazed by how good she was. After the game, Lacy went to Hannah's. Mary, Maggie, Billy, and I went to the lake house. Billy stayed the weekend and Maggie went back to Cherokee to attend to Little D. Billy wanted to make sure no one was lurking in the woods, waiting to shoot me.

On Monday, Jim Doak flew me to Connecticut—actually, New York, since we landed at White Plains. A Fleet Industries vice president who doubled as a bodyguard accompanied me.

"It never hurts to have a second set of eyes," Roy said.

I didn't protest. A second set of eyes was never a bad thing, especially if they belonged to Roy Husky. Roy was like Billy. He didn't miss much.

It was nice to have friends who cared.

49

I rented a Chevy Traverse from Hertz. We drove north on the Merritt Parkway to Exit 36, then into the Springdale section of Stamford, obediently following Hilda's directions. Lacy has insisted I take Hilda, and I didn't argue, since Hilda knew the area better than I did. A right, a left, a couple more rights, and we found the Prudence Drive address—a baby-blue split-level in an upscale neighborhood. I parked on the street in front of the house.

"Wait here," I said to Roy.

"Try not to get shot before you reach the front door," Roy said.

"Not funny," I said as I got out.

I climbed the few steps to the front landing and pushed the doorbell. A few seconds later, a woman opened the door. She was in her early to mid-sixties and about five and a half feet tall and had dyed blond hair and a trim figure. She wore tennis whites. She did not look happy.

"What is it?" she said. "Whatever it is will have to wait. I'm late for my game."

"This is the last address I have for John Francis Kelly," I said. "I'm looking for him."

"Why?" she asked, annoyed.

I made a quick decision. If this woman knew I was a private investigator, she might well tell me to get lost or call the cops. And then they'd tell me to get lost.

"I'm a reporter," I said. "I'm doing a story on Silver Star recipients. I want to interview John."

She looked past me. "Who is that person in the SUV?" she asked.

"My photographer," I said.

"Well, John doesn't live here anymore. He lives in Illinois."

I was unable to disguise my surprise. "He's alive?"

"Of course he's alive," she said. "He's a priest, big Catholic church in Evanston. Now, I really must go."

"Thanks," I said.

I don't think she heard me. She slammed the door in my face. As I walked back to the car, I heard the garage door go up. A few seconds later, a silver Volvo backed out of the driveway and into the street, laid some rubber, and sped away.

"How'd that go?" Roy asked as I got in and started the engine.

"I think I just interviewed the Wicked Witch of the North," I said.

"That well, huh? The old Youngblood charm not working?"

"Any Youngblood charm was lost on that woman," I said. "But it doesn't matter. According to her, whoever she was, Father John Francis Kelly is alive and well in Evanston, Illinois."

"He has kids?" Roy asked.

I wasn't sure whether he was kidding or not.

"Apparently, a whole church full."

◆ ◆ ◆ ◆

We drove back to White Plains and turned in the rental. Before we jetted off to Tri-Cities, I called Gretchen.

"Go online and search for Catholic churches in Evanston, Illinois," I said. "See if any of them lists a priest by the name of John Francis Kelly."

"Will do," Gretchen said. "Are you coming in today?"

"Yes," I said. "Probably after you're gone. Leave me a note on what you find."

"It'll be in your inbox," she said.

"Any messages?"

"Sister Sarah Agnes," Gretchen said. "She said to tell you the client arrived and that things are progressing positively."

"Good," I said. "Anything else?"

A decided pause followed.

"That vamp from Florida called."

"Alexandria?" I asked with some surprise. I hadn't expected to hear from her again.

"She wanted to touch base."

"Uh-huh," I said. "Why don't you send her a bill? Inflate it, if it makes you feel better."

"Love to," Gretchen said.

◆ ◆ ◆ ◆

A grinning Oscar Morales was waiting for us with the Fleet limo to take us back to Mountain Center. I had not seen Oscar in a while.

"How's it going, O-man?" I asked.

"Life is good, Mr. Youngblood," Oscar said as he opened the back door. I noticed he didn't call me "boss."

We made a quick exit from the airport. The day was cold and gray. A few snowflakes danced in a light breeze. I wondered if heavier snow was in our forecast.

A half-hour later, we dropped Roy at Fleet Industries before heading into Mountain Center.

"Watch your back," Roy said as he shut the limo door.

"I'll do my best," I said, thinking of the absurdity behind that idea.

Oscar dropped me in front of the Hamilton Building a few minutes after four o'clock.

"We were not followed," he said, turning to face me in the backseat.

"You know about the shooter?"

"Roy told me," he said. "If you need a bodyguard or backup, I'm your man."

"Thanks," I said. "But I believe I'm covered."

I didn't know whether I really believed that or not.

"Do you need me for anything this week?" Oscar asked.

"Don't think so, O-man," I said. "I'll be in touch."

◆ ◆ ◆ ◆

I came off the elevator with my hand on my Ruger, remembering the time I was surprised by a crazed killer near my office door. Today, however, no surprises were waiting for me. I made it inside, left the outer door unlocked, and went to my desk.

I looked at my messages, most of which I already knew about. The one that I didn't was from Joseph Fleet, who rarely called unless it was important. I rang his private number. Roy answered.

"Mr. Fleet called me," I said.

"Hang on, gumshoe."

"Donald," Joseph Fleet said. "Roy informed me about this nasty business you're mixed up in, and I wanted to tell you the jet is at your disposal until you get this cleared up."

"I appreciate that," I said. "I think I need to buy part interest in it."

"Nonsense," he said. "It's a business expense."

"God bless the IRS," I said.

Joseph Fleet was still laughing when I hung up.

50

The next morning, Jim Doak flew me to Chicago Executive Airport, a regional airport fifteen miles from Our Mother of the Divine Catholic Church in Evanston. I had coffee and a cheese Danish and read the printout Gretchen had pulled from the church's website. Our Mother of the Divine consisted of an old church, a new church, and a school spread out over fifty acres. The staff was large, which I guessed meant a large membership. Highlighted in DayGlo yellow was Father John Francis Kelly, senior pastor.

I picked up a rental from Hertz and drove to the church, following directions from Hilda, with whom I seemed destined to have a relationship. I parked in the main lot and with little difficulty found the entrance marked "Church Offices." I went through the glass door and past the restroom area looking for a live body. An office on my right was unoccupied. In the next office, a pleasant-looking, dark-haired woman around thirty years old was doing some word processing on her computer.

"Excuse me," I said.

"Can I help you?" she asked, looking up.

"Yes, please. Can you tell me where I can find Father John?"

"His office is on the right at the end of the hall," she said. "If he's not there, he's probably in the sanctuary."

Father John's office was empty, so I continued down the hall and through a door to a T-intersection with another hall. A small plaque with the word *Sanctuary* and an arrow pointing left was on the wall. As directed, I took the left and at the end of that hall went through a set of double doors to find myself in the back of a large sanctuary. The place was cool and quiet and full of shadows, though candles burned and a few lights were on. The atmosphere demanded quiet and reverence and dredged up some distant childhood memory of sitting alone in an empty sanctuary and enjoying the solitude. I had the urge to sit and take a deep breath. The lights at the front of the church were on, and I saw a man who appeared to be polishing various item around the altar. He was dark haired and about five-foot-ten and looked to be fit. I walked down the aisle toward him. He looked up and saw me coming.

"I now know what 'man of the cloth' means," I said.

He laughed. "That's good. I may have to use that in my next sermon."

"Don Youngblood," I said, extending my hand.

"Father John Francis Kelly," he said. "Call me Father John."

"Father, I'm a private investigator," I said, showing him my ID. "I need to talk to you about a group of men—seven, in fact."

He didn't answer for a moment.

"The Southside Seven," he said softly, as if recalling something long forgotten.

◆ ◆ ◆ ◆

We were in what Father John referred to as his "old office." We sat in worn but comfortable chairs in front of an ancient desk.

"I still come here from time to time to get a little peace and quiet," he said.

"I understand. I often go to my office early in the morning for the same reason."

"Tell me why you've come," he said.

"Walter Crane died recently for no apparent reason," I said. "His widow asked me to look into his death. At the time, I thought she was just being paranoid. Now, I'm not so sure."

"I'm sorry to hear that," Father John said. "Walter was a good man. I didn't know him well, but I could tell."

From the inside pocket of my jacket, I pulled a smaller version of the picture I had found in Walter Crane's basement and handed it to Father John.

"Recognize this?"

He took it from me, studied it for a minute, and slowly nodded.

"So long ago," he said. "The Southside Seven."

"Do you know you're the only one in that picture who's still alive?" I asked.

"No, I didn't," he said, surprise showing on his face and in his voice.

"Want to hear all of it?" I asked.

"Yes, of course," he said. "Tell me."

I went through my investigation step by step, trip by trip, including the attempt on my life. When I finished, he was quiet while he processed the information.

"So you think all the deaths are connected?" he asked.

"I think maybe someone has a reason to want all the men in that picture dead," I said. "I think you might know who or maybe why."

He looked away and remained silent.

"One thing I forgot to mention," I said. "I found an old note in Walter Crane's desk dated 1994. It read—"

"'Seven die one by one and no one knows when their time will come,'" Father John said, as if repeating a chant.

"You got one?" I said, stunned.

"Yes."

"Do you know who sent it?"

"No."

"Do you know why?"

"I think so," he said. "Retribution."

"Did it involve the mission that led to your receiving the Silver Star?" I asked.

"Yes," he said. "I think it must have."

"What happened over there, Father John?"

He took a deep breath and stared at the floor. He rubbed his chin and turned his dark eyes on me.

"We weren't supposed to talk about it," he said. "But it's been a long time. Maybe talking about it will give me some peace."

"I've got all day," I said. "Take your time."

"It was a black ops mission in early January 1991. We hadn't sent troops in yet," Father John began. "I was surprised I was chosen, but officially I volunteered. I could have turned it down, but no Ranger would turn down a black ops mission. We lived for that kind of thing in those days. We were all from different units, didn't know each other. I guess that's the way they wanted it.

"Walter was the team leader, and a good one. We trained together for a week or so, and then we were coptered at night from Kuwait into an area of Iraq that was considered unfriendly. There were eight of us. We were never told exactly where we were, but it was a few miles from a decent-sized town. We were on a rescue mission. I didn't know who we were rescuing at the time, but I heard rumors later."

"What rumors?" I asked.

"That the mission was all about oil. A favor for some bigwig who controlled much of the supply in Kuwait." Father John paused a moment. "We went into the town after midnight. Walter had a map of the location where the captive, who had been kidnapped, was being held. We located the building, and then all hell broke loose. Somebody inside must have been on lookout and started shooting. We were receiving fire, then we were returning fire, and it was like World War III. In less than a minute, we stopped receiving any return fire. Then we heard the screams. Walter yelled for a cease-fire. All we heard then was the screaming and the crying. We crashed through the front door, weapons ready, but there was no need. The gunmen were dead—and so were a dozen children. Others were huddled in a corner with a few adults, whimpering like wounded animals. Unknown to us, the kidnappers were hiding the captive in a schoolhouse. Why kids were there at that hour, I don't know. Maybe they were hostages.

"A young man, late teens or early twenties, was tied up in the basement unharmed. He babbled on and on, thanking each of us and telling us his father would make us rich. I was surprised at how good his English was. Walter finally told him to shut up. We took him and got out of that schoolhouse as fast as we could, leaving the wounded to fend for themselves. Walter was mad as hell that the intel hadn't mentioned the schoolhouse and the possibility that kids were inside."

He paused and took another deep breath.

"We returned to our units without talking about what happened, but I knew we'd all be haunted by it. The next time we saw each other was when we received the Silver Star and had the picture made. That was later in 1991. None of us wanted the medal. We just wanted to forget the mission ever happened and to get home. We were sent stateside soon afterward. As far as I know, nobody planned on reenlisting."

We both sat silently while I assessed what he had said.

"You mentioned eight Rangers," I said. "Only seven are in the picture. What happened to the eighth man?"

"Walter sent him back in the copter. The guy had a stress attack or something. Could hardly talk, uncontrollable stuttering. He was mad as hell that Walter kicked him off the mission."

"Do you remember his name?"

"Tommy Bell," he said. "Seemed like an okay guy until he went to pieces."

"Do you know what happened to him?"

"Randy Butler told me at the medal ceremony that he heard Bell was given a medical discharge," he said.

"Do you know anything else about him?"

"Nothing," Father John said.

"Did you stay in touch with any of those guys?"

"No," he said. "Like I told you, we didn't know each other, and we all went back to our own units. I didn't want any reminders of that night, and I'm guessing none of them did either. I prayed for forgiveness and absolution, and then God called me to the priesthood. I pray every day for the souls of those we killed. Now, I'll add the names of the others on that mission to my prayer list."

"I'm sorry I dredged up such a bad memory," I said.

"It's not your fault. I'm glad you came, though I wonder if you can make any sense out of this. Tell me what you think about all these deaths."

"I do think they're connected to the mission," I said. "I think someone wants revenge for something—the dead children, maybe. Or maybe Tommy Bell was upset about being sent back and then finding out that all of you received the Silver Star. I think all seven of you got the note. I think Randy Butler got it and decided not to wait to be murdered. What's really puzzling is the gap between Randy's apparent suicide and the disappearance of Armand Priloux. Why did the killer wait so long? And I think Armand Priloux, Bobby McMullen, Thomas Barry, and Walter Crane were murdered. I think Frank McCurry died of cancer because that was worse than being murdered. I think you're still alive because you're a priest." I paused to consider. "I think Tommy Bell is my best suspect."

"So what do you do next?"

"I need to find Tommy Bell."

"Be careful," Father John said.

"I will. But it won't hurt if you add me to your prayer list."

"Consider it done," he said.

◆ ◆ ◆ ◆

I was back in the office late that afternoon. Daylight was almost gone, and I was beat. I scanned my messages from Gretchen and found nothing important enough to make me stay any later than I had to.

I called Jessica Crane.

"I found one alive," I said when I got her on the phone.

"Good Lord," she said. "Did he know anything?"

"He knew a lot."

I told her all of it.

"So you're going after Tommy Bell," she said.

"As soon as I get his last known address."

51

The following afternoon, Mary and I took the dogs for their weekly romp. Jake and Junior raced around the Little League field like birds fleeing a cage. Their exercise was usually on leashes and occasionally on the tennis courts at the condo, but the surface there was hard on their pads, and some of the players objected to paw marks on the courts. The basketball goal had been removed and a No Dogs sign posted. The board of directors had no respect for the famous private investigator. I was ready to sell and move to the lake house permanently.

Christmas was approaching, and the days were short. This particular afternoon was overcast and cold. I wore boots, cords, and a ski jacket. The temperature was in the thirties, but a mild breeze made it feel colder. The dogs didn't seem to notice. They ran and nipped at and chased each other. I knew that if they could talk, they'd thank me for what a good time they were having.

The field was surrounded by fencing, so the dogs were contained. I sat in the aluminum bleachers outside the fence and watched the show. My butt was freezing.

"I'm worried about you," Mary said, huddling close.

"I know," I said.

"You need to back off this thing before it gets you killed."

"Too late," I said. "I need to find Tommy Bell. He's either trying to kill me or knows who is. Either way, I'm too close now. The only way to stop this is to end it."

I had left a message at the Pentagon for Lieutenant Colonel Bradley Culpepper to call me. I needed him to get me the last known address for Tommy Bell.

On the field, Jake was tiring and Junior was still racing around.

"Then I have a list of demands," Mary said. "If they are not met, I'm going to throw you in jail until you agree."

I smiled. *Ain't love grand*?

"Okay," I said. "Let's hear them."

I listened and watched the dogs. Jake trotted over to the fence and lay down by the gate, signaling that he was ready to go. Junior came over and tried to get Jake interested in playing again. Jake was having none of it. Junior gave up and raced away.

Mary finished.

"Well?" she said.

"Agreed," I said.

She turned and took my face in her hands and kissed me passionately.

"I love you," she said.

"I know." I smiled and paused. "Want to go underneath the bleachers?"

"You're hopeless," Mary said.

◆ ◆ ◆ ◆

That night, after a dinner of Chinese takeout, I was in the bedroom working on my laptop. The Street was sagging; the Dow was under twelve thousand. Mary and Lacy were two floors down in the den watching a supposedly authentic forensics show on one of the cable channels. Lacy had decided she wanted to be in law enforcement, and forensics was one of her interests, especially if it involved computers. Mountain Center High School offered a criminology class, and Lacy was constantly quizzing Mary regarding procedure.

I was looking at the charts on a particular stock when my cell phone rang. Caller ID was blocked. Normally, I would have let the call go to voice mail, but with the Crane case heating up, I decided to answer. I was glad I did.

"Youngblood, is that you?"

I knew that voice.

"Yes," I said.

"Bradley Culpepper here. I'm returning your call."

"Working late?"

"No," he said. "I'm home in my study with a brandy. I'm curious why you called."

"The mission we discussed," I said. "Did you know it had an eighth man?"

There was a pause on the other end.

"No, I didn't." He sounded genuinely surprised.

"His name was Tommy Bell," I said. "I was told he was medically discharged soon after the mission. Apparently, he was sent back before it was completed because he had some kind of breakdown."

"Hang on a minute," Culpepper said.

I heard a drawer open and shut.

"Okay, you said Tommy Bell. I'm guessing you want his last known address," he said.

"It would help."

"Tell me what you've found out so far."

"Six of the seven are dead," I said.

"Jesus Christ!" he said. "What the hell is going on, Youngblood?"

I thought the brandy might be working its magic. Bradley Culpepper was a little less military than when I saw him at the Pentagon. He listened as I hit the highlights, then was silent after I finished.

"No wonder they didn't want the Silver Star," he said, sounding like he was talking to himself. "So you think this Tommy Bell is your killer?"

"He's the best lead I have," I said. "He may be the killer, or he may know who is. Or he may not know a damn thing."

52

Early the next morning, I took Jake and Junior to the office. Never hurt to have bodyguards. I entered the outer office, closed the front door behind me, and looked around. No one was waiting to shoot me. While the dogs sniffed the premises, I locked the front door and made coffee. I had dumped my old coffeemaker and bought a Keurig, since Dunkin' Donuts was now making K-Cups.

Satisfied that everything was as it should be, Jake and Junior went to their beds, circled a few times, and lay down. I took a drink of coffee and called Sister Sarah Agnes Woods.

"How is the patient I sent you?" I asked after the usual hellos.

"She is doing quite well," Sarah Agnes said. "She wants to be a nun and work here at Silverthorn."

I laughed. "She thinks she's found herself and doesn't want to leave."

"That often happens in the early stages of treatment," she said. "Usually, they get past it and realize they want to go back to life in the real world."

"What's the prognosis?" I asked.

"Treating addictions is not an exact science," Sarah Agnes said. "But I expect we'll be successful. She's tough and fragile at the same time. I'll let her stay as long as she needs to."

"Send the bill to Carlo Vincente on this one," I said. "He can afford it."

"Gladly," she said.

"How is business?"

"Booming," Sarah Agnes said. "Addictions are all the rage. The newest one is sex addiction. We're treating some high-profile cases—mostly athletes and politicians. If I could clone myself, I'd build a second Silverthorn."

"You can do only so much," I said. "Concentrate on the here and now."

"I can always count on you for good advice," she said. "Now, tell me what's happening in your world."

"It's a long story," I said.

"I've got time. You always have such good stories."

So I told her all of it.

"Mercy!" Sarah Agnes said when I finished. "Bulletproof glass. Did you get your new car back?"

"It's a sport utility vehicle," I said.

"Of course it is," she said. "How foolish of me."

She was messing with me, just as all the important females in my life did. As far as Sarah Agnes was concerned, if it had four wheels and took you places, it was a car. All the other details were inconsequential.

"You're as bad as Mary and Lacy," I said. "Anyway, I did get it back, as good as new and ready to stop more bullets."

"Will you have to deal with more bullets?"

"I certainly hope not," I said.

We talked awhile longer before someone interrupted her with a crisis and she had to go. I finished my coffee, left the dogs sleeping peacefully on their beds, and walked to the Mountain Center Diner. I had a quiet breakfast and didn't see Roy or Big Bob, which didn't happen often.

◆ ◆ ◆ ◆

Shortly after I got back to the office, the phone rang. It was the call I was waiting for.

"Culpepper here," the voice said.

"Good morning, colonel."

"Thanks for the thought, but it's still lieutenant colonel," he said.

"Matter of time. What've you got?"

"Tommy Bell's last known address is in your backyard."

"Mountain Center?" I asked, incredulous.

"Not quite," he said. "Asheville, North Carolina. Got a pencil?"

After we hung up, I ran the address he gave me through MapQuest. Tommy Bell, if he was still there, was sixty-six miles from my office. Was that a bad omen?

◆ ◆ ◆ ◆

Fifteen minutes and one phone call later, I left the office. I knew Gretchen was going to be late, so I took the dogs back to the condo and then headed for Asheville. I swung south and picked up Interstate 40. A half-hour later, I crossed into North Carolina. I got off the interstate at Exit 20 and pulled into a service station. Swain County Deputy Sheriff Billy Two-Feathers was waiting. He was in uniform and packing a Glock 9.

"Look at you," I said.

"Shut up, Blood," Billy growled.

"Sorry, Chief," I said. "On second thought, the uniform's not such a bad idea."

"What's in Asheville?" Billy asked.

When I called, I had told him only that I was going to Asheville and might need some backup. Billy wasn't one for asking many questions. He told me when and where to meet him, then hung up. Now that I had him face to face, I filled in the blanks.

"Probably long gone," Billy said.

"Maybe, maybe not. But I need to find out."

"*We* need to find out," Billy said.

"We do," I said.

◆ ◆ ◆ ◆

Tommy Bell's last known address was in an old upper-middle-class neighborhood where the houses were close together and shaded by ancient oak trees. The homes were in good repair and the small yards well kept. The house we were looking for occupied a corner lot at a four-way stop. I parked on the street in front. It was almost lunchtime, and I hoped to catch someone home—probably not Tommy Bell, assuming he was working.

"Stay in the Pathfinder," I said.

"No," Billy said.

"I don't want him to see the uniform."

"I do," Billy said. "And I want him to see the Glock if he's here, which I doubt."

It was useless to argue, so I didn't. We went up the walk to the porch. I rang the ancient doorbell and waited. Nothing. I rang it again and waited some more. Nothing.

The porch went around one side of the house, so that it faced both streets. I walked to my right and stared through my reflection into what looked like a den. I saw no one. Billy walked around the left side and disappeared.

A few seconds later, I heard him call out.

"Blood!"

He came fast back around the porch toward the front door, Glock out. Billy with a gun in his hand just didn't compute. I drew my Ruger.

"What?"

"Body on the floor," he said.

I tried the door. It was unlocked.

"Me first," Billy said.

Again, I didn't argue. Billy went through the door, and I followed, scanning right as he scanned left. Nothing. The house was quiet. Somewhere, I heard water dripping and a small motor running—the sounds of an empty, or at least lifeless, house.

A woman lay on the living-room floor on her stomach. She looked to be in her early sixties. She wore running shoes, jeans, and a white pullover. I could see the left side of her face. The eye stared unseeing toward a side window. There was no sign of blood.

Billy knelt to check her pulse, looked at me, and shook his head.

"I'm calling it in," he said. "Let's wait on the porch."

"I'd love ten minutes to look around," I said.

"No," Billy said. "Outside, Blood."

I nodded, and we went back out the door and waited on the porch.

53

The first of Asheville's finest on the scene was a patrol car with one uniformed officer. Billy said he'd do the talking, and I let him. I smiled to myself as I walked to the far end of the porch and half leaned, half sat on the railing; Billy usually hated doing the talking. He was taking this deputy sheriff thing seriously. The uniform didn't seem much interested in why we were here—only that we had found the body.

Next on the scene was a black unmarked car. Two plain-clothes detectives came up the walk and onto the porch. I heard them introduce themselves to Billy as Riggs and King. Riggs was older, shorter, and thinner than King. King talked to Billy for a minute, and then Riggs walked over to me.

"I'm Riggs," he said. He didn't offer his hand.

"Youngblood," I said.

"The big Indian says you're a PI," Riggs said.

He might as well have said *dog shit* as *PI*. I didn't like his attitude.

"The big Indian's name is Billy Two-Feathers," I said. "And he's a deputy sheriff."

"Right," Riggs said.

I watched over Riggs's shoulder as Billy and King went into the house.

"You're from Mountain Center," Riggs said, like it was an outhouse.

"Right," I said. If he hadn't been a plain-clothes detective, I would have bitch-slapped him.

"So what brings you to Asheville, Youngblood?"

"I'm working a case," I said, annoyed and letting it show.

"And what brings you to this house?"

I played it straight, even though I found it hard not to be a smart ass.

"I wanted to interview someone who might still be living here," I said in my hard-as-nails private detective persona.

"Who?"

"Tommy Bell," I said.

Riggs was making notes in a small notebook.

"And you just walked in and found the woman dead on the floor?"

"We rang the bell, then looked in the windows," I said with some attitude. "Billy saw the body. We tried the door, and it was unlocked. We went in and checked to see if she was still alive. She wasn't. We came back out and called it in."

"So you didn't touch anything?"

I answered as if it was the dumbest question I had ever heard. "Of course not."

Riggs nodded. "Of course not," he said sarcastically.

I was ready to throw him off the porch.

"Okay," Riggs said. "That's all for now. Stick around."

Riggs walked over to King, who was now back on the porch, and they had a quiet conversation, no doubt comparing notes. Another patrol car arrived. Neighbors milled about in their yards, wondering what was going on. Riggs and King split up and went to conduct interviews. Billy was in a conversation with the uniform. I scanned the neighbors and noticed a guy across the street on the opposite corner. Looking right at me, he made a slight movement of his head. I got off the railing, slowly walked around the corner of the porch, and descended another set of stairs to avoid Riggs and King. I went across the street and up to the corner and across the intersecting street. The man watched me come. He was probably in his late fifties, fit looking, maybe five-foot-eight with short gray hair and a close-cropped beard. He had on jeans and a lightweight black jacket.

"You're Donald Youngblood, right?" he asked.

"How did you know that?"

"Saw your picture last year when you cracked that serial-killer case," he said. "Very interesting. What's going on over there?"

I glanced toward Riggs and King, who were otherwise engaged and had not spotted me leaving the porch.

"Is there somewhere we can talk out of view of the cops?" I asked.

"Around back," he said. "Follow me."

As I did so, I noticed another car arriving. *Medical examiner*, I thought. We went around the corner of his house and into a screened porch that was winterized. While not exactly warm, it was warmer than outside, which was about fifty degrees.

"Ned Blount," he said, extending his hand.

"My partner and I found a woman dead in that house," I said. "Who lives there?"

"Miriam Bell," he said. "Is it her?"

I described the woman.

"That's her," he said, shaking his head. "What happened?"

"I don't know," I said. "Did she live alone?"

"Yes, she did. Her husband died of a heart attack a couple years ago."

"What about her son?" I asked. "Do you know where he is?"

"Which one?" he asked. "She had three, and a girl."

"Tommy," I said.

"Dead," he said. "Killed in a car wreck. Pulled out in front of a truck, I think. Damn shame."

"When?"

"Long time ago," he said. "Back in the nineties. I don't remember many of the details. Died on the scene, I think."

"In Asheville?"

"I guess," Ned Blount said. "I really don't remember."

"Christ, have mercy," I said, more to myself than to him. I'd reached another dead end, literally.

◆ ◆ ◆ ◆

I thanked Ned Blount and walked back across the street, having gone unnoticed by Riggs and King. I returned to my previous place against the railing and watched another car pull up. A suit got out. The suit received a lot of attention from the uniform. Riggs and King made a beeline to him and did most of the talking, with some pointing thrown in. One of the points went in my direction, another in Billy's. The suit did a lot of nodding. Then Riggs and King left to talk to more neighbors while the suit headed toward the porch. *This ought to be fun*, I thought.

The suit came up the front steps and turned in my direction. He was a little overweight and had an air of importance about him. We made eye contact as he approached.

"Youngblood?" he said.

"That's me."

"Jack Dillard," he said.

"Chief of police?"

"Yeah," he said. "How'd you know?"

"The anxiety level among the troops went up a notch or two when you arrived."

"Yeah," he said. "That tends to happen. I called Big Bob Wilson when I heard a Mountain Center PI found Mrs. Bell's body. I've known Big Bob awhile. He said you were the only PI in town, and a damn good one, and not to tell you he said it."

"Sounds like him," I said. "We were best friends in high school."

"What can you tell me about this mess?" he asked.

Behind Chief Dillard, I saw the crime-scene unit arrive.

"Not much," I said. "I came to interview Tommy Bell, and we found Mrs. Bell dead. Billy was with me as backup, since someone took a few shots at me last week. I've subsequently learned Tommy Bell is also dead, so I'd like to get back to Mountain Center for dinner with my wife and kid, if that's okay."

Before he could respond, the M.E. came shuffling up. He was a thin, bald older man who didn't look to be in good health. *Smoker*, I thought.

"Murdered," he said to Chief Dillard, not even acknowledging my presence. His voice was gravelly, as if he needed to clear his throat.

"How?" Dillard asked.

"Sharp instrument to the base of the skull above the hairline," he said. "Maybe an ice pick. Practically no blood, and what blood there was the hair soaked up. Clean and efficient. Damn lucky I found it. A pro, I'd say."

"Okay," Chief Dillard said. "Take her downtown as soon as the crime-scene unit gives you the okay." He turned back to me. "What aren't you telling me?"

"I can't be sure," I said, "but I think she might have been killed to prevent her from telling me something. What that might have been, I don't know. Who might have killed her, I don't know either."

"So you think your investigation might have gotten Mrs. Bell killed?"

"I sure as hell hope not," I said.

But in the back of my mind, I knew better. *You got that lady killed, Youngblood*, I thought. *Way to go.*

◆ ◆ ◆ ◆

Billy came over a few minutes later but stayed quiet.

"Bad business," he said finally.

"It is," I said.

"You've pulled something dark into the light," Billy said. "And it doesn't want to be there."

The way he said it sent a chill down my spine. Something evil was cleaning up after itself, and it wasn't Tommy Bell. It didn't seem to matter now. I had no one else to talk to. Tommy and his mother were my last hope. The thing that bothered me most was how the killer knew I was on my way to the Bell residence. Was my phone tapped? Was Father John Kelly not what he seemed to be? Was Tommy Bell really dead?

"Let's get out of here," I said.

"Not yet," Billy said. "King asked for us to wait a few minutes in case they have more questions."

The cops let us stew a bit before King came over and said we could go. By the time we walked to the Pathfinder, my watch showed three o'clock. We got in, and I sat there with my hands on the wheel and a feeling I was missing something. I stared trancelike at the stop sign.

"What?" Billy asked.

"The guy across the street," I said. "I need to ask him a few more questions."

I watched as Riggs and King got in their car and departed. I drove around the block and came back down the other side of the street and parked in front of Ned Blount's house.

"Come with me," I said to Billy.

We went up the front steps and knocked on the door.

54

We sat at Ned Blount's kitchen table. What I could see of the house was neat. I learned that Ned had done two tours in the army in Vietnam and had lived in the neighborhood since 1970, the year Tommy Bell was born. His wife had died of cancer a few years back. He missed her but liked living alone. He fixed all of us a glass of iced tea and sat across from me. Billy was on my left.

I took a drink. The tea was perfect, freshly brewed with real lemon.

"How well did you know Tommy Bell?" I asked.

"Not very," he said. "He did talk to me about the Rangers, though. That surprised me."

"Tell me what you remember about Tommy," I said.

"He was a shy kid growing up. He stuttered when he was younger and got teased. You can imagine. Judith and Skipper were his only friends. They looked out for him and stuck up for him. Judith lived in the house directly across the street from me, and Skipper was in the house across from the Bells."

"Is either family still there?"

"No," Ned said. "They both moved sometime in the nineties. Skipper de Soto was killed in Desert Storm before Tommy Bell died in that car accident, and his family moved soon after that. Judith's family moved after she graduated from college."

"What college?"

"Georgetown," he said. "Her parents were very proud."

"What was Judith's last name?" I asked.

"Minor," he said. "M-i-n-o-r."

"Do you know where she is now?"

"No," Ned said. "Last I heard, she had a government job, but that was a long time ago."

"Do you know where the family moved?" I asked.

"I'm not sure," he said. "Florida, maybe."

"Did they call her Judy?"

"No," he said. "If you called her Judy, she would correct you. 'My name is Judith,' she would say."

I sat and thought and drank more tea. I realized I was out of meaningful questions. I drained the glass.

"Thanks. You were a big help," I said. "Anything you want to ask?" I said to Billy.

He shook his head. "I think you covered it."

"I don't want to know now," Ned Blount said. "But when this is over, give me a call and let me know what was really going on."

"I will," I promised. "If I can ever find out."

◆ ◆ ◆ ◆

Back in the Pathfinder, I retrieved a notebook from my briefcase and made notes on my conversation with Ned Blount. Billy placed a call on his cell phone. By the tone of his voice, I was pretty sure he was talking to Maggie. I wrote down "Judith Minor" and underlined it twice. I also wrote down "Skipper de Soto" with a question mark. I needed to make a couple of calls myself, but Billy was still talking, so I slid out of the Pathfinder and shut the door.

I called Gretchen.

"Where are you?" she answered.

"Very professional," I said.

"I knew it was you. Caller ID."

"Wonderful," I said.

"Why didn't you leave me a note or something?"

"Hey," I said, "who's the boss of this operation?"

"Me, of course," Gretchen said.

"Okay, boss. I need you to do some research. See what you can find out about a Judith Minor from Asheville, North Carolina. She graduated from Georgetown University in Washington, D.C."

"I know where Georgetown is," Gretchen said.

"Sorry," I said. "Of course you do." I gave her Judith's last known address. "She'd be early to mid-forties now. Next, see if you can find a death notice for a Skipper de Soto, also from Asheville and about the same age as Judith. I was told he was killed in Desert Storm."

"Anything else?" she asked. I heard excitement in her voice.

"I need to confirm that a Tommy Bell died in a car accident, probably in North Carolina, around 1992 or 1993," I said.

"How old was he?"

"Probably early twenties, give or take a couple of years."

"Okay," Gretchen said. "Is that all?"

"For now," I said.

"Are you coming back today?"

"No. I'll see you in the morning."

I disconnected from Gretchen, called Scott Glass, and found out he was in Washington, tied up in meetings for a couple of days. So I called David Steele.

David Steele was the special agent in charge of the Knoxville office of the FBI. I had met Agent Steele at Quantico, Virginia, where he trained new recruits for the bureau. Scott Glass and I had been among those recruits. My relationship with David Steele had been rocky. After basic training, I decided life in the FBI was not for me. Scott stayed, and I landed on Wall Street. David Steele and I reconnected years later when I was working the Walker case, which became nationally known as the Three Devils case. We formed an unfriendly alliance that became considerably friendlier as the case progressed. I hadn't seen him since the day I married Mary.

"Youngblood," he said. "It's been awhile. How's married life?"

"Most of the time, it's great," I said. "The rest of the time, it's still good."

"Glad to hear it," he said. "That Mary is something else."

"She is," I said. "But she can be a ball breaker sometimes."

"Can't they all," David Steele said.

"I thought you were retiring," I said. Scott had told me, but I never got the details.

"Yeah, well, I went to turn in my papers and say adios, and they offered me a big raise. From their point of view, I was the golden boy who cracked the Three Devils case. I tried to tell them it was you and not me, but they weren't about to listen to that."

"You got it reopened and backed me up," I said.

"Still, it was your instincts," David Steele said. "But we saved that girl and maybe a lot more. We have to feel good about that."

"We do," I agreed.

"Anyway, so they offered me this big raise, and I talked it over with Betty, and we agreed I'd stay a few more years and put some money away. It'll make retirement a hell of a lot easier."

"Good for you," I said. "Listen, Dave, I need a favor."

"Thought you might," he said. "I know Scott's tied up in Washington. What do you need?"

"See if you can find a Judith Minor in any government database. She'd be early to mid-forties. Grew up in Asheville, North Carolina. Went to Georgetown University and supposedly had some kind of government job."

"Will do," David Steele said. "I'll call you back."

But he never did.

◆ ◆ ◆ ◆

We were sitting at the kitchen bar eating Italian takeout. I was feeling depressed and being way too quiet. I was picking at my food and had just opened my third beer—one over the norm for me—when the females picked up on my mood.

"What's wrong?" Mary asked.

"Yeah," Lacy said. "You haven't said two words during dinner, and you haven't eaten much, and you're on your third beer."

Miss Observant.

"Just tired," I said.

"Bullshit," Mary said. "Most of the time you're tired, you can't shut up about how tired you are."

"Tell us," Lacy said.

I took a deep breath. "I think I got a lady killed today."

The kitchen got funeral-home quiet.

"Tell us," Mary said.

I told them about finding out where Tommy Bell was from and about going to Asheville with Billy. I told them about finding the body, about how Miriam Bell had been murdered, about the dickhead detectives, and about how guilty I felt.

After I finished, they were quiet, processing.

When she spoke, Mary chose her words carefully, talking like a cop comforting a victim. "You have to understand that when you take a case, things like this can happen. You were just doing your job. You didn't kill her, and you're only guessing as to why she was killed. Forget the guilt, and get the bastard who did it."

Lacy put her hand on mine. "Don, you're the best person I know. You cannot control other people's actions. You had no way to know where your investigation would lead or who it might affect. It's not your fault."

"How'd you get so smart?" I asked.

"Living around Jake and Junior," she said.

55

The next morning, I went straight to the Mountain Center Diner. I had gotten up late. The reason I had gotten up late was because Mary decided last to get me out of my depressed state. Sometime during the act of being reinstated to the land of the living, I had reached another level of consciousness or broken the sound barrier or achieved zero gravity, or maybe all three. When it was over, I was convinced it could never be that good again. Mary promptly made me promise to make it my life's work to make it that good again. After I agreed, she gave me a little white sleeping pill and one last kiss goodnight. The next thing I knew, it was daylight, my bed was empty, and I was starving.

Big Bob Wilson was at my table when I arrived at the diner. I'd expected he might be. He would want the details on my Asheville adventure.

"You look . . . ," he started.

"What?" I said as I sat.

Then he smiled. "Pussy-whipped," he said.

"Please, no vulgarity before my first cup of coffee," I said.

Doris hustled over, poured coffee, took our order, and scurried away.

"Tell me what happened in Asheville."

I told him all of it, including the part about my guilt at getting Miriam Bell killed.

"That's bullshit," Big Bob said. "Hell, witnesses get killed sometimes. It goes with the territory. We're trying to shut down the bad guys. You're one of the good guys. Don't forget it."

"That's basically what Mary said. But it really pisses me off. I want to catch this guy. I want to kill the bastard."

"I understand," he said. "But you need to calm down and relax."

Our food arrived.

"And enjoy your breakfast," he added.

I smiled. Big Bob was usually not the voice of reason. Our roles had temporarily reversed. I took a bite of home fries, and my mood improved. Then I took a bite of feta cheese omelet, and it improved further. We talked sports, family, guns, cars, and movies and left the bad stuff in the gutter. The big man had a sense of what I needed, and I rolled with it.

◆ ◆ ◆ ◆

I beat Gretchen to the office by a few minutes. Once she settled in, she came into my office and took residence in one of the chairs in front of my desk. She flipped open her notebook.

"I have some answers," she said.

"Okay, let's hear them."

"First, I found a Tommy Bell, twenty-one years old, who died in a car accident in Durham, North Carolina, in 1991."

"Durham?"

"Yes."

"Nineteen ninety-one?"

"Didn't I just say that?"

"Sorry," I said. "I think I just made a connection. Go ahead."

"Next, Eduardo 'Skipper' de Soto from Asheville, North Carolina, died in Desert Storm in 1991. He's buried in Arlington National Cemetery."

"Okay," I said. "I figured Ned Blount had it right, but it never hurts to check. What else?"

"Judith Minor of Asheville, North Carolina, was a high-school jock in basketball and gymnastics. She won the state gymnastics all-around title her senior year. Then she went to Georgetown and graduated with highest honors in political science."

"Sports?"

"Not at Georgetown," Gretchen said. "Now, the interesting part." She paused for effect.

"Okay," I said. "Give."

"I found no record of Judith Minor after Georgetown. I checked Facebook, LinkedIn, Google, and a bunch of other sources and found zip. And I don't think she's dead. It's like she vanished."

"Interesting," I said. "Maybe she ran away with Armand Priloux."

"Cute," Gretchen said.

"Sorry, that's all I've got."

"I have a picture of Judith Minor in her senior year at Georgetown," Gretchen said.

"Let's have it."

Gretchen handed me a picture she had run on our office printer.

"I enlarged it," she said. "Those yearbook pictures are awfully small. The quality is not the greatest."

But it was good enough. Judith Anne Minor was a dark-haired, dark-eyed beauty. She wasn't smiling. She reminded me of someone, but I couldn't quite pull it up from the basement of my memory.

"Pretty," I said.

"She is," Gretchen said. "Or was."

"Anything else?"

"Nope, that's it."

"Okay, then," I said. "One other thing. See if you can find any more details about Tommy Bell's death."

She wrote in the notebook. "Is that all?"

"It is," I said.

She stood, turned, and headed toward the outer office.

"Good job, Gretchen," I said.

She paused at the door, looked over her shoulder, and smiled.

"Thanks, boss."

◆ ◆ ◆ ◆

I sat for a long time and thought. Unless David Steele came up with something on Judith Minor, I was out of leads. Was Walter Crane murdered? My gut said yes—too many coincidences. Somebody had targeted the Southside Seven. Why? The killer had left Father John Francis Kelly alive. Why? Could the priest be the killer? I didn't think so. He was too forthcoming, and I had a nose for people who lied to me—except for women, of course.

I buzzed Gretchen on the intercom.

"See if you can find a telephone number for Ned Blount in Asheville," I said. I gave her the street address.

A few minutes later, I was talking to Ned Blount.

"I have a question," I said.

"Shoot," Ned said.

"Was the Minor family Catholic?"

Ned paused. "How did you know that?"

"Just a guess," I said.

"They were the only Catholic family in the neighborhood," he said. "Is that important?"

"Maybe," I said. "At this point, I don't know what's important and what isn't."

Another coincidence.

I need to find Judith Minor, I thought.

56

I was having an afternoon cup of green tea with local honey when my intercom buzzed twice, a signal that Gretchen was on her way into my office.

"Three gentlemen are here to see you," she said rather softly after shutting my door behind her. "All wearing suits. One of them says his name is David Steele."

"David Steele is FBI," I said. "The other guys are obviously feds. Go ahead and send them in."

I stood as Gretchen opened my door and invited them in. David Steele was the first one through; followed by a tall, lean man and a shorter, stockier one. Gretchen was right behind them with a conference-table chair. I rarely had three people in my office at once.

"Anyone need coffee?" Gretchen asked—rather sarcastically, I thought.

No one did.

David Steele introduced Jared Gray, assistant director of the CIA, and Charles Morrell, special agent of the CIA. *Judith Minor has a following*, I thought.

The two CIA guys took the comfortable chairs—big surprise. Jared Gray was the tall, lean man. He had dark hair graying at the temples. He looked distinguished, like a judge or a high-priced attorney. He wore an expensive suit. Charles Morrell looked confrontational, like a middle linebacker going after a quarterback. He had short sandy-colored hair, brown eyes, and a freckled complexion. His suit was not expensive.

"Why are you interested in Judith Minor?" Jared Gray asked, pleasant but direct.

"It's confidential," I said, a little annoyed that they had shown up unannounced.

"It's a matter of national security," Jared Gray said calmly. "In such cases, nothing is confidential."

"Why do you ask?" I said, figuring my question would not go over well. I was right.

"We're asking the questions," Charles Morrell said, coming down hard on the *we*. Charles was less calm than Jared Gray.

I looked at David Steele. He gave me a slight shrug as if to say, *Don't look to me for help. This is your ball game.* Or maybe he meant, *It's useless. You might as well answer the question.*

"I'll talk to you one on one," I said to Jared Gray.

"You'll talk to all of us," Charles Morrell said, his role, no doubt, that of bad-guy enforcer.

Gray looked at Morrell. "Wait in the other room," he said flatly.

Morrell opened his mouth to protest, then closed it, got up, opened the door to my outer office, and walked out. David Steele followed without a word. The door closed.

Gray looked at me as if to say, *I'm waiting.*

I looked back at him, hands steepled in front of my face. *Youngblood, the great thinker.* He sat patiently, knowing that sooner or later he'd get what he came for. I let him wait a bit.

"I'm working a murder case," I began. "Judith Minor knew a man named Tommy Bell, who I wanted to interview. Tommy Bell is dead. Judith Minor was a childhood friend of Tommy Bell. Bell's mother was murdered yesterday. I want to interview Judith Minor to see what I can learn about Tommy Bell and maybe get a lead on who killed Mrs. Bell."

"Okay, I'll buy that," Jared Gray said. "But that's not all of it. Start from the beginning and tell me everything."

"Quid pro quo, assistant director?" I said.

The famous quote from *The Silence of the Lambs* was not lost on Jared Gray. He smiled and nodded. "One of my favorite movies," he said. "Okay, you tell me all of it and I'll share some things you don't know. Some of it is classified, but I have the clearance to share with discretion."

"Agreed," I said.

He removed a small recorder from his suit pocket and handed it to me. I had one myself in my top right-hand desk drawer, where it kept my Ruger company.

"Push this button when you're ready," he said.

"How long will this one record?"

"An hour," he said.

I pulled some notes from my laptop backpack and some other notes from my desk drawer. I took a minute to organize my thoughts. When I was ready, I drew a deep breath, pushed the record button, and began.

Half an hour later, I pushed the stop button and handed the recorder to Jared Gray. He remained quiet for a moment.

"Bulletproof glass," he said, impressed. "Unbelievable foresight, Mr. Youngblood."

"Stuff works," I said.

"Indeed it does." He paused, thinking again. "Impressive work," he said. "And a very good verbal report. You're a good investigator, Mr. Youngblood. Want a job?"

"No thanks," I said. "I tried that once a long time ago."

"I know," he said. "I read your file."

"Your turn," I said.

"From everything I've read and heard, you can keep your mouth shut," Jared Gray said. "So please treat what I'm about to tell you as extremely confidential."

I nodded while silently sliding my top right-hand drawer open and pressing the record button on *my* machine.

"Judith Minor was an agent for a rather obscure subdivision of the CIA," he said. "The name of the group is not important, and you wouldn't recognize it even if I told you. It operates overseas."

"Spies," I said.

"Operatives," he corrected.

A rose by any other name, I thought.

"Some time ago, Judith Minor went off the grid, disappeared," he continued. "She told a contact that she had some things to take care of and would be in touch when she was finished. She reappeared a few months later, took a severe tongue-lashing, and was reinstated. Then, a year or so later, it happened again, with the same result. Apparently, she was very good at what she did."

"Killing people," I said.

"Who knows?" Jared Gray said. "About a year ago, she went off the grid for a third time and did not come back. And she took something she should not have taken. If you find her, let us know and we'll handle it. We would owe you one."

"Might help if I know what she took," I said.

"At this point, you don't need to know that," Jared Gray said. He handed me a card. "Day or night, it doesn't matter. Call."

I nodded.

"Be careful," he said. "She's highly trained and dangerous. My guess is she killed Mrs. Bell so Mrs. Bell couldn't talk to you."

"You could have passed on saying that," I said.

"Sorry, but it's not your fault. No way could you have known. Collateral damage, as we say in the business."

He stood, and we shook hands. I liked the man. He was calm and calculating. Whether I trusted him or not was another story. But it certainly wouldn't be a bad thing having the assistant director of the CIA owe me a favor. He nodded, walked out, and shut the door behind him.

A minute later, my intercom buzzed.

"Agent Steele is still here," Gretchen said.

"Tell him to give me five minutes and then come in," I said.

◆ ◆ ◆ ◆

David Steele made himself comfortable in the oversized chair closer to the window. Outside, the light was dimming and a few snowflakes danced. I was a lover of snow; unfortunately, an accumulation was not in the forecast.

"I'm sorry you got blindsided," he said. "They just showed up at my office and wanted to know why I was interested in Judith Minor. I told them I was doing it for one of our consultants, since you're listed as one. Naturally, they asked who and I had to tell them. Then they ordered me to follow them. I checked with my superior and was told to cooperate. When we got close to Mountain Center, I guessed your office was our destination."

"What did you find when you looked up Judith?" I asked.

"I drew blanks everywhere. I finally found her in the CIA database. When I tried to open her file, I got a classified screen that required a password. I didn't have the clearance, so I gave up. I was going to call and tell you I didn't have any luck, but they showed up before I could. You should have told me this was a hot potato."

"I didn't know it was," I said.

"What did you tell Gray?" David Steele asked.

"Almost everything," I said. "He recorded it."

"And what did he tell you?"

"Quite a bit, actually," I said. "I recorded that."

"You didn't," he said.

"I did."

"How?"

I pulled my miniature recorder from the drawer and showed it to him.

David Steele smiled widely. "Good for you," he said. "Never hurts to have leverage. Anything you can share?"

"I promised I wouldn't," I said.

"Anything you think I need to know?" he asked.

"No," I said. "If I find Judith Minor, I'll call Jared Gray. I don't think he cares whether she's dead or alive."

"Be careful, Youngblood," David Steele said. "These CIA chicks are deadly."

"So it would appear," I said.

57

Gretchen had left the office, and night had arrived. The flurries had turned to a light snow. I was five minutes from leaving when the phone rang. I wasn't going to answer, but caller ID told me it was Jessica Crane.

"Cherokee Investigations," I said, thinking it rude to let on that I knew who was calling.

"Mr. Youngblood, it's Jessica Crane."

"Hello, Mrs. Crane. What can I do for you?"

"I found something you need to see right away," she said.

"Can it wait until tomorrow?"

"No, it cannot," she said. "Please come now."

She sounds stressed, I thought.

"Okay," I said. "I'll be there in an hour or so."

I disconnected and called Mary.

"I'll be late for dinner," I said. "If I'm not home by seven, eat without me."

"What's going on?" Mary asked.

"Jessica Crane wants to see me."

"About the case?"

"I would guess so," I said. "She was vague."

"Remember your promise," she said. "Be careful."

"Don't worry," I said. "I'll call you on my way back."

◆ ◆ ◆ ◆

Heading up the long driveway to the Crane Mansion, I noticed that the house seemed dark. A porch light was on, but nothing else. But I had never visited at night, so I had no point of reference. Still, I felt uneasy.

You're getting paranoid, Youngblood, I thought.

I walked up the stairs to the front door and rang the bell. The wind chill was noticeable as I stood on the porch. Looking around, I noticed a dusting of snow on the ground. I rang the bell again.

A few seconds later, Jessica Crane's voice came over the intercom. "The door is unlocked," she said. "Come on back. I'm in the dining room."

I opened the door, stepped through, and shut it behind me. I took out my Ruger and moved toward the light, holding the gun out of sight behind me. I didn't want to alarm Jessica Crane if it wasn't necessary, but something didn't seem right.

She was sitting at the far end of the dining-room table. An overhead recessed light spotlighted that end of the room.

"I'm sorry," she said as I moved toward her. "She made me call you."

"Who?"

"Put your gun on the table," a female voice said. "Now!"

I did as instructed; laying the Ruger in the center of the table in front of Jessica Crane, close enough to make a lunge for it if I got desperate. Maybe Judith hoped I would. Why not tell me to slide it across the table?

She moved out of the shadows from the far end of the room, stopping at the end of the table. In her hand was a 9mm Sig Sauer. Her hair had been up the last time I saw her, and I really hadn't paid much attention to how pretty she was. Seeing her now explained a lot. Jessica Crane's housekeeper, Anna, was Judith Minor.

"You've been a real pain in the ass, Mr. Youngblood," she said. "And that goddamn bulletproof glass. Fucking unbelievable."

"Give me your address, and I'll send you a bill for replacing it," I said.

"You're not going to live long enough for that," she said.

I heard a gasp from Jessica Crane. I turned my body so I squarely faced Judith Minor. I was gambling she wouldn't take a head shot and hoping my Kevlar vest would give me time to get to the Ruger and fire a shot.

"Going to kill me like you did Miriam Bell?" I asked.

The image of Mrs. Bell lying dead on her dining-room floor flashed through my mind. I felt the anger rise inside me.

"I do feel bad about that," she said. "I should have known one of the neighbors would come up with my name. Which one told you about me?"

"Answer some questions first, then I'll tell you." I had no intention of telling Judith Minor anything, but I did want to get her talking.

"Why not? You won't be able to share what you learn."

"How many of the seven did you kill?"

"You probably figured that out," Judith said. "Bobby McMullen, Tom Barry, and, of course, Walter."

"How did you give Bobby anthrax?"

"I put it on the glue of a self-addressed return envelope," she said. "Made it look real official with a letter that said to confirm a few things to get more benefits. Lick the envelope and you die. Clever, don't you think?"

"You should be proud," I said, sarcastically.

She smiled and took a little bow.

"What about Walter?" I asked.

"An undetectable synthetic poison created by the CIA," she said. "Three drops was all it took in his drink. Three deadly drops."

"You fucking bitch!" Jessica Crane screamed.

Her outburst startled me. I didn't think she had it in her.

"Shut up or I'll shoot you now," Judith Minor said.

"Why did you do it?" I asked. "For Tommy Bell?"

"Tommy Bell," she said, as if reminiscing. "Sweet Tommy Bell, who never did a bad thing in his life, driven to write a death list because he was mocked for stuttering and was denied the Silver Star. He died before he could kill any of them, though I have my doubts he would have followed through. I don't think it was in him. Tommy sent me a letter a long time ago with the list and why he was going to kill them. I was overseas. Someone was taking care of my mail, and the letter got mixed in with some magazines and catalogs, and I found it about five years ago when I was cleaning out. Imagine my surprise. I miss Tommy. We understood each other."

She seemed sincere but not overly saddened, like she was talking about the death of a pet.

"But I don't kill for revenge," she said. "I kill for profit. So I did some research and discovered Operation Dark Recovery. I had to dig deep. It was highly classified. The site where the kids were killed was a private school for children of wealthy families. So I got the idea that one or more of the families might be interested in retribution. I have contacts in that part of the world, so I put out some feelers and got a nibble. We agreed on terms and a price."

"Why so long between kills?"

"Part of the contract," Judith said. "My clients wanted to savor every kill. They paid me for each one, with a big bonus at the end. Waiting between targets made it easier for me, gave me time to plan. I found out Randy Butler was already dead, but they paid me anyway. I never could find Armand Priloux. I'm guessing Katrina got him. That's what I told my employers. I didn't get paid for Priloux. The next year, I got paid for Tom Barry, and then the following year for Bobby McMullen. When I found Frank McCurry, he was dying a horrible death from pancreatic cancer, so my employers agreed to leave him alone. I got paid for him as soon as he died and I sent them a copy of the death certificate. I'm having second thoughts about the priest. I'm going to hell anyway, so I might as well do Father Kelly. I don't get the bonus until they're all dead."

She was on a roll, almost manic, reveling in the chance to tell somebody how good she was. I wanted to keep her going, to distract her long enough to make a play for my Ruger. I was intent on making her pay for the death of Miriam Bell.

"One thing I don't get," I said. "After you killed Walter, why didn't you just take off?"

"I was ready to," she said. "I wanted to make sure the autopsy was clean. Then Mrs. Crane hired you. I researched you on the web and decided you were trouble. So I stuck around to see how much you could turn up. Very impressive, I have to admit. Then I decided to take you out. That didn't work either, but now I can finish the job."

A low rumble came out of the shadows. "Not likely."

It was hard to tell exactly where he was. No way could she get a shot off and hope to hit him.

"Put the gun down," the voice said.

Judith Minor hesitated, obviously surprised. I heard a hammer cock.

"Two seconds," Billy said.

Judith Minor carefully placed the Sig on the dining-room table and moved away.

"Doesn't matter," Judith Minor said. "I'm CIA. I'll never go to jail."

The next sound I heard was my Ruger. Loaded with .357 Magnum hollow-point shells, it sounded like a bomb exploding in the dining room. Judith Minor was knocked backward like she'd been hit by a truck. Blood mushroomed on her chest. I had no doubt she was dead before she hit the floor.

Jessica Crane put the Ruger gently on the table and looked at me. "So much for the CIA," she said calmly. She sat back down and was quiet, almost in a trancelike state.

I turned to Billy with a puzzled look.

"Mary called me," he said. "Said she had a bad feeling."

I nodded. *Thank God for Mary*, I thought.

"You should have called me, Blood," Billy said, his face hard. I could tell he was angry that I had been so careless. "I had to drive like a bat out of hell to get here. One of these days, I won't make it in time and you'll get yourself killed."

"Sorry," I said. "At least I'm wearing a vest."

He shook his head as if lamenting my hopelessness.

58

"You said day or night."

"That was damn quick," Jared Gray said. "You got her?"

"I did," I said.

"Dead or alive?"

"Dead," I said.

"Tell me about it."

I told him most of it, with some alterations. In my version, I had shot Judith Minor. I saw no reason to get Jessica Crane hung up. After all, it was my gun. But that didn't matter much. I had no doubt the death of Judith Minor would never see the light of day.

"I'll have some people there in a few hours," Jared Gray said. "Don't let anyone near the place."

◆ ◆ ◆ ◆

I went over our version of the shooting with Billy and Jessica Crane, then led Mrs. Crane upstairs.

"Take a shower before you go to bed," I said. "Pay particular attention to your hands and arms. Put all your clothes in a bag and give it to me."

"Why are you doing this?" she asked as she sat on the edge of her bed. "I killed that woman, and I'm glad I did."

"It sounds more believable if I did it," I said. "I have a history of shooting people. Anyway, I'm sure nothing will ever come of it. The feds will clean this up, and it will all be forgotten. I'm just being careful."

"Thank you," she said weakly. She looked exhausted.

"Do you have anything to make you sleep?" I asked.

"Lunesta," she said.

"What milligram?"

"Two," she said.

"Take two of them," I said. "When you wake up tomorrow, this will all be a bad dream."

"I'll do it," she said. "Thank you again."

I left her sitting on the bed, went back downstairs, and called Mary on my cell phone.

"I'll be a little later that I expected," I said.

"You okay?"

"I'm fine."

"Is Billy there?"

"He is," I said.

"Did you need him?"

"I did," I said. "Thanks."

"Don," she said, "don't you think it's about time you quit risking your life and settled down with your new family?"

I was in no mood to have this discussion. "As soon as you decide to quit being a cop," I said.

She was silent on the other end.

"Get your butt home as soon as you can," she said finally. "I'll keep your dinner warm, and we'll talk."

"My butt and all that goes with it will be home as soon as possible."

◆ ◆ ◆ ◆

Before anyone arrived, I took Jessica Crane's clothes to the Pathfinder and hid them underneath the backseat.

David Steele was first.

"I've got a couple of guys at the driveway entrance," he said. "Nobody gets in who Jared Gray didn't send."

He walked to the other end of the dining room and looked down at the body of Judith Minor. She was sprawled face up, arms extended, eyes staring at the ceiling. Her chest was soaked in blood.

"Jesus," David Steele said. "What did you hit her with?"

"A .357 Magnum loaded with hollow points," I said.

"Blew her up."

"Big time," I said.

"How'd it go down?" he asked.

"She had the drop on me, then Billy had the drop on her. I went to pick up the Ruger, then she decided to go for her Sig, and I shot her before she shot me."

"Well, that makes sense as long as you were standing here," he said, pointing to where Jessica Crane had sat.

"How do you figure that?" I asked.

"Angle of the body," he said. "She was hit straight on and would have fallen straight back."

"That's where he was standing," Billy said, eyes staring hard at David Steele.

"Good," David Steele said. "I don't think anyone will care, but it never hurts to have the details clear."

"You're right," I said. "Thanks."

We heard sounds from the front of the house. Three men appeared, looked around, and got right to work.

An hour later, they were gone. So was any trace of Judith Minor.

"Those guys are good," David Steele said. "No crime-scene unit in the country would ever know a shooting took place here tonight."

"Did a shooting take place here tonight?" I asked.

"Not that I know of," David Steele said.

◆ ◆ ◆ ◆

I sat at the kitchen bar with Mary eating leftover pot roast with mashed potatoes and peas and drinking a Sam Adams Light. It was after midnight, and I was still amped up from the events of the evening. I had told Mary everything that happened.

"I'm going to have to meet Jessica Crane someday," she said. "She sounds like a woman after my own heart."

"She sure surprised me," I said.

"I'll take care of the clothes," Mary said.

I nodded and drained the bottle of beer. Mary went to the refrigerator and brought me another.

"You still took a chance," she said. "She could have shot you in the head."

"I know," I said. "And I felt something wasn't right, but I went in anyway. I wanted a confrontation. I wanted questions answered. I think my need to know everything about a case is an addiction. Maybe I need to check in at Silverthorn."

"Checking in at Silverthorn wouldn't change who you are," Mary said. "You're a damn good PI, and you get obsessed with a case once you're into it. I knew that when I married you. It goes with the territory. And I understand because I'm a cop." She put her hand on mine. "You're the love of my life, Don. If anything ever happens to you, I'll never survive it."

You would survive, I thought. Mary was too tough not to and had too much to live for. But I kept that to myself.

"I'll make sure that never happens," I said.

"Promise?"

"Promise," I said. "And you know I never break a promise."

◆ ◆ ◆ ◆

Waiting can be exhausting. Mary succumbed to her tiredness and went to bed soon after I finished eating, leaving me in the kitchen. She understood that I needed to wind down.

I unloaded my Ruger and tossed the spent shell in a box of other empty shells. As I cleaned, polished, and reloaded, I reflected on the Crane case.

Jessica Crane's instincts had probably saved Father John Kelly's life. She had believed from the start that Walter was murdered. *Never discount the grieving widow*, I thought. Had I been busy on another case, I would have sent Jessica Crane on her way and never would have been pulled into the labyrinth of death surrounding the Southside Seven. In the end, justice had been served, and that was what mattered to me. That I felt good about.

I carried the Ruger upstairs to our bedroom and quietly placed it in the drawer of the nightstand on my side of the bed, hoping it wouldn't kill anyone in the near future. Mary didn't stir.

I undressed, went to the bathroom, put on my pajama bottoms and T-shirt, flossed, gargled, and brushed my teeth. The tiredness was descending rapidly as I slipped into bed.

Mary rolled toward me. "Good night, my love," she whispered.

59

When the Houston Oilers decided to move to Nashville, they didn't find a whole lot of interest in East Tennessee, where college football ruled. The Oilers had not been good for a while, and a real push was on in Nashville to sell season tickets. It was a rare opportunity to get good seats to NFL games. I had a chance for four seats in the lower section near the fifty-yard line about twenty rows from the field. Knowing that I'd never go to eight games a season, I gave the opportunity to a lawyer friend in Nashville, who in turn let me have a couple of games a year at face value.

The franchise was in search of a new nickname, and I was convinced I had the perfect one—the Tornados. It made perfect sense, since a tornado had visited the stadium while it was being built. And the stadium could be nicknamed Tornado Alley. But cooler heads prevailed. An old AFL nickname was resurrected, and Tennessee's NFL team was nicknamed the Titans. In hindsight, I guess the powers that be felt that naming a team for a destructive force of nature was not such a good idea. Tennessee Titans did have a nice ring to it.

I mention this because the Sunday after the Judith Minor incident, Mary, Lacy, Biker, and I drove to Nashville to see the Titans and Mary's son, Jimmy, play Tom Brady and the New England Patriots. I desperately needed to put the Crane case behind me, and a weekend immersed in football was just the ticket.

Game-time weather was overcast with a light wind and temperatures in the thirties. Biker and I thought it was a perfect day. The blondes thought it was cold. Jimmy Sanders threw for three hundred yards and two touchdowns, but the Patriots prevailed 24–21.

Afterward, we went to Jimmy's house for an early dinner. Jimmy had purchased a big house in an area that was home to many of Nashville's country-music stars. His six-bedroom mini-mansion sat on a large parcel of land enclosed by a high fence and an electronic gate at the driveway entrance.

The dinner was catered. The caterer brought aged filets mignons and grilled them to perfection on Jimmy's outdoor gas grill. I got the idea it was not the first time the caterer had been to Jimmy's.

Ah, the life of an NFL quarterback, I thought.

After dinner, Jimmy and I retired to the den while Mary and Jimmy's wife, Diane, stayed in the kitchen. Biker and Lacy went to the game room to play pool or darts or do something I didn't want to know about.

"Tough loss," I said as we settled in with our beers.

"We came close," Jimmy said. "The Patriots will always be tough as long as they have Tom Brady. Tom and Peyton Manning are the only opposing quarterbacks I watch during a game. If you blitz them, they'll find an open receiver. And if your front four doesn't put pressure on them, they'll pick you apart."

"How long do you dwell on a loss?" I asked.

"Not long," Jimmy said. "I'll replay the game in my head tonight to see what I could have done better. When I wake up tomorrow, it will be all about our next opponent. It's not like college. It's a job now. Win or lose, I have to take my emotions out of the equation."

We drank some beer.

"Mom seems happy," Jimmy said. "And she looks terrific. You must be doing something right."

"Just going with the flow," I said. "It's two against one. I don't have much say."

He laughed and then turned serious. "I'm happy for her," he said. "Dad had problems. I'm beginning to realize life with him couldn't have been easy."

I didn't know how to respond to that, so I drank some more beer. The silence was a little uncomfortable.

"Heard from Susan?" I asked.

Susan was Jimmy's younger sister, who also graduated from Wake Forest. She had then promptly moved to San Francisco. Mary was less than enthusiastic about that.

"I talked to her yesterday," Jimmy said. "She always calls the day before a game. She loves San Francisco and hopes Mom will go out to visit her."

"I'll work on that," I said.

Jimmy shifted his weight on the couch and let out a low moan. He had been sacked four times and had also taken a couple of good hits while running the ball.

"I need to spend some time in the hot tub," he said.

We heard laughter coming down the hall from the game room.

"Lacy seems like a nice girl," Jimmy said. "You and Mom did a good thing."

"She deserved a break," I said. "I think Lacy will prove to be exceptional. She's wise beyond her years."

"Is she serious about that boy?"

"I don't think so," I said. "Not too many high-school romances last."

Mary poked her head in the den door. "We need to get going," she said.

Twenty minutes later, we were rolling. Mary no doubt set a record for travel time by car from Nashville to Mountain Center, somehow avoiding the Tennessee Highway Patrol. Biker McBride looked a little pale by the time we dropped him at his house.

60

I thought the Crane case was over but soon learned a few loose ends remained. My Monday-morning visitor at the office opened it up again. All I wanted was to zero in on Christmas. Mary was trying to convince Susan to fly in from California, but it didn't look promising. Christmas was less than two weeks away. I had shopping to do and maybe a tree to decorate. I was tired of private detecting.

He was waiting for me when I arrived. He followed me in and made himself comfortable in one of my oversized chairs. I sat behind my desk.

"Mr. Gray," I said, emphasizing the *Mr*. "To what do I owe the pleasure?"

"How did my boys do the other night?" he asked.

I had no doubt he knew how they did. This call was about something else. He would eventually get to it.

"The dining room looks as if we were never there," I said.

"Good. I appreciate your help in all of this. We owe you one. But I want to ask you a few questions."

"I'm listening."

"Do you remember I told you that when Judith Minor went missing the last time, she took something that didn't belong to her?"

Sure, I do, I thought. *I have it recorded.*

"I remember," I said.

"Did she mention anything about that?"

"The synthetic poison?" I said.

Jared Gray was silent for a moment. "How did you know?"

"She told me that's how she killed Walter Crane."

"Why would she tell you that?" Gray asked, surprised.

"We were exchanging information," I said. "She thought I'd be dead in a few minutes and was bragging about her kills."

"What else did she tell you?" Gray asked.

"Who she killed, and how," I said.

He didn't seem the least bit interested in that. "Did she mention where the poison is?"

"No," I said.

Jared Gary looked perplexed.

"It's probably well hidden somewhere," I said. "Since she's dead, it will stay hidden."

"You don't understand," he said. "It's a prototype. She took the vial and the formula. She somehow wiped if off our computers and killed the scientist who came up with it."

"Why would she do that?" I asked.

"Obviously, she wanted to sell it," Gray said. "I think she tested it on Walter to be sure it worked."

"Maybe it's already been sold."

"We don't think so," he said. "We would have picked up some intel on that. But we believe she was in the Middle East recently negotiating a deal. We think the vial is hidden in an airtight metal box designed to keep the poison at a certain temperature. The compound breaks down if it gets too hot." He hesitated and looked away. "Only a few people know it's missing. I want to keep it that way."

He was covering his butt. His job was probably on the line.

Jared Gray handed me a picture of a gunmetal gray box with a lock.

"I think you're better off if the box stays hidden," I said. "That kind of killing power could be devastating in the wrong hands."

"Yes," he said, standing. "You're right about that. If you ever want a job, Mr. Youngblood, I'd love to have you on my team."

Not in a million years, I thought.

"I'll keep that in mind," I said.

He and I both knew his people were looking for the box. I hoped they struck out. Nothing good would come from finding it.

61

Wednesday morning, my intercom buzzed.

"Jessica Crane to see you," Gretchen said.

I got out of my chair, went to my office door, and opened it.

"Come in, Mrs. Crane," I said. "Please sit down. Would you like coffee?"

"That would be nice," she said. "Black."

I looked at Gretchen, and she nodded. Jessica Crane followed me into my office and sat in the chair directly across from me. She carried a shopping bag, which she placed on the floor on the left side of the chair. Gretchen came in with coffee, exited, and shut the door behind her. Mrs. Crane took a sip of coffee and seemed to approve. She looked clear eyed and well rested.

"How have you been?" I asked.

"Very well," she said. "Those two pills really knocked me out. That was a good idea. I didn't wake up until after noon. And you were right. It all seemed like a bad dream. Downstairs looked like no one had ever been there. I would like to get whoever cleaned up to do my whole house."

I laughed. Maybe Jessica Crane was still in shock, or maybe she felt she had vindicated her husband's death. Either way, she seemed to have recovered nicely.

"I'll see what I can do," I said.

I waited. I knew there was more.

"I want to thank you for everything you did," she said.

"That's not necessary."

"You saved my life," she said.

"My partner saved us both."

"Yes. Please thank him as well," she said. "But you came when I called, and you knew it was a trap. Otherwise, you would not have had your gun out."

I shrugged. "I was just being cautious. She still got the drop on me."

Then Jessica Crane finally got around to the reason for her visit. "Have you ever killed anyone, Mr. Youngblood?" she asked.

"Yes," I said.

"Did you feel guilty about it?"

"No."

"They were bad people, I suppose."

"Yes," I said. "They were."

"I don't feel guilty either," she said. "I didn't have to kill her, but I did. I executed her."

"The woman you knew as Anna was not a nice person," I said. "She killed at least four people I know of and would have killed you and me if my partner hadn't shown up. You did the world a favor. I'm sure you saved a few lives."

"Thank you for that," she said.

She stood and picked up the shopping bag.

"I don't know why, but I felt compelled to go through Walter's trunk," she said. "I found this."

She reached into the shopping bag, pulled out a gunmetal gray box with a lock, and set it on my desk with a thud. I was stunned.

"I think Anna hid it there," she said.

"She must have hid it there recently," I said. "The box wasn't there when I went through the trunk. Did you find a key?"

"No," she said. "And I looked for quite a while. Do you know what this is?"

"Yes," I said.

"Do I want to know?" she asked.

"You'll be better off if you don't," I said.

"Very well," Jessica Crane said. "I'll trust your judgment on that."

I nodded. "I have something for you," I said.

I went to my closet and brought back Jessica Crane's clothes from the night of the murder. They were clean and neatly folded inside a plastic grocery bag.

"These are yours," I said, handing the bag to her.

She smiled, took the bag, and extended her hand. "Thank you for everything," she said. "I'll expect a hefty bill, the sooner the better."

"I'll see to it," I said.

At that, Jessica Crane turned and left my office. I haven't seen or heard from her since.

◆ ◆ ◆ ◆

I sat and stared at the box and thought about what to do with it. It was about the size of a cigar box with a rather substantial lock on the front. It was well made, almost seamless. I picked it up. It was heavy—lead, maybe. *Maybe the poison is radioactive*, I thought. I put the box down and stared at it some more. I knew I was not going to give it to Jared Gray. No one else was going to die from the contents of that box. Of course, the box might be empty. If it was, it didn't matter, as I'd never find the vial. But I knew it wasn't empty. My gut told me so. Judith Minor would not have wanted to be far from that box.

Something Jared Gray had said sparked an idea. I went online and did some research. I was pretty sure the box was lead. I found out that lead melts at around 640 degrees. I was fairly certain the oven of a crematorium was hotter than that.

I called Thaddeus Miller, the owner of the local funeral home that had handled my parents' burial.

"Don," he said. "Is everything okay?"

"Everything is fine, Thaddeus. I have a question."

"Ask away," he said.

"Do you have a crematorium?"

"Yes, we do," he said. "On site."

"How hot do you run the oven?" I asked.

"Around eighteen hundred degrees," Thaddeus said.

"I'd like to rent some time," I said. "I have something I need to destroy in a very hot oven."

"My goodness, Don," he said. "We just cremate dead bodies."

"But it could be done," I said.

"Well, I suppose so, depending on what it is."

"A lead box that I want to melt to a puddle," I said. "And in the process destroy what's inside."

"And what's inside?" he asked.

"Something dangerous," I said. "But heat renders it harmless, and your oven would totally destroy it. You'd need to keep this between us."

"Tell me this is for the greater good, Don," Thaddeus said.

"It absolutely is," I said. "Destroying this box will save lives."

"Bring it over tonight around six," he said. "Come to the back. Call me on your cell when you get here, and I'll unlock the back door. I'll get the oven prepped."

◆ ◆ ◆ ◆

At exactly six o'clock, I pulled into the back parking lot of the Mountain Center Funeral Home and called Thaddeus Miller. I carried the metal box in a canvas bag.

Thaddeus, a tall, slender, bald man, greeted me at the door. "The deceased, I presume," he said.

Funeral-home humor, I thought. "Yes," I said, handing him the canvas bag. "Dead as lead."

Thaddeus removed the box from the bag and hefted it. "Definitely lead," he said. "It will be one big puddle when I'm finished. What would you like done with the remains?"

"I don't care," I said. "Put them in the bottom of one of your caskets, or toss them out with the garbage."

"Are you going to stick around?"

"At least until it's in the oven," I said. "Then I'd like to view the remains."

"Okay," he said. "Since you seem to be the only family."

And they say funeral directors don't have a sense of humor.

62

The next morning, I stared at what was left of the box.

"Any problems?" I asked Thaddeus.

"None," he said. "When it's completely cooled, I'll break it into small pieces and toss it in the dumpster."

"I appreciate your help."

"I know you're on the side of truth, justice, and the American way," he said.

"True," I said, smiling. "But I'm not Superman."

"Close, I hear," Thaddeus said. "At least that's what the papers say."

"And you can always believe everything you read in the papers."

◆ ◆ ◆ ◆

I parked in my spot behind the office and went to my right down the alley almost to the end of the block and through the back door of the Mountain Center Diner, marked "Employees Only." I slipped silently to my table and sat.

Doris was on me in two seconds with coffee. "Slipped in the back, huh?"

"Nothing gets by you," I said. "I've been up for a while, and I'm starved."

"Want to order now?" Doris asked.

"Give me a few minutes," I said. "Got a local paper?"

"Sure," Doris said. "Be back in a sec."

It was more like twenty seconds, but who was counting?

Doris set a slightly used *Mountain Center Press* on the table. "One owner," she said.

I picked up the paper and looked at the front page. It must have been a slow news day. "Lone Squirrel Causes Power Outage," the headline read.

A terrorist squirrel, no doubt, I thought. The squirrel had blown a transformer and gotten fried to a crispy critter for its efforts. I went to the sports page.

Fifteen minutes later, Big Bob Wilson showed up and made himself comfortable in his usual spot at my table.

"How'd you know I was here?" I asked the big man.

"I saw your SUV in the parking lot, and a suspicious-looking character was reported going down the alley. I'm guessing you came in the back."

"You don't miss a thing, do you?"

"Try not to," he said.

Doris hustled over, and we ordered—a ham-and-cheese omelet with home fries and rye toast for me, half the menu for Big Bob. We talked sports until the food arrived and then Big Bob changed the subject.

"How's your case going?" he asked.

"Finished," I said, taking the first bite of my omelet.

"Was it murder or bad luck?"

"A little of both," I said.

"Tell me."

I took a drink of coffee and ate some home fries.

"One dead from an accident or maybe a suicide, one guy missing and probably dead but not murdered, one dead from cancer, and three definitely murdered."

"That's six," he said. "What happened to number seven?"

"A priest," I said. "The killer was Catholic and decided to give the priest a pass, but she was having second thoughts."

"Did you say *she*?"

"She," I said.

"Where is she now?" Big Bob asked.

"Dead."

"How?" he asked as the food arrived.

"Shot," I said, taking another bite of my omelet.

"You?" Big Bob asked, working on his eggs Benedict.

"No."

"When?"

"Last week."

"I didn't hear about it," he said.

"You won't."

Between questions, we were both doing a good job of disposing of our breakfasts.

"Who shot her?" Big Bob asked.

"Can't say."

"Feds," he snorted.

I smiled. "I'll tell you about it sometime."

"Yeah, that's what you said about the Fairchild case," he said. "And you still haven't told me about that."

"Let's just say that, as far as the Fairchild case is concerned, justice was served. Rather unconventionally, but served just the same."

"Meaning you caught the bastard and you or someone else killed him," Big Bob said.

"Something like that," I said.

"And the same holds true for this female assassin."

"More or less," I said.

We were almost finished. The big man had more to eat, but he ate faster than I did. I guess growing up with three brothers will do that to you.

"How much more dangerous did this thing get?" he asked.

I didn't answer. He already knew about the parking-garage assault. I finished my last bite of toast and drank some coffee.

"That's what I thought," he said.

"It was under control," I said.

"I'll bet," Big Bob said as he finished his last bite of home fries. "Damn, that was good."

"On me," I said. "My contribution to your crime-fighting efforts."

"You're just trying to avoid a lecture."

"That, too," I said. "But Mary already took care of that."

"I don't doubt it," he said.

◆ ◆ ◆ ◆

As soon as I reached the office, my phone rang.

"I heard you had some excitement recently," Scott Glass said.

"Where did you hear that, Professor?"

"Sources," Scott said.

"I guess David Steele wasn't sworn to secrecy."

"The FBI loves to talk trash about the CIA," Scott said. "Especially when we help clean up their messes. Word around FBI headquarters is that you outed a rogue agent."

"More like my investigation led the rogue agent to try to kill me," I said.

"Whatever it was, you earned another gold star," Scott said. "You're becoming sort of a cult hero. I'm earning points just knowing you."

"Enough bullshit, Professor," I said. "Why did you really call?"

"Well, I wondered if you, Mary, and Lacy might want to come out for the holidays and ski your legs off. I have two guest bedrooms with private baths. It'll be a blast."

"Not a bad idea," I said. "Let me get back to you."

◆ ◆ ◆ ◆

A few minutes before ten, I left a note on Gretchen's desk and walked down the hall to Rollie Ogle's office. Estelle Huff was at her desk, ever vigilant for irate husbands. Rollie was basically a divorce lawyer. He liked to represent wives. It was easy to make husbands look guilty, he once told me. That was not a comforting revelation.

"Hi, Don," she said. "How's the family?"

"They're good, Estelle," I said. "Thanks for asking. Is Rollie in?"

She nodded and pressed her intercom.

"Yes?" Rollie said.

"Don's here to see you," Estelle said.

Seconds later, Rollie's door opened. "Hey, cowboy," he said. "Come on in."

I took a spot on his couch as he sat in a chair facing me, a coffee table between us. His desk was tucked in a corner near a window.

"Thanks for sending Jessica Crane my way," I said.

"How'd you know it was me?" he asked.

"She said the word *attorney.*"

He smiled, unashamed. "How did that work out?"

"Nearly got me killed," I said.

"You're kidding."

"Nope."

"Jesus, Don, I'm sorry," Rollie said. "Are you here to shoot me or something?"

"Relax," I said. "I need you to do some legal stuff for me, and then we have to take a trip. You'll have to clear a day on your calendar. The sooner, the better."

"Okay," he said. "We flying or driving?"

"Flying," I said. "Probably on one of Joseph Fleet's jets."

"Hot dog!" Rollie said. "Tell me what you need."

I told him.

When I finished, he looked at me, smiled, and shook his head.

"You know, Don," he said in that sophisticated Southern drawl of his, "you're the only rich guy I know who doesn't like being rich."

63

We sat at an out-of-the-way table in the cafeteria at St. Jude Children's Hospital. Four of us were present: Rollie Ogle, Charlene Barry, Ross Dean, and me. I had asked Ross to come along because I wasn't sure Charlene Barry would believe what we were telling her, and also because it gave me the chance to fill Ross in on the highlights of the Crane case. Rollie had all the documents. Ross and I sat back and listened as he explained to Charlene the college trust fund I had set up for her two children.

"Any more questions?" Rollie asked.

"I don't think so," she said, a bit confused.

"By the time your children go to college, the amount in trust will be much larger," Rollie said.

She looked at Ross, then at Rollie. "Could I have a word alone with Mr. Youngblood?" she said.

"Certainly," Rollie said, standing. "Detective, let me buy you a cup of coffee."

Ross looked at me as he stood. "A lawyer buying me a cup of coffee? Now, there's a first."

I laughed as they walked away.

Charlene Barry turned her gaze on me.

"Why are you doing this, Mr. Youngblood?" she asked. "This makes me uncomfortable, although I know it's a godsend."

"First, I have more money than I'll ever need, and I'm making more each year," I said. "Second, it feels good to be able to help you. Third and most important, it's for Thomas and all those brave men who've served our country. I was never in the service. Your husband was. He was part of a mission that went bad, and I have a feeling it haunted him. It certainly seemed to haunt the rest of them. His children have a right to a quality education."

"I don't know what to say," she said, tearing up.

"You don't have to say anything. It's only money."

"No," she said. "It's more than that. Plenty of rich men out there would never give my children a second thought." She put her hand on mine. "Thank you. I'll pray for you and your family every night."

◆ ◆ ◆ ◆

Ross Dean drove us back to the airport. He had insisted on picking us up when I told him why we were coming. When Ross stopped the car in front of the private hangar, Rollie said his goodbyes and got out. I lingered, sensing Ross had something to say.

"It's been a pleasure working with you, Don," he said, extending his hand.

We shook.

"Thanks for your help," I said.

"That's one hell of a thing you did for Charlene Barry," he said. "If you ever need anything in Memphis, you know who to call."

"Thanks," I said. "You never know."

64

The Monday before Christmas, I showered and left the condo before woman or beast stirred. I had awakened in the middle of the night to go to the bathroom and get a drink of milk. I was sitting at the kitchen bar with my glass when it hit me. There was one small mystery for which I didn't have an answer. I recently had the opportunity to get it but was so distracted that I completely forgot. I needed to make a phone call but had to wait until morning. I went back to bed and tossed and turned until five-thirty, then got up.

In the office, I made coffee, went online, and waited. At nine o'clock, I logged off the Internet and made the call.

"Our Mother of the Divine," the female voice said.

"Father John Kelly, please."

"Father John is in the confessional right now," she said. "May I have him call you back?"

"Yes, please," I said. I gave her my name and number.

"It may be awhile," she said.

"That will be fine."

I had plenty to do. Doubling as a private investigator and an investment counselor meant one or the other had to suffer. Lately, it was the investment side. Gretchen handled the maintenance accounts well enough, but she didn't buy and sell. My client list, which I intentionally kept small, was growing now that I had a full-time assistant. The irony was that I was making plenty of money I didn't need—a big reason I shared it from time to time for worthy causes, causes I could monitor.

I went back online and looked at a number of stocks I had in my watch folder. There had been an October sell-off for profit taking, and I knew that certain stocks would be excellent buys sometime after the first of the year. The trick was figuring out the bottom. Guess right and I scored big. Guess wrong and it could get ugly.

The phone rang, and then the intercom buzzed.

"I have a Ned Blount on line one," Gretchen said.

"I'll take it," I said. "Youngblood," I answered.

"Mr. Youngblood, it's Ned Blount over in Asheville. I'm sorry to bother you. I just wondered if you ever found Judith Minor."

"There doesn't seem to be any trace of her," I said. While not exactly the truth, that also wasn't an out-and-out lie. "I've closed the case and moved on to other things. I do appreciate your help, though."

"Sure," he said. "It was a pleasure meeting you. If you're ever this way again, come by and see me."

"I will," I said. "Take care of yourself, Mr. Blount."

◆ ◆ ◆ ◆

I kept busy throughout the morning, waiting for Father John to call. He didn't.

For lunch, I went across the street to Dunkin' Donuts and bought a medium coffee and a sesame seed bagel with cream cheese and brought them back to the office. I ate slowly. The phone still didn't ring. Gretchen went out to lunch with a friend. I played a game of chess on my laptop and then a miniature-golf game I had discovered online. To pass the time, I called the Orangeburg, South Carolina, chief of police, Tyler Davis.

"What can I do for you, Mr. Youngblood?" He sounded hesitant.

"Relax, chief. It's not bad news."

"That's a relief," he said.

"Bobby McMullen was murdered," I said. "I thought you'd like to know."

"How did you confirm it?"

"Got it from the horse's mouth," I said. "I can't give you the details. The feds are involved. The anthrax was on an envelope that Bobby McMullen licked."

"Son of a bitch," Tyler Davis said. "That sure as hell will make you think twice about licking any more envelopes, won't it?"

"It will," I said.

"Thanks for calling," Chief Davis said. "If you're ever this way again, stop in and see me."

"Will do," I said.

Not likely, I thought.

◆ ◆ ◆ ◆

After lunch, the phone started ringing. None of the calls were Father John Kelly. Most of the time, the intercom stayed quiet, which meant Gretchen was handling things. Every now and then, somebody actually wanted to talk with me. By midafternoon, I was convinced I would not be talking with Father John that day.

Five minutes later, the phone rang, and then the intercom buzzed.

"Father John Kelly on line one," Gretchen said.

O ye of little faith.

"Father John," I said. "Thanks for ringing me back."

"I was glad to hear you called," Father John said. "It meant you're still with us. How do things stand?"

"Can we treat this phone call with the confidentiality of the confessional?" I asked.

"Rather unorthodox, but I see no reason not to."

"So I can take that as a yes?"

"You may," he said. "This conversation will remain between you, me, and God."

I told him about finding Tommy Bell's mother and about Judith Minor being Tommy's best friend. I told him about the confrontation with Judith Minor, and that she had already tried to kill me once. Then I told him that Judith Minor had been shot and killed.

"May she rest in peace," he said. "I hope you didn't have to kill her."

"No," I said. "This time, it wasn't me."

"You've killed before," he said. It was a statement, not a question.

"I have," I said. "Once in self-defense and twice to save another life."

"Have you asked forgiveness?"

"Not really," I said. "I thought I was justified."

"I'm not sure killing another human being is ever justified," he said. "But everything is forgivable by God, if forgiveness is truly sought."

I was starting to feel uncomfortable. This was not the conversation I wanted to have with Father John. To this day, I have never felt guilty about the people I killed and would do it again if the circumstances were the same. I didn't want to debate it with a priest.

Father John must have sensed my dilemma. "Sorry," he said. "Once a priest . . ."

"It's okay," I said. "If it means anything, Judith Minor did say she was having second thoughts about not killing you."

"Then I guess our heavenly father was watching out for both of us," Father John said. "Did you call to give me an update, or do you have something else?"

"Just a little mystery I want to clear up," I said. "How did your black ops Ranger group get the name the Southside Seven?"

Father John chuckled. "Randy Butler gave us that name," he said. "We were all left-handed, which we thought was really weird. Randy was a baseball player in high school and loved baseball history, talked it all the time. He said we were all southpaws, which meant we threw from the south side. Something about the way baseball parks are laid out. I never played baseball, so I didn't understand all of it. Anyway, after Tommy Bell was sent back, Randy said, 'Now, we're the Southside Seven.' And it stuck."

"Thanks," I said. "I should have figured that out myself."

"Call me sometime and let me know how you're doing, Don," he said. "I'll be praying for you."

"Thanks, Father John," I said.

When we hung up, I felt something about me had changed, though I wasn't sure what. And it was never a bad thing having a person—especially a Catholic priest—pray for you.

Epilogue

Two days before Christmas, Jim Doak flew Mary, Lacy, Hannah, and me to Utah to visit Scott Glass. Susan, Mary's daughter, loved the idea, since she could see us without having to fly cross-country. Somehow, Hannah had convinced her mother to let her come with us, which was fine with Mary and me, since it meant more time alone for us. Not surprisingly, Mary hit it off immediately with Scott's girlfriend, Deena. They fast became friends. Deena was slender, dark haired, around five-foot-eight, and attractive. She and Scott seemed to like each other a great deal.

Friday, Christmas Eve, we skied Brighton. We took Christmas off and did all those things families and friends do that day—open presents, eat, drink, listen to Christmas music, and be of good cheer. It was exhausting.

Sunday, Monday, and Tuesday, we skied. Monday evening, we checked into a two-bedroom suite at the Cottonwood Residence Inn. I figured four nights imposing on Scott was enough. Neither Scott nor Deena complained about our leaving. Fish and guests—after a few nights, both started to smell.

By Wednesday morning, my legs were dead; a condition Mary found amusing, since she had warned me it would be futile trying to keep up with two athletic teenage girls. Scott and Deena had to go back to work, so Mary and I took the day off. We dropped the girls at Solitude Ski Resort and went to the nearby Silver Fork Lodge for breakfast. The place was maybe a third full. We sat at a corner table for four by the window. A fire crackled in a nearby fireplace. The scene was made even cozier by the blowing snow outside our window. Breakfast was terrific, and I ate with gusto.

Afterward, in no hurry to leave, and with nowhere to go, we sat and talked over coffee.

"This is a perfect moment," Mary said.

"It is."

"I really like Utah."

"Me, too," I said.

"I wouldn't mind having a place out here," she said. "You know, for spending the winter."

"You're confusing me," I said.

"Well, I was just thinking," Mary said. "In a little over a year, Lacy will be off to college, and I'll have twenty-five years in law enforcement."

She paused and took a drink of coffee.

"I'm listening," I said. I really liked the direction this conversation was taking.

"What if we sold the condo downtown and bought a place out here? We could divide time between the slopes, the beach, and the mountains."

"I like it," I said. "What about Cherokee Investigations?"

"We keep it," Mary said. "Take a few cases and work them together. You still do your investment thing, and Gretchen runs the office and takes care of the routine stuff. We can afford it, right?"

"Right," I said. "When did you come up with all this?"

"I've been thinking about it for a while," Mary said.

"Sounds like a plan."

"Maybe we should sleep on it."

"Okay."

"Like now," Mary said, raising an eyebrow.

"You mean right now?"

Mary smiled. "That's what I mean, cowboy."

Author's Note

Most of the places in this story are real. Mountain Center, however, is not one of them. I chose a wide-open space on a map of East Tennessee and decided that's where Mountain Center should be. You might recognize places from Gatlinburg, where I reside, and Johnson City, my hometown. I have transplanted them to Donald Youngblood's Mountain Center.

Don's lake house is very much like my mountain home in Gatlinburg, except that below my bottom deck is not a lake but hundreds of acres of undeveloped land. Just over the ridge is Ober Gatlinburg, Tennessee's only ski resort. At night, when it's cold enough to make snow, I can hear the snow guns from my back deck.

I have the greatest respect for the men and women who serve our country. When I started this novel I did not intend for it to be a story about Army Rangers, but I went where the story took me; that's how it goes sometimes. This story is pure fiction and any resemblances between actual missions and participants are purely coincidental.

I spend a several months of the year on Singer Island enjoying the beautiful beach, playing tennis, eating great seafood and working on the next Donald Youngblood mystery. As I write this, book five is well under way; as always, I have no idea where it is going.

Stay tuned.

Visit the Donald Youngblood Mysteries website at:
www.donaldyoungbloodmysteries.com

You may write the author at:
DYBloodMysteries@aol.com

Acknowledgments

My thanks to:

Meri Saffelder, web master, for attending my web site @ www.donaldyoungbloodmysteries.com

Buie Hancock, master potter and owner of Buie Pottery who has given Donald Youngblood and friends a spotlight in the Gatlinburg community.

Larry Wolf, a Gator fan (I forgive him) who has a vast knowledge of Harleys and shared some of it with me.

My wife, Tessa, proofreader extraordinaire, who catches mistakes others cannot.

Mary Sanchez, my publicist, who continues to surprise me by the number of events she lines up.

And finally:

Steve Kirk, my editor at John F. Blair Publisher, who really put me through my paces on this one. Great job, as always.

Praise for Keith Donnelly's Donald Youngblood Mystery Series

"*Three Deuces Down* and *Three Days Dead* are as rich in texture, charm, and personality as the East Tennessee mountains in which much of the action is set. The well-written, fast-paced novels are full of engaging characters and compelling plots and are so entertaining that you'll be disappointed they have to end."

—**Bill Noel,** author, the Folly Beach Mystery Series

"It is difficult to find entertaining, fast-moving, can't-put-it-down mysteries, but Keith Donnelly accomplishes it all in the Donald Youngblood Mystery Series. *Three Devils Dancing* will again prove Donnelly's genius as a true storyteller."

—**Larry Reid,** talk-show host, WBGZ

"Keeps the reader alive, and wanting for more . . . Although [*Three Days Dead*] stands well by itself, a wise reader would pick up *Three Deuces Down* to get the full flavor of the characters. A perfect pair of books for those snowy days ahead."

—**Edward Clarkin,** *New Britain Herald/Bristol Press*

"Keith Donnelly's . . . *Three Deuces Down* and *Three Days Dead* are well-written, enjoyable tales that blend elements of the traditional PI novel with the flavor of the present-day South. Donnelly's Tennessee private investigator, Don Youngblood, is realistically portrayed as competent, likeable, and flawed, as are the supporting characters, such as business partner and best friend Billy Two-Feathers and the mysterious and dangerous Roy Husky. Don's standard poodle, Jake, adds another dimension to the books, providing an opportunity for the tough-guy PI to show his sensitive side."

—**Jaden E. Terrell,** author, *Racing the Devil*

"Donnelly puts the reader at ease. Nothing complicated, just a comfortable read that leaves you asking when his next book will be finished. He continues to develop the characters in the series, and you will soon feel you have intimate knowledge of them... His books don't come with a money-back guarantee you will like them, but they should."

—**Joe Biddle,** sports columnist, *The Tennessean*